THE MEMORY ARTIST

Katherine Brabon was born in Melbourne in 1987 and grew up in Woodend, Victoria. *The Memory Artist* is her first novel and won the 2016 *The Australian*/Vogel's Literary Award.

THE
MEMORY
ARTIST

KATHERINE BRABON

ALLEN&UNWIN
SYDNEY · MELBOURNE · AUCKLAND · LONDON

For my parents, Nina and Martin,
and my sisters, Emily and Meredith

First published in 2016

Allen & Unwin
83 Alexander Street
Crows Nest NSW 2065
Australia
Phone: (61 2) 8425 0100
Email: info@allenandunwin.com
Web: www.allenandunwin.com

Cataloguing-in-Publication details are available
from the National Library of Australia
www.trove.nla.gov.au

ISBN 978 1 76029 286 7

Set in 13.25/17 pt Adobe Jenson Pro by Bookhouse, Sydney
Printed and bound in Australia by Griffin Press

10 9 8 7 6 5 4 3 2 1

PART I

If you ask me, 'Did this happen?' I will reply, 'No.'
If you ask me, 'Is this true?' I will say, 'Of course.'

Elena Bonner, *Mothers and Daughters*

CHAPTER 1

I was born in Moscow in 1964. Our apartment was a *dvushka*, two rooms and a small square of kitchen, in a Khrushchev-era concrete block. In that apartment of my childhood, uneven towers of paper, a precarious city, sprawled across the living room floor. On a glass-fronted bookshelf, photos of old dissidents, exiled writers and dead poets leant against the volumes and journals, looking out with silent faces. A narrow balcony faced the street.

Every child has their window, and from mine, in the kitchen, I could see only a narrow street, the tops of hats or umbrellas of people passing below, slanting shadows on the walls of the tower opposite and identical to ours, rain bouncing off bitumen, piles of snow and sometimes the old woman who cleared it away. On the windowsill were a few of those old meat tins—from the war years, my mother said—that now held pencils and fake flowers.

Life was our kitchen table. Rectangular, not very big, metal legs; draped in a cream cloth with latticed edges, stitched flowers in orange, brown and yellow. It was mesmerising, for me as a boy, to see how our rooms could transform between morning and late evening. In the morning, the table, and therefore the apartment, had a certain stillness; there were only a few ripples in the tablecloth where the vase or a plate had nudged the material out of place. I could hear my mother's slippers on the linoleum floor, the tick of the gas boiler on the wall, the soft knock of tea glasses placed on the wooden shelf. Pasha, drink your tea, my mother would say to me.

By evening our kitchen table would be another place, crowded and always, it seemed to me, made more colourful by the noise and the people gathered there. Rather than a first memory, I grasped a first feeling, an impression of those evenings in my childhood.

Oleg would usually arrive first. He had broad shoulders but was thin, the sinews of his neck stretched as if to their limits. The veins on his hands resembled river lines on a map. His hair, neatly parted, was slightly wispy, and his eyes were a striking shade of light blue. There was one night, or many, when I was very young and Oleg was talking as usual with the adults gathered in our kitchen. From my seat I watched as he casually reached for a cloth to dry the very plate from which I had moments ago eaten my dinner, that my mother had washed in the sink. In its ease, the unspoken closeness of old friends, it was a gesture that comforted me. We had probably lost my father by then. Perhaps I craved the figure of another parent that Oleg seemed to embody.

And then the others would arrive for the gathering—or underground activist meeting, as I would later learn to call these evenings in our apartment. They greeted one another, taking glasses from the table or shelf, some talking loudly as they walked through the tiny entranceway from the hall, pausing by the door to take off their boots, others quieter, patting me on the shoulder. I could smell *makhorka* tobacco as if it drifted in with those tall figures, riding on the warmth of their wheezing laughs or the cold of the draught from the hallway. Since the table was so small, most stood leaning against the wall, the doorway, or the edge of the sink. Certain papers were sometimes lifted from beneath the linoleum on the floor. Oleg would turn the radio on, wink at me and say, Let's find out what's happening to us today, Pasha. And then voices from Radio Liberty, Voice of America, or the BBC would speak from the shiny mint-green Latvian radio that was moved to the table for those gatherings—another object, like the kitchen table, that became so deeply woven into events of those years that it was something of a character in my memories. Such things seemed to hold an emotional personality as real as those of the people who, after all, would themselves become only memory objects of a kind.

And usually the typewriter, which spent its days either covered and hidden in the wardrobe, or on the kitchen table with my mother hunched over its keys, surrounded by papers, would take its heavy place on the table. The adults would grow serious; laughter would die down and I'd notice the sharpness in the air as they looked to the typewriter, the waiting white paper. Darya, someone would say to my mother, Darya, make sure this is said . . . include that name . . . no, say it this way. My mother's long hair would be pulled back in a silken black bun, though a few strands always seemed to get in the way and she would push them aside, touch the frame of her glasses with forefinger and thumb. Her back made an incline as she leant over the typewriter—like a mountain, severe and strong.

5

I'd wander over sometimes, tired or wanting attention, and stand next to her while she typed.

Yes, Pasha, she would say, even if I hadn't asked a question. Sometimes one of her arms would find me, wrap around my waist, and she'd let me hover at her side. I loved to follow the words as they appeared from nowhere on the expanse of white, like tiny figures running across a bare landscape. Standing there at the typewriter with her, surrounded by our friends, at the kitchen table that was our life, I was home.

Others would spend the time writing by hand, usually making *samizdat* copies of the same document—perhaps a banned poem or article. At the time, I wouldn't have known the meaning behind those typed and scrawled words, nor the weight between the lines. But listening to the care the dissident aunts and uncles took with each line, I learnt to revere them all the same.

Often I was allowed to sit on someone's lap and listen, though at times I would be sent to bed on the divan behind a screen in the living room. The radio's hum would reach my ears faintly, and murmurs or shuffling feet blurred into the edge of my sleep. I liked to see the yellow light thrown from the kitchen to the ceiling above me; it was forever connected in my mind to the dissidents' presence there.

In the morning after those meetings, the apartment was always charged with something, a lingering vigour; the scent of tobacco, brandy, the winter dampness of coats; the sight of something left behind, a hat or an unfamiliar flower-patterned plate. Each was evidence of the night and the very different place our rooms seemed to become in those hours.

Years later, when I was no longer the little boy with fair hair and wide brown eyes, I would wonder what the dates were, or even the years, when shades of tension, sadness and anger seeped into the mood of those gatherings. It wasn't the dates or events I absorbed as a child, but the sightless shifts in the air, which harnessed themselves to memory and came to define my recollections.

Once, a woman whose name I never knew, or eventually forgot, entered the kitchen, sat down heavily on a chair and looked away from the table with wet cheeks. I was struck by the way her hands lay, upturned and inert, on her lap. My mother sat with the woman while others brought out bottles, crystalline vodka or golden brandy, and asked me where extra glasses were kept. A man I didn't know washed the biscuit plates at the end of the night because my mother did not leave the sad woman's side.

Another time, Oleg looked at me with clouded red eyes and such an unfamiliar tension around his mouth (since it seemed to me he was always smiling) that I actually hid, pretending to read, on the floor by the couch in the other room. His sadness frightened me.

And sometimes, certain friends stopped coming. Perhaps the young man with black hair who left his hat under the chair at the back of the room, or the woman who was known for her good *kotleti* patties; they would be reduced to names I heard, still spoken at the table, but now turned into stories, or a telling expression on another's face. Gradually, I forgot what they looked like. Sometimes even the names vanished from the air and were only scribbled on paper, handed across the table with a knowing look, before nervous hands tore up the paper and threw the pieces in the stove. Those people became slightly unreal to me. I knew that the men and women attached to those unspoken names were not dead, exactly. Yet they had disappeared from the two rooms that were my real world. Like characters in a long-lost book, I could scarcely picture them in prison or a labour camp or exile. Perhaps that was how I came to think, even when I was no longer a child, that those who disappeared were not gone forever, but went to some other place, in the present or the past or somewhere else entirely, where terrible truths hid.

Of all the dissident aunts and uncles in the apartment of my childhood, Oleg was the one I worried about most. I feared he wouldn't return one day, like some of the others; that he'd disappear into the void of a name unspoken. Oleg was always full of smiles for me; wrinkles splayed from his blue eyes and over his forehead even when he was a young man. In his thin, veined hands he would always be holding something for me to read: a book or loose sheets of paper. Though the discussion at our kitchen table was rarely explicitly denied to me, I had a sense from an early age that they were communicating in ways I was missing, in a language I didn't properly understand. As I grew older, and entered my teens, Oleg welcomed me into that world. When he handed me books, single sheets of onionskin paper, copies of the *Chronicle of Current Events*, smuggled journals and other banned authors (for I really felt he was introducing me to the person—*Here is Brodsky; There you go, meet Platonov*), it was as though he was acknowledging that I could understand, that I perceived the world around our kitchen table as a universe different to the Moscow outside and that I was, with them, something of an outsider.

I clung to those scuffed journals and blank-faced books, especially as a teenager—not so much for their censored content but because they came from him, and if I collected enough, had enough evidence of his many visits, then Oleg's presence would be solidified somehow, and it would not be possible for him to disappear.

CHAPTER 2

I was thirty-four and living in St Petersburg when my mother died. It was 1999 and for six years I had lived there, in Primorsky District where the streets are wide like grey rivers, so far from the city centre that the buildings suddenly end where the Gulf of Finland begins, as cliff edges meet the sea.

The phone rang at three in the morning. It was Oleg. He told me the news and said he would help organise the funeral. I hung up the phone, lit a cigarette and stood at the window in my bedroom. As though I was trying to remember her all at once, I saw my mother as I knew her when I was young, in the apartment where we had lived in Moscow; and then as a woman I didn't know, a young dissident in the sixties, writing and publishing illegal articles. Her life in the underground. Emerging through those images, like film developing in a darkroom, was the face of my mother in the present, or as she had been the day before, when she was alive. A woman aged sixty-two. She'd spoken of doctors' visits and some health problems, but I didn't know—maybe she didn't either—that things were serious enough for her to die. It was strange, but those old moments and images, like the apartment in Primorsky where I lived alone, were soundless. I thought of that nearly silent moment when a piece of music is almost over, the piano resonance is both there and not there, in a moment that is, perhaps, like the moment of comprehending death.

It was July, the height of summer, with a gold, bluish sky hiding the fact that it was really still night. From the sixth-floor apartment where I lived I could see the gulf as a broad quicksilver sheet through the window of my bedroom. My mother was born in Chudovo, a town partway between St Petersburg and Moscow. I'd visited once as a boy, but my grandparents had died when I was young so we hadn't been there since. I would have to call the cemetery there. And buy a train ticket. I would have to go back to Moscow soon, too, to the apartment, and sort through whatever was left behind. It was reassuring, to have some noise come back to my mind as I thought of those practicalities, as things asked for my attention.

After staring at the gulf for a while I went to the other window, in the kitchen, where three pale grey and cream apartment towers formed a wall of rectangular windows. Like row upon row of mirrors, depending on the time of day those windows sent back countless images of my own apartment building, a grey day, or the sun. Seeing the odd yellow rectangle at night-time never failed to offer me a kind of distant company. But it was four in the morning, now, and they were all lightless.

I wasn't sure what to do. I opened my mail that lay forgotten in a chair: a list of summer classes from the school where I taught Russian to foreigners; from the new bar on

Korablestroiteley Street nearby a waxy, coloured advertisement sang of Baltika beer.

I lay on my bed but could only drift uneasily around sleep, so instead I spent the rest of the white night, and the start of the new day, sitting and smoking, or pacing from one window to the other.

In the early afternoon I made tea, ate some bread, then went out. In Primorsky I lived in a chosen solitude. If I left the apartment early enough, before the families had left for school or work, or later, after the old couples had gone for their walks, I could slip out, down the elevator, across the car parks and wide grey roads, board the *marshrutka* and sit at the back of the bus, unnoticed except to pass my coins to someone up front.

But that afternoon I felt like walking. As I crossed the dual lanes of Korablestroiteley, the sun beat down and the air was humid, heavy with fumes of the melting city. I cut through a few side streets. In a ragged yard around some old apartment buildings, four or five dogs, strays, barked as I passed by. Waiting at the Nalichnaya Street intersection, I heard faint music and bleary summer revelry float over from the bar on the corner.

I continued, passing over Smolenka River bridge, over Maly Prospekt, Sredny Prospekt. Eventually I reached the edge of Vasilyevsky Island. The air felt immediately clearer, close to the water, away from the concrete thicket of apartment blocks. The wide sunlight cast sharp shadows on the pavement and across the grand buildings painted beige, pink, pale yellow. A young couple walked with a pram covered by a white blanket against the sunlight. An older woman, round and blonde, stood in a girl's dress, all blue dots and frills, on the embankment beside the Neva River. Her husband wore a naval shirt, blue and white striped, over his round belly and murmured something to her as an ancient-looking cigarette clung to his lip.

From Vasilyevsky I took a metro, with the idea that I would go to Moscow station to find out about train tickets. In the subway it was cool, a relief from the heat, though a warm, metallic breeze fluttered down as I rode the escalator up to the station exit.

As I crossed over a busy intersection onto Vosstaniya Square, I saw a beautiful bride at a memorial obelisk, probably ready to lay her bouquet there, like so many brides before her since the end of the war. A few other bouquets already wilted in the heat. With the groom at her side she posed for a photograph beside the granite body of the obelisk. I stopped at the edge of the square, caught by the sight of the bride. As she stood there, still and statuesque, an almost spectral white light reflected from her dress in the glare of the day. I couldn't help thinking that the burst of red across her chest, from the bouquet in her hands, had the appearance of a grievous crime. The bridal couple smiled, almost grimacing in that intense sunlight, at the photographer who stood a few metres away.

At the sight of her, the bride, I felt something vaguely familiar, like an old longing or maybe just the appeal of a pretty face.

I watched as she held out a long white-sleeved arm, as she bent down, graceful as a lady in paintings of the past, to let the flowers fall from a small height. The couple left soon after, stepping into a polished white car.

From the square it was just a short walk to Moscow station. The foyer was full of ornate plaster carvings, white sculptured faces and curves like smooth snow. A few tourists milled about, their voices low or lost in the towering ceiling. A statue of Peter the Great stood in the place where Lenin's was a few years before.

The woman at the cashier desk blinked long and carefully, showing a light purplish glitter on her eyelids, then told me to come back on the day I actually wanted to travel.

I sat down in the foyer. The passage between St Petersburg and Moscow, a journey of some five hours by train, was for me once the road from Moscow to Leningrad. But then the name of the city had changed, and I had moved cities, so those small shifts took place. I had a strange feeling, then. As though I was only just realising I would never again travel to or from Leningrad. I stayed in the foyer for a while; I must have looked like a man pinned to my seat.

I went to a public phone and called Yura, an old friend who lived in the city, on his office number. He offered to come to Chudovo with me for the funeral. I said no, I wouldn't be there long.

I could have a beer now though, I said.

I finish at six.

Thanks, brother.

It's nothing. I'll see you.

I had two hours to fill somehow. I crossed the road and from a stall outside a metro station bought a bunch of flowers, they might have been carnations, mostly yellow, red and pink, wrapped in white paper. I took a tram away from the city centre to Volkovskoye Cemetery. I'd gone there many times before. My sanctuary among the dead. Through the large grounds by Volkovsky River, through the heavy woods, past immobile stone faces on plinths. As I walked I thought it must have been winter when I'd been there last, because I kept imagining an old coldness, bare trees, pastel clouds and hanging fog, whereas on that afternoon it was warm even in the shade.

I read the headstones. There were some familiar names. Alexander Popov, a pioneer of the radio, resting embraced by vivid green leaves. I'd always had an attachment to radios. As a boy I loved their strange ability to bring faraway words to me in our small rooms in Moscow. Oleg once told me that in 1942 a performance by twelve-year-old piano prodigy Lazar Berman, playing Liszt's 'La Campanella', was broadcast out of Leningrad all the way to the United Kingdom. Whenever I thought about that astonishing broadcast, I connected it to the reverence my mother, Oleg and their fellow dissidents had for the bodiless wisdom that came from our radio speakers, which had left me with a similar devotion to the tiny lattices of metal. I would sit so close my breath would leave wet warmth on the speakers. In our enclosed world of whispers, hidden from the Moscow outside, the radio seemed to say that it knew me, knew our hidden world, that it knew I existed.

Not far from Popov's grave was that of Vladimir Bekhterev, the famous psychiatrist. I stared at the statue of his bearded face; there was something severe and challenging about his expression. Bekhterev was said to have been the first to make a link between the brain's hippocampus and memory. During an autopsy on a patient with severe memory impairment, Bekhterev noticed lesions in a certain part of the brain, and so found the connection. The psychiatrist had died in mysterious circumstances the day after he met Joseph Stalin. I'd long had an interest in, and unpleasant associations with, psychiatric hospitals in Moscow.

At the end of a bright green canopied path of very old graves lay the writer Alexander Radishchev. In 1790 he wrote *A Journey from St Petersburg to Moscow*, describing a trip from one city to the other after the death of his mother. Everything he saw along the way disgusted him as gradually he realised the state of the country, the poverty and decay. So he wrote about it. Our earliest dissident, who also thought he could change the world with words.

I let the flowers, yellow and red and pink, fall down together to the ground at Radishchev's grave. All of my dead were in Moscow.

Yura was waiting for me at the bar, two full glasses of beer on the table. He wore a sky-blue business shirt and had thick-rimmed glasses. He worked at St Petersburg State University but we'd met years before, in Moscow. We'd both wanted to leave that city, for our own reasons, though Yura seemed to have settled in our new city far better than me. I told him how my mother had been ill for a while, with blood pressure problems, but it hadn't seemed life-threatening and so her death was a shock.

Mostly we spoke about Moscow. The longer we were both in Petersburg, the more it seemed that our old city was the main thing we had in common. In the six years since I left, I'd been back three or four times, but each visit was less than three days. Yura hadn't been back at all.

We probably wouldn't recognise the place now, he said. He looked down at his beer. Yura somehow still had a young face, though his light brown hair was thinning and his eyes seemed a little tired.

Well, I'll know soon enough, I said. I looked down at my own drink. I'll have to go back to sort out the apartment. Maybe I'll move back there.

It was a throwaway line, but the thought wasn't completely unappealing. Sometimes when we had a drink I would mention to Yura that I never really felt comfortable in Petersburg. It was as if the city was hostile to me, though I'd never said it in those words. Secretly I'd always admired, even envied, Yura's ability to detest the city of his birth. He had been stuck there in the eighties, when Moscow's Jews were trying hard to leave but they were repeatedly denied exit visas. It was particularly hard for well-educated Jews; Gorbachev maintained they were causing a *brain drain*, trying to leave all at once. So when he finally left the city, even though he stayed in Russia, it was surely like breaking the bars of a prison. But me, I was never sure.

Well, you know what I've said before . . . Yura held up his beer glass, tilting it at me. You left the city on bad terms. Left things unfinished. If you're like me, you make a clean break: goodbye, Moscow.

Yura pressed four fingers, hard, into the table and drew an invisible line across the marbly white laminate. I've never been back. But you, he said, you were never sure. You left so quickly and had those few trips back. Short flings. Like a lover you can't leave behind.

We nodded and drank.

Well, I'll let you know, I said.

I had to teach a class the next day. It was an easy one, just two businessmen from Rotterdam who both wore neatly pressed light green shirts and were always polite. I taught fewer classes in recent years, working more on organisation, marketing, helping to manage the language school business. After making a few phone calls, I went home.

I sat at the square wooden desk in my bedroom, smoking and looking out the window to my right. I watched the gulf, the water silvery and still from this distance, though it would have been rippling with a current. Sometimes the endless daylight was jarring. It seemed unnatural to me, that we were put in charge of the hours like that.

I went to the kitchen, made a meal of lamb and potatoes, opened a beer, and sat reading a newspaper, absorbing not a word. Yellow rectangles had appeared in the view from my kitchen window, though it was still sunny. I wondered if the residents of those towers turned on their lights just out of habit, since according to our watches and clocks it should have been dark.

That night, as though hoping to make sense of something through the effort of recording it, I began to write about Moscow. Though with the sky still light at midnight it was really no night at all.

CHAPTER 3

Chudovo, my mother's hometown, was one hundred kilometres south of St Petersburg in the Novgorod region. Trains departed from Moscow station, as if something was determined to remind me of that city. As I purchased a ticket, I remembered Yura telling me I hadn't properly parted with the city of my birth.

The train carriage was old but the seats were comfortable. The air was close, the heat trapped in there, so I took a can of beer from my bag. As I took a cooling, bitter sip, the train coasted out of the city, and for a while I followed only the shifting view of thinning towns.

My thoughts flickered back to that walk through Volkovskoye Cemetery. I saw the vivid green canopies protecting the graves. I imagined that the trees, as they grew, would one day lean right down and caress the faces of those walking by. One of the old Russians there, Radishchev, wrote in *A Journey from St Petersburg to Moscow* about the people he met on that oppressively hot summer trip back home after his mother died. It wasn't lost on me that I was making a trip under similar circumstances. Along the way the writer met peasants and townspeople who told him of their problems and all the things awry under the government of Catherine the Great. Radishchev, who had thought himself far removed from the small-town life he'd left behind, was haunted by a question from one of the poor souls he met on the trip. A man asked Radishchev whether he thought the peasants had been treated right by the leaders they had never met. It was a question Radishchev couldn't answer. One of those without a question mark, that are asked again and again like a never-ending echo.

I looked out the window, thinking we couldn't be far from Chudovo. Oleg had arranged to meet me at the station. When I thought of Oleg I often saw him looking down at me, kind eyes, a smile, or I was observing him from a small distance, as he stood near the kitchen table in our apartment, maybe with his arms folded across his chest, talking or laughing with someone I couldn't see or had forgotten. They were all child-hood images, as though my perception was fixed in those early years.

Now I could see powerlines, untended green fields, a few wooden buildings as we passed by quickly. I finished my beer. A girl maybe twenty years old got in at one of the stops and sat across from me. She looked quietly out the window while her pretty reflection looked back. We arrived at Chudovo station about twenty minutes later. It was a yellow classical-style building, bordered in white and topped by a sloping maroon roof. *A yellow house.* Dostoyevsky often put those in his settings, when his characters roamed uneasily around St Petersburg, a hint for readers who knew about the yellow-painted Obukhovskaya Hospital, a mental asylum. His characters often verged on the point of madness, tormented by delusions, thinking their actions sane. I almost turned to the girl in the carriage, as we were leaving, to explain to her the significance of the yellow building. But she slunk out of the carriage before I could say a word. She walked ahead of me and didn't turn back. I slung my rucksack over one shoulder and walked out onto the platform.

Oleg was there. His thin hair was wispier, whiter than in the image I had ready in my head, though his eyes were the same bright blue. He seemed thinner, even shorter, or maybe I just wasn't used to being taller than him. Hanging from his shoulders was a rucksack, which I remembered him carrying any time he was outside.

We hugged and said a quiet hello, then we walked along a wide road behind the station. A trio of black birds arced overhead.

As we walked in silence, I thought of the apartment where I grew up. Moscow. Our feet crunched on the gravel. I remembered that transformation at our table, from morning to evening. The adults who came in, each patting me on the shoulder, as if they were giving me something as they walked by, and I'd find myself almost nodding in thanks. Though I had kept in contact with Oleg, there were so many of those dissident aunts and uncles who seemed to disappear along with the world of my childhood.

Oleg had arranged everything for the funeral. There was a short ceremony in a small wooden community hall. At the burial itself, as if emerging from my childhood, voices I thought I recognised read poems and spoke briefly but earnestly about my mother's role in the dissident movement in the Brezhnev years, especially her campaign for the release of political prisoners incarcerated in psychiatric institutions. I couldn't really reconcile the old, wrinkled faces and grey heads of the people who were speaking with any concrete remembrance from childhood. I closed my eyes and imagined they reached me, those voices, from the faraway, comforting static of the radio on our kitchen table in the apartment in Moscow.

Afterwards we went to the home of a local family for drinks and *zakuski* snacks. Like the voices at the funeral, the house felt known to me, distantly, in that way rooms we've never before been in manage somehow to reach out to us. Simple brown carpet covered the living room floor except for the stone around an enormous old-fashioned stove. A large sideboard of dark red wood held painted plates on the upper shelves and, below them, rows of books behind glass, photos leaning against the books. A few women bustled around with food. I could smell the spice-scent of ginger biscuits, the tartness of vinegar; I saw the tumbling steam clouds from a boiling samovar. I poured a glass of brandy, finished it and had another. The intense familiarity of it all made me feel a bit weightless.

A man, perhaps in his sixties, came over to talk to me. He wore a thin short-sleeved white shirt tucked into trousers belted high at his waist. When I was a boy I knew that the dissidents' day jobs included translating, accounting, book-binding, even tombstone engraving, but their real work had been for the underground movement. Sergei Ivanovich was a geologist, and he told me stories of Siberian expeditions and taiga land studies, and described his admiration for the geologist and famous anarchist writer Peter Kropotkin. I tried hard to concentrate on his sentences. I explained that I didn't see much of the countryside; I was usually in the city, my concrete-and-bitumen suburb.

He had a *dacha* near St Petersburg, he told me; just a small cottage in a forest. It's yours anytime, he said. I like to see the old group—he waved an arm to encompass the people in the room—like to see them using the place.

I felt somehow validated to be included in the old group, that old life in the apartment of my childhood.

Oleg introduced me to a few more people, I had a little to eat, more to drink, and the afternoon blurred into a sunny evening. During the darkless night I stepped outside and walked some way down the wide rubbly road. A green field stretched out before me; its vastness was a freeing sight after so long in the city. I looked as far as I could into the distance, until the green merged with loose, bluish clouds. The next morning, I returned with a headache to St Petersburg.

CHAPTER 4

O nce back in the city, though, I was feeling strange—perhaps because I hadn't slept in a while. When I was a boy our friends would say that my mother never slept. I thought it was just a figure of speech because she was always working late. Of course she sleeps, I would say, too young then to comprehend the worries that might keep one awake at night. After the funeral I was often hit by such fragments of conversations.

The funeral was on a Tuesday, and I went back to work Thursday. On Saturday I went to the city centre. In the metro carriage, every noise was excessively loud. Sound seemed to physically touch me, and the yellow light was harsh on my eyes. Insomnia brought about a kind of loneliness, as though nobody else in the world felt that way. It was like watching the world through glass. In the train carriage I had the sense that people were looking, staring, as if they knew things about me that I didn't know myself. At those times, I felt just a trip on the pavement or an elbow on the metro away from madness. Gestures were obscene, buildings malign.

I called Yura, arranged to meet for drinks, but then phoned back an hour later and cancelled. I ended up calling Sonya, a woman I sometimes saw. She had two children, sons, and a husband who had died. She had a long oval face and eyes that always seemed to look away, mournfully, out a window or across a room. Her hair was bright blonde and her dyed eyelashes were long and very dark. The building where she rented a one-bedroom apartment was on the other side of St Petersburg to my place, and she worked at a travel agency near Griboyedov Canal. We would sleep together sometimes but, like me, she favoured solitude; my lonely Sonya who for both practical and emotional reasons never wanted me to stay for long.

When I visited, Sonya's sons stayed at their grandmother's. Her bed was a low mattress, the softest I'd ever lain on. The room was sparse, just a small chest of drawers, light orange curtains, a low bedside table with a few magazines and always a glass of water and vitamins or tablets. And her lingering smell, a muted perfume. That night we were both very quiet, though Sonya pulled me towards her with a sad strength in her palms and fingers, and at one point she cried out loudly. It was on those nights I knew she was particularly lonely, her dead husband closer to her than I.

I didn't tell Sonya that my mother had died. I rarely talked to her about Moscow and my previous life. I preferred to be solitary in every way, and clung to the feeling that I had no defined story. As if I had no edges.

We lay in that soft bed, and Sonya told me about her sons, how she had taken them to a church ceremony. She had been attending services for the past few months. I hadn't ever met her children—she was strict about such a separation, always making sure I arrived after they had left—a choice that was part of her desired solitude, I always assumed.

It was very moving, Pasha, she said. To see my two little ones holding out their candles for lighting, and carefully following the words in their little songbooks. A languid smile passed over her face. I like to see them care about something, she said.

I listened, touched her blonde hair. She knew I didn't believe in any god.

I left Sonya's and went home, though I couldn't sleep. The hours changed but not the light. At two in the morning, I stood watching the silky gulf water. The wind picked up, as though ready for the approaching, premature day. It sounded high and very close, right at my window and almost like waves; I imagined that the gulf had broken its banks to leak over the suburb, leaving only the concrete tower island of the apartment. The sky was stone grey.

The next morning, I left the apartment. The wind persisted and it was hot already. I never knew what to do on a Sunday, such a quiet, cavernous day. I wandered, lost in thought, to the metro and boarded a train that was empty. Primorskaya station was the end of the line, though in the morning it was more like the beginning. I was often indecisive, prone to seeking out diversions, and that morning even more so. At first I went to the city centre, walked along Nevsky, turned to walk alongside Griboyedov Canal and then down past Yusupov Gardens and along Sadovaya. It was busier there in the narrower streets, or maybe the wide boulevards in the centre gave an illusion of thinner crowds, greater calm. Around Sennaya Square the mood was brittle, the heat close. Teenagers sat on steps or stood in those fractured circles of the young, where the attention is usually on one or two players, laughs are uneven or mocking, and nobody ever seems to be still. Mothers pushed prams. Soldiers, young men but old veterans, drank on the edges of the throng. I walked down a lane and emerged at the end into another crowded square, people pooled into these cramped spaces. Vendors called out from stalls in the square.

I'd walked in those parts many times, especially when I first arrived in the city and knew nobody. So many repetitions. If someone inked in our footsteps, and the footsteps of those who came before us, there might be only a series of widening and constricting circles, endless turns and corners. My aimless walk gave me nothing but the decision to take some time away from the city.

In the afternoon I returned to my apartment and called the language school. I explained that I would need a couple of weeks off work. The school was owned and run by a young Dutch guy, Joran. He had moved to Russia the year before, with the view that with our wretched economy it was a good time to start a business with foreign money, teaching Russian to businessmen and students, about which he was probably right. He was easygoing and didn't seem to mind the prospect of my absence, since there were plenty of university students looking for summer work.

I had little money or direction, but I wanted to leave the city for a while and find a place to write whatever it was I had started since my mother died. I called the man I had met at the funeral, Sergei Ivanovich, and arranged to stay at his *dacha* for a couple of weeks.

Since moving to St Petersburg in 1993, I had not struggled with life so much as with death, the allure of it. I would go to work, function like the machine I needed to be, but then on the weekends I'd lie staring at the ceiling and feel myself turning to stone. An inner silence lived in me. Life had a dreamlike texture. Perhaps at the highest point of melancholia you exist in the silence and truth of dreams. Dreams are, after all, something of which we are the bewildered authors; we don't know what we have created with that blend of what we have lived and what we haven't, what we desire and what terrifies us.

I looked back on the last six years since I'd left Moscow and felt that nothing filled them. One of the few things I'd read in the years after I'd moved, and I read it quite often, was Kafka's short story 'A Hunger Artist'. An artist starves himself and people come to watch. His art is their entertainment. But the authorities dictate that he can't starve himself for more than forty days, because after that time he starts to look gruesome and the public find it too confronting.

Perhaps I read it over and again because of my own thoughts of dying. Or maybe I kept going back to the story because it seemed to tell me different things at different times. I sometimes thought it was Kafka's way of saying that people don't know what they really want; they have to be shocked into appreciating the new because nobody ever knew that the greatest works of art or song or literature were coming. To dictate art is to rob it of its very definition.

At other times I wasn't sure of the point of the story. I couldn't understand what the artist was doing it all for.

Perhaps, I thought, the story symbolised the very act of making art: there would never be the satisfaction of attainment. He couldn't say, *Yes, I did it, I starved to death*. The artist doesn't, and perhaps shouldn't, truly know what it is they have created.

At the end of the story, the hunger artist says that he didn't eat because he couldn't find a food that he liked. That made me feel uneasy somehow, to think there was no real inner need behind his art, or that the cause we expected, creative desire itself, wasn't really there. Maybe Kafka was saying we never know the true roots of our need to create. Maybe we destroy, just a little, a work of art when we try to touch it, to shape it into words. According to this view, what is important is the hell of the attempt to create.

My fixation with that story, at a time when I wanted to read nothing, was likely because I'd reached a point where I doubted I could ever be a writer and, by extension, doubted the point and power of art. Since I was a boy, the knowledge that I was an outsider, a holder of certain truths, gave me a reason to exist. I wanted to carry on the work of the dissidents who raised me and preserve, through my writing, the memories of oppression they'd fought so hard to keep afloat in the mire of repression.

But Moscow had undermined me, and since I'd left I'd felt I had no reason for being, no meaning. And the truth was that my mother, her life, had indirectly stopped me ever trying to be rid of my own. My father had died when I was very young and it would be too great a tragedy, I reasoned, for her to lose her son as well. In that summer of 1999, the wall between myself and death, a wall I'd constructed and maintained for six years, fell when my mother died. I had to meet with whatever was on the other side of that wall.

All of my dead were in Moscow, and in my memory they thrived, an especial ability of the absent. They left a resonance, faint wind chimes haunting my consciousness, and in that sound I strained to hear some kind of meaning.

Just as I didn't know why that artist starved himself—a question that dogged me—so I didn't understand my own need to write about the dead, to preserve their memory. Once one person dies, their memory beats in others as though it is a life. Not just the memory you have of them, but their own individual memories that they have passed on by words or other means. If that knowledge falls away, is forgotten, it exists nowhere. I was so long estranged from art, from the desire to remember, that I knew I had a tough task in front of me.

The writer Andrei Bitov said that writing was a state of being. He had to find time for expeditions to places ideal for writing—escapes, he called them—where there was no time and no information. That summer in Petersburg, in that overheated, overthought place, I craved a similar state of being.

CHAPTER 5

From our apartment to the street was a walk of five floors downstairs, there being no elevators in the new sixties buildings with their apartments comprising two rooms and kitchen, or sometimes only one room and kitchen. The street was lined with other five-floor blocks—Khrushchev had had them built all over Moscow—as well as a post office, a small shop, and a bus stop at the end.

On the first of September every year, like every Soviet child, I clutched my bunch of flowers and, holding my mother's hand, walked in my uniform shirt and jacket with the murmuring mass of colour through Moscow's streets to school.

I was a quiet boy. With my friends Artyom and Dmitry I played in the playgrounds in apartment yards or sailed boats in the streams formed by clogged drains in the street. To me the water flowed as beautifully and as fast as any clear blue stream you might find in the countryside. We tried our first cigarettes as twelve-year-olds, sitting on the cold bars of an outdoor gym in the snow.

At school my class teacher, a man with a broad chest and receding hairline, stood beneath the red banners, the colourful posters, and the portraits of leaders past and present. He spoke with eerie reverence about the Great Patriotic War. Years later, it occurred to me that perhaps his own father was one of the dead. He told us about the Tomb of the Unknown Soldier in Moscow, which held the remains of some unidentified soldiers killed between 1941 and 1945. Those unknown dead were once buried in a mass grave at the forty-first kilometre of the Leningrad Highway, at the city of Zelenograd, precisely resting at (almost guarding, I thought) the place the Nazi armies reached on their march to Moscow.

And I was horrified, sitting at my school desk, to learn that in 1966 the remains were dug up out of the earth. They were moved to Moscow, buried at the Kremlin Wall by the Alexander Garden, with the words *Imya tvoyo neizvestno, podvig tvoy bessmerten*—Your name is unknown, your deed is immortal—inscribed in bronze. I wondered what the scene might have looked like when the grave was unearthed at Zelenograd; the remains, I supposed, were skeletons, but I also pictured crumpled remnants of clothes, a belt buckle, weapons.

I wondered who was assigned the task of unburying the dead, and how they went about transporting them (probably by train, I eventually decided). And I was struck by the strangeness of reburying bodies long dead with names never to be known. I had also, more than once, thought of the old burial place in Zelenograd. I wondered what it might have looked like in the silent years after the unburial, whether it was recognisable for what or whom the earth once held.

For me there was an enormous silence in those classes. The people, places and events that existed within the walls of my home were not mentioned at school. The Gulag prison camps, the mass shootings under Stalin, the dissidents locked away in psychiatric hospitals, those things were present only upon the precious, dangerous, hidden papers at our apartment, or in the bodiless words drifting from the mint-green radio, from Radio Liberty or the BBC, or in the looks between the adults who came to meetings in our apartment.

There was a line to follow in the world outside and a different one at home, and I understood that those lines stood for two very different stories. And so I only really felt like my true self at home.

Though I could never remember being told, I somehow always knew that silence and secrecy kept us safe. I understood that I could not tell the other story at school. I knew I couldn't say that as the vodka flowed and cheeks grew red, my mother's friends laughed as they spoke of *kopchushka*, the smoked fish, when really they meant Lenin, or his body preserved forever in his tomb in Moscow. Maybe sometimes my mother whispered, Not for school, Pasha, or maybe I imagined that loving censure when later trying to grasp how I knew the things I did. The importance of silence. The existence of a parallel, invisible line running beside the official one, as real to me as the unseen passages of blood in our veins.

Sometimes I didn't want to hold the silence in me anymore. After school one day I showed Dmitry a record that was pressed *on the bones*—made by underground musicians on old X-rays. It was probably a copy of some jazz or rock album from the West. *Look at it!* It was too impressive not to show him. We knelt on the floor in front of the divan where I usually slept and I held it up between us. You could see the skeleton of some unknown person and you knew that the music was somehow, impossibly, *inside* the image of those bones. I could just see Dmitry's face, his chubby chin and blond mop of hair, through the large circle of shadowy film.

The danger of what I did only shocked me in retrospect. At the other end of that act could have been the interrogation, surveillance, even arrest of my mother, Oleg, the musicians themselves. But in return, at Dmitry's place, we took some forbidden brandy from his dad's shelf. His parents both worked in a factory and usually left for work as he arrived home from school. Standing at the window, which looked straight at a white-walled building, we passed the bottle between us. The brandy warmed my throat and thrilled me. I didn't really like it but I loved it all the same. We sealed our pact with a glance and never mentioned those things—the record or the brandy—again.

It was my first sense of knowing, of creating myself, a secret space separate to the one of my mother's dissident life. Firsthand, I grasped how something could form between two people, only known because of certain contingencies—a look, an encounter, a decision not to speak. It was probably the first time, too, that I unknowingly learnt—felt, more than anything—that there could be an entire universe of spaces like that.

CHAPTER 6

The view from my childhood window in the kitchen didn't change much over the years, only through the seasons. A few more buildings grew up in the narrow gaps I'd never noticed existed until they were gone, and so a few more shifting drifts of smog appeared, like winter breath in the schoolyard, as did a few dozen more squares of light in the evening and most of the day in winter. During my high school years, the dissidents still gathered in our apartment and I became more interested in following their activities, rather than simply absorbing them in that subconscious way a child takes on the things their parent knows.

There seemed to be something about the new leader, Mikhail Gorbachev, a suggestion that his time in the Kremlin might have a different hue from the unchanging grey of all the other leaders. I saw him speak on television after he took over. He was young. He had no cue cards, no prepared monotone speech. There was the faintest hint of uncertainty behind his neat suit, the microphone, the wall of comrades nearby. His appearance and manner coloured the image on the television, as though the picture was clarified, the sound amplified; I sat up on the divan and watched closely. Even my mother was listening, instead of turning up the radio as she usually did when the Central Committee were droning on the television. She had stopped whatever she was doing and stood behind me in the living room. I glanced back once or twice and saw her eyes on the screen, lips compressed and arms crossed. Though Gorbachev mostly parroted the usual lines—about strengthening socialism, about the bright future ahead—he also spoke about taking off the rose-coloured glasses, about the need for change. The era we would call *glasnost*, openness, had begun.

In 1985, after a few years of working boring odd jobs because I wasn't sure what I wanted to do after high school, I started studying at the Gorky Institute of Literature in Moscow. There was some tension at home when I said I wanted to study at the Gorky Institute. Because of who my parents were, there was doubt as to whether I'd be admitted in the first place. Probably, too, my mother was worried that I would run into trouble if I studied at university. That's where things go wrong for people, she had always said. So when the Gorky Institute question arose, she called in help. Oleg came over and there was an uneasy meal at our apartment during which they tried to convince me not to apply.

You cannot study humanities in this country, my mother said. There's no truth in *those* novels. You can't call them real Russian literature when they just write what that Writers' Union decrees is acceptable.

I've decided, I said. I'm going. I was young and stubborn.

Oleg leant in, calm and serious, his vivid blue gaze on me. He pushed back his thin hair. But Pasha, he said, they might give you a hard time. More than others, given your background.

They'll crush you because you can think for yourself, said my mother. She had long forgotten her soup. Her arms were folded across her chest, her voice unsteady in a way that made me feel guilty. To her, true writers existed between the official lines; censorship was the highest form of praise. But I didn't want to be an above-ground accountant and underground writer. I was sick of being split: I wanted to just be.

And so I went. It wasn't as bad as they feared. I studied Bitov (some of his works were banned, others were deemed acceptable), who had been at the Gorky Institute some thirty years before and was a tutor there after I left. He was Russian enough for my mother. She seemed to grow used to the fact that I attended Gorky after the first few months went by and nothing sinister happened to me, though I was never sure what she was expecting.

I had a girlfriend in my first year, Tatyana. We would meet at boring culture clubs, dance awkwardly over the wooden zigzag pattern of the parquet floor that looked the same in every Soviet culture hall. We'd go to the cinema or kiss in parks like all the other students, and we had sex in her friend's dorm room a few times. The excitement of the new lasted maybe five months before we drifted apart, saw each other less and less, kissed other people, and eventually went our separate ways.

I spent three years at Gorky, sometimes writing my own stories or sketching out chapters for a novel, but mostly writing studies of other authors. I always associated the start of college with change. Since Gorbachev's first year, the life of the city had felt different. A new law allowed public groups to form—everything from drama groups to car enthusiasts to garden appreciation clubs—groups that were not connected to the Party. The dissidents of my childhood began to make contact with other underground groups. They formed the Memorial Society, and words previously unspeakable in public rose up from underground. The society's objectives included the release of political prisoners and the creation of a memorial to victims of Stalin's Terror. It was silence, my mother always said: silence enabled the murder of millions under Stalin. Breaking that silence would ensure that the terror would never return. And that was how, slowly, the people and ideas around our kitchen table became a solid presence in the Moscow outside.

By 1986, when I was in my second year at Gorky, people were taking to the new freedoms in their own ways—even those who learnt conformity at home. Borya, whose parents were Party members, walked around wearing a USA t-shirt, and Elena, once a leader in the Komsomol Communist Youth League, now wore her hair short and dyed black, her eyes lined with black pencil, and as we sat in class chewed a silver cross she wore on a chain around her neck.

It was during my second year that I met Ilya. If I was the solitary aspiring novelist who sat up the back scribbling, Ilya was the brash poet who would have stood on the desk to recite his work if he could have got away with it. He was always late for class, forever wearing that leather jacket, his black hair messy; he was likely not long out of bed. Ilya could be confronting, loud; he worshipped Hemingway and Yevtushenko, and had a restless energy about him—each time he walked into a room he would sit in every chair, talking all the time, before stretching out in the chair he'd started with.

Some of our classmates lived in the filthy dorms at the Gorky Institute, and we would often meet there to drink on the weekends. Or we would lose hours in front of the TV watching all the concerts that suddenly began to be broadcast then—The Beatles or the Velvet Underground, anything out of London or Liverpool or New York. I longed for an electric guitar, and wondered if I could pull off an ear piercing.

It was through music, above all, that the new Moscow flooded our lives. Ilya always knew where the latest, best, realest shows were going on. In the red darkness of concerts we could literally scream every thought, every want. We went to the Yolka Festival on New Year's Eve 1986. Five hundred people filled a Moscow culture club; and there were ten live bands, and people crawled up the windows trying to get in—they could hear it, the sounds and the life; they wanted to *be* there, to *reach* that freedom.

This is *it*, Pasha, Ilya called out to me, shoving my shoulder. This will wake *the fuck* out of the country!

In the sweating crowd, a girl with long dark hair kissed me so forcefully I grasped her shoulders in my hands, then just kept holding her. As quickly as she'd appeared she vanished into the smoky darkness of the club, hands drifting above her like some swaying underwater plant, and I never saw her again.

Near the end of my degree, I applied for a job at the Gorky Institute library and, when I graduated, accepted a position there. It was steady, methodical work, processing loans and helping researchers. Each day I had lunch at a workers' cafeteria nearby. This was, I reasoned, how I'd make a living before making my way as a writer. Ilya found a job with a stock delivery driver and so spent each day hauling boxes and chatting with his boss, the truck driver, Timofey. It was 1988, June had finally brought summer heat, and we were free young men ready for the world *glasnost* had brought us. We had weekends and most evenings off work, so Ilya and I spent every possible moment of that summer out in our city that felt like a new city.

Though memories don't always have words, they usually have a place, and for me those years were one and the same with the Arbat. In 1986 they turned it into a pedestrian street, paved and lined with streetlamps. It became the stage of central Moscow, filled with milling shoppers and people strolling in any season, though the summer of 1988 was different. Thick crowds slowed the pace and new scenes slid by with the heat: the punks all pierced in their black leather, hair shaved or spiked like barbed wire. The man with long stringy hair cooing over his guitar while people threw him a kopek or two. Young guys in tracksuits dancing, falling to the ground and twisting on their backs before bouncing up again; a little further on a group of teenage girls swaying to music coming from somewhere, maybe a cassette player, one of them flicking her hair as though she liked the way it moved so freely. The tourist with a silver camera, and socks beneath her white high-heeled sandals.

We would walk and watch, listen to the music, bask in the wide sun. Ilya in his leather jacket despite the heat, squinting as he blew smoke rings to the sky. I even wore a *New York* t-shirt that I had bought from a seller at Izmaylovsky Market.

In the afternoons we would cool down in parks or beside fountains, with Pepsi or *kvass* sold from those large yellow barrels. We'd read or listen to music on Ilya's black-market Walkman, Billy Bragg cassettes turned up loud. Sun-sleepy, hazy music, broad blue skies. Usually Ilya was breaking a girl's heart somewhere in Moscow and he would tell me about this or that beauty he had just met or lost. I, on the other hand, usually fell for girls from a distance.

From the Arbat we would walk to Pushkin Square, along the green-lined boulevard of Tverskoy. The *stengazety* wall newspapers were posted on glass-covered noticeboards outside the news offices in Pushkin Square, so we would often go to read them. In April of 1988, the papers had reported that the square would be the site of the first McDonald's in the Soviet Union. People laughed at the idea of *fast food* or fast anything in the city with a twenty-minute queue for eggs at Tagansky Gastronom, or thirty minutes if you wanted the Bulgarian deodorant.

Gorbachev's *glasnost* loosened censorship's grasp. He said it was time to fill in the blank spaces of history. Our favourite saying in those years came from the Belarusian writer Adamovich, who said it was more interesting to read than to live. In the *stengazety* papers at the time, there were articles about mass-grave investigations, reports on alcoholism and prostitution, stories on promised reforms, and letters from workers complaining about their bosses. Victims of the Gulag were writing their stories and sending them to the newspapers. And the newspapers were publishing them. *Glasnost* was supposed to open up society and *perestroika*, reconstruction, to change it. We read out this or that article to each other, or just stood silently with a cigarette hungrily reading the latest. Crowds vied for a spot in front of the noticeboards.

Also, in 1988, the Memorial Society started collecting signatures for a petition calling for a monument to Stalin's victims. I volunteered with Ilya and a few other friends and we took to the Arbat, explaining the goal—a public monument, a statue of some kind, in central Moscow to commemorate the dead—to watchful and eager, if very quiet, groups of Muscovites. After seventy years of Communist silence, people were emerging like survivors of a storm, looking gingerly up and out, squinting in the light of the morning after, uncertain if the walls of remaining buildings might suddenly collapse.

We saw little difference between the mass graves of the dead and the mass of the living, the people. Indifference to the former would simply shift to the latter. How the state and citizens alike acted towards history would determine how anyone cared, or not, about people in the future. But it would not always be the case. History's reach and its lessons would only emanate so far from the event. Over time, the impact would fade; knowledge would be lost after one or two generations. Then what we went through would simply become events; it would become something that happened to some people long ago.

CHAPTER 7

The only people our age Ilya and I knew who had an apartment of their own were Sukhanov, an artist, and his wife Lena. When she and Sukhanov married, Lena's parents gave up a two-room apartment in exchange for two one-room apartments, so Lena and Sukhanov had their own place, unlike most newlyweds, who lived with their parents or in-laws.

Sukhanov, a tall guy with wavy blond hair, was adamant that he needed noise and company after a day with his art. And so a never-ending stream of guests was invited over to their apartment every weekend evening. Sukhanov's face would have the feverish look of someone in the midst of creative ecstasy, when everything is possible and the intangible in the mind will be touched in a future moment that is wonderfully close. He got by working at a desk job somewhere, though he so rarely mentioned it that I never could remember what he did there. Lena always seemed pretty glamorous; she was a sound technician at a local TV station and had an incredible ringing laugh.

Sukhanov's style was varied: sometimes he painted abstract images—waves of colour or stunning metallic-looking sheets like oil on water—or he made the familiar uncanny, guitars and violins with their strings set loose, floating in the air, or a single term like *glasnost* or *perestroika* with the letters jumbled or put down in uneven jagged lines, as if they'd fallen out of their words.

Music, either from someone's guitar or the cassette player, filled every space in their apartment. The place was tiny but decent. Their bed was the couch, usually folded out with several people lying or sitting on it. Scents of cheap Armenian brandy and bitter tobacco smoke old and new hung in the air. Even with a window open the air was close; there was something full about it, as though nothing from outside could intrude upon our loud oasis.

I met Anya one night at the Sukhanovs' place. Anna Mikhailovna. On that night, or many, Anya wore a white t-shirt belted into jeans—it was 1988, most of us were wearing jeans. She stood by the sink in the kitchen—really a few cupboards and a stove just off the main room—pouring red wine into a glass, her head tilted to one side. She had a round, pretty face and blonde hair to her shoulders. We got talking and she said she was studying philosophy.

I went to Gorky with Ilya, I said. I looked over to where my friend was laughing and talking loudly at the other end of the room, drink in hand.

She nodded, raised her eyebrows. I heard there were a few writers here, she said. My friend from class kept talking about your group. Painters and poets and novelists.

We want to be, anyway, I said.

Yeah, I want to write, she said. But everything feels too constricted here. I'd love to leave. Move to Berlin or Paris or somewhere.

She spoke about her idol, Lou Andreas-Saloméa, a Russian-born woman said to have been the first female psychoanalyst. Lover of the poet Rilke, friend of Nietzsche and Freud.

She was really interesting, said Anya. Something made her feel separate from the people around her, alone in company. Even as a child she preferred to talk to flowers and made up stories about people she saw in the street. She was all about her ideas. I want to write books that are good *thinking*, not just good stories.

Anya had a kind of hard confidence about her and didn't smile much. She had ashy-looking dark circles under her eyes, but rather than make her look tired, they gave her face a beautiful weariness. I was hooked.

We were all struck by a deep longing for art. From Kandinsky we all took on the idea of inner necessity—that there is something inner that drives you to make your own art. We were all trying to create something of our own, to paint the canvas given to us by *glasnost*. It felt like an inheritance, in a way, from the underground, the repressed artists and writers who came before us. A thing we could only make together but that came from our individual inner lives.

This country suffocates me sometimes, Anya was saying. Like something is wrong with the air.

I said something ridiculous, only half serious, about how great art is made under repression. Look at the greats, the poets, I said. They fought back with their art. Look at music today—that's all about working against the system.

She shook her head. Saying art thrives under suffering gives some kind of excuse to the things that cause the suffering. Illness is illness. Pain is the beginning and the end. Political killings are murder.

We moved from the kitchen to sit against the wall below the windowsill in the lounge room. Anya seemed interested in my parents' lives, Oleg and the dissidents, in my writing or at least my impatience to create. It was as though we both sensed we were on the verge of something, of art maybe, and like the others in that apartment, cramped yet free, we stood there, at the edge, together. Really it was an unknown abyss in front of us, but we were tired of Moscow's state-sanctioned life—boring culture clubs, monotonous working days at grey jobs, eating the same food every day and barely able to afford the black-market clothes and music we wanted—and so the abyss was, like any freedom, full of both fear and beauty.

Anya and I began to see a lot of each other. She said the group at the Sukhanovs' place inspired her. I hoped that she also wanted to be around me. I was never as confident as Ilya, but it must have been obvious that I liked her: I gave her books that I loved, and we tentatively shared our writing, our ideas. Like many Soviet couples desperate for space of their own, we took each other to our favourite spots—walks in parks and through narrow suburban streets, finding places to sit on the river embankment or on park benches. In novels and in life, it seemed every couple in Moscow had a story of their favourite bench, their beloved park, and that over time we all shared the same embankments and benches and grassy parks as our parents and grandparents.

The city was our canvas. Our lives that summer were all about loud, smoky gatherings in the Sukhanovs' apartment, shouted political demonstrations on the Arbat, and the dimly lit, thumping world of rock concerts in basements or abandoned shopfronts. From the bustling, musical Arbat to Novopushkinskaya Park, rippling green with dashes of colour where people lay or walked, and then to the crowded crimson-brick desert of Pushkin Square.

Summer heat, summer sun. A thin breeze. We stood on the Arbat. Anya reached out to hand me a placard. We held them in the air: HELP FILL THE BLANK SPOTS OF HISTORY, SUPPORT THE MEMORIAL FOR STALIN'S VICTIMS, or something similar. Ilya stood on a wooden box, calling out to the crowds. Slowly we collected signatures on single sheets of onionskin paper. Our placards shuddered in the breeze. The importance of words felt unbounded, and their repression the strongest method for locking away the horrors of the past: *To keep alive the memory of the victims of political repression* was the Memorial Society's motto.

I understood early on that Anya's aversion to the Soviet Union, her desire to leave, was not a fleeting thing. She had been drawn to the West for as long as she could remember. One night that summer, we were sharing a cigarette on a bench in Novopushkinskaya Park. The heat was pressing. In the humidity, Anya's cheeks, neck and chest had a thin shine of sweat that made me wish our bodies were close. The park hosted a shifting crowd, a summer crowd: mothers with pigtailed girls, kids kicking cans or soccer balls, grandfathers with ice cream and cigarettes.

Germany, said Anya. That's where. When I was little, I had this picture of somewhere in Germany. It was probably the East, but right now anywhere is fine by me. From there I could get to the West. I don't even know where we got it, but it was a postcard with nothing written on it. I'd seen something about Germany on TV, and just had this strange feeling, knowing there was this other place where, right now, people were living lives I knew nothing about. It was like this strong desire.

Germany, I said.

Germany.

We sat for a while longer, an easy quiet between us. The sun lowered, our silence smooth as the easing heat and the drifting, indistinct voices collecting in the heights of the air over Novopushkinskaya Park.

In a way it attracted me, knowing she wanted a world away from the one we lived in. I didn't need to think too far ahead. Young summers always feel endless.

Anya made me want to stop sitting around talking about writing and actually finish something. When she asked me what I was working on, what my plans were, it was with the expectation that I'd actually do something. I felt high on anticipation.

After a few weeks Anya invited me over. She lived with her parents in an apartment not far from Frunzenskaya Embankment. It was a Moscow I didn't know well: affluent, leafy, with neoclassical mustard-and-sand buildings looking to both Neskuchny Garden and Gorky Park. Her parents weren't home. Anya said they were away in Leningrad visiting relatives.

Beyond the kitchen I could see a living room and doors leading from it into other rooms. There were bookcases of dark wood with a few neat volumes, a leather chair in one corner, another chair and a divan against the wall. On the wall was a large painting, in the shadows, and curtains that looked plush in their heavy, mountainous folds.

In Anya's room I saw the postcard of the unnamed German town on the windowsill, resting against the glass as though it was a substitute for the mustard-yellow building seen through the real window. She had another print taped to the wall. I walked over, hands in pockets, and looked at it closely.

Sveshnikov, she said, nodding. I love his work—though I don't know if love's the right word for that kind of art.

After a moment she said, I admire him.

I knew Boris Sveshnikov's works. He had spent years in Vetlosian, one of the labour camps in the Urals. At first he wasn't able to get hold of materials to paint or draw, but eventually, on changing camps due to a friend's help, he was able to access paper and pen to keep his art going. His works were marked by their melancholic faces bathed in tense, stormy colours, the elongated, reaching hands of pearly green, the cloaked grey figures, skeletal yet somehow still alive.

The print on Anya's wall showed a city view formed of teal, dark purple, aquamarine and light pink square dashes, almost like rainbow-coloured fish scales. A female face looked on from a strange perspective, as if the artist was standing with her on a hill somewhere above the city. Her lips and eyebrows were thin and her eyes were clouded with greenish shadows. The title was *Recollection*. I couldn't see any roads, but the longer I stared, more faces emerged from the city.

There was an eerie sound to it in my mind, like a musical violence inside the image.

It's odd, said Anya, with a serious expression now familiar to me. After he was released, Sveshnikov's style changed. The drawings he did in the camp were very realistic—depictions of torture, or dead bodies lying on the ground while people walking by look the other way. But his later paintings are more surreal, almost distorted. The figures look less and less like any recognisable human form.

I think I've seen some of those, I said. Sveshnikov said he didn't paint for any political reason, he painted for the grave.

Anya nodded slowly. But maybe because his art changed so much, she said, that's what was political about it, even if he didn't want it to be.

We were quiet for a moment. I thought it was almost as though, during his time in the camp, the rules of expression had undergone a mutilation of their own in the deep recesses of the artist's mind.

Since Gorbachev's call for openness, the press had begun to carry revelations, memories, stories—horrors in an endless stream—and Anya told me that she had become obsessed with these stories of the past.

My mother hates it, she said. She can't understand why I would want to read it all, let alone why I'd want a picture like Sveshnikov's in my room. Whenever I ask her about her own past, she insists there's nothing to tell. *I've got no stories*, she says. But she lived through Stalin's years. Everyone's got a story. This whole city's a story.

I watched Anya as she went to stand by the window, looking at the postcard or maybe just through the glass at the building opposite. She lit a cigarette and turned around.

My father's is a more complicated story, she said. Slowly a thin smoke plume dissolved in front of her. I'll tell you about it sometime.

I walked over, touched her hair, soft blonde reeds, repeating the motion as though committing the act to memory. To be in a room of our own, Anya's bedroom, had a silence and freedom about it. Usually you found a few minutes at a friend's university dorm or the living room divan in the apartment where you grew up—having that place of our own felt like an entirely new space, almost a new life.

CHAPTER 8

A week after my mother's funeral, I took a train from St Petersburg in the direction of silence and the *dacha*. It was August 1999. Lenin's bronze arm still reached out over the square at Finland Station. As the train left the city behind and the railroad cut through forests, the tracks were enfolded by walls of deep green. There were few towns along the way. As we passed into the Kurortny District, some grey wooden buildings and old farm plots emerged here and there like the remnants of a village wiped away by a storm the previous day or half a century before.

Scenes appeared like set pieces. A grey-haired woman waited at a bus stop that had lost its walls except for one, on which was scrawled *Mama, Happy Birthday!* in green paint. An old couple entered a wooden house so slowly they might have been approaching it for hours already. At an unknown train station, someone stood tossing crumbs to a flock of pigeons while the birds all flapped their wings, stepping to and fro like a confused crowd. Then each view disappeared as if it had never been.

Through the window I saw clouds gathering weight and darkening. A few heavy flecks of rain hit the glass. In the seat across from me, two women tied plastic bags over their shoes as we gained on Repino station.

Less than an hour after leaving the city, I stepped out onto the platform at Repino. As the train pulled away, I saw rows of passengers sitting still as though frozen, their faces indistinct through the rain-blurred glass. At the station's edge, the forest began immediately. I knew the sea was nearby. I had seen the Gulf of Finland as a serrated blue ribbon on the map folded somewhere in my belongings. The eastern arm of the Baltic Sea, it joined Finland, Estonia and Russia in uncertain watery borders. I had read that below the waters, on the silent sand of the gulf floor, was one of the largest known ship graveyards. Since the gulf sea was especially cold, and the salt levels low, some two thousand broken vessels were preserved down there as if time didn't bother with them.

Near the station was a small shop, a few houses and a weary-looking bistro. Two boys in Adidas tracksuits shared a cigarette beside the grey road. I went to buy a newspaper and some food. A man with clumpy brown hair stood speaking to the cashier. He held a plastic bag, a newspaper under his elbow, but stood to one side, continuing to talk as though not ready to leave. The new prime minister, they were saying. Vladimir Vladimirovich Putin.

The woman nodded and held up a newspaper, her polished purple nails tapping at the edges of the page. And maybe president for him next year, so I hear. Out with old Yeltsin before he falls over, in with a strong man again, please, said the woman, and she rolled her eyes up to the ceiling, where plasterboard sagged like the billowed sail of a boat. I picked up a paper and read the first lines: *In one year, for the first time in the country's history, the first president of Russia will transfer power to a fresh, newly elected president,* Yeltsin said. *In any case, he will be your president, respected Russians, he who has won in honest and clean elections.* He went on to speak of his trust in the new prime minister.

I bought bread, jam, a few apples. I decided not to buy a newspaper and left the *produkti* shop soon after.

Walking on, after half an hour or so I reached the outskirts of town, where the roads were frayed at the edges with crumbling tar. There was one bus stop, still and lonely as though abandoned. I left the main street and followed a wide dirt road into a forest. A few houses seemed to watch my passage, like timid forest beasts, through the tall pines and draping willows. The leaves dripped. I read again the instructions scribbled on the paper in my hand, looked up and saw that I had reached the small *dacha* where I was to stay. The house had vertical weatherboards of the lightest green, almost white. I found the key hidden underneath a red brick, as Sergei Ivanovich had told me it would be.

I opened the front door and, feeling heavy with city heat, I let my two bags fall to the floor. The *dacha* was cool and smelt of dust, so I left the door open and took a few steps in. The wooden floorboards were softly worn. There was a sense of peace in walking through rooms I knew nothing about. I didn't know the front window view or how it might change across the seasons, and I didn't know the scents in the thin cotton bedsheets. In the kitchen there were three unmatched chairs, a somehow diminished number, which held no mark of past occupants. On the walls were several small paintings, of valley views, the Neva River in another time. A few books on a high narrow shelf. There were no photos. On the kitchen table were two empty vases. As I moved them to a shelf, the glass felt cold. There was no samovar but I found a heat coil, a glass, then warmed water for tea.

I left the kitchen and stood at the front window of the *dacha*, slowly drinking tea. There was a desk, a chair and little else in the front room. An ideal writing room, I thought. Over a view of pale road and countless birch trees, the clouds grew darker still. Heavy drops gathered speed, a liquid canter at the window. For a few minutes the rain eclipsed all other sounds with its heavy fall, but soon left an unlikely silence.

Like St Petersburg, Repino was much further north than Moscow. In that gaping midsummer day, twilight came well after midnight. A bare hour of semi-darkness coated the trees in blue before treading an unseen boundary to another day. I walked through the house. The thinning curtains, the whitewashed walls, made the dusty and near-empty rooms glow. I slept little.

In the morning I went outside early. The grass was wild and overgrown, flattened here and there by a few pots and wet with yesterday's rain. In the yard behind the house were the remains of a vegetable garden, some lettuce or cabbage hanging on. From where I stood in the backyard, to my right was a house, to my left a grassy, empty block, and ahead of me, the forest.

I heard children's voices drifting, hitting at the walls of the houses or the underside of leaves high in the air. Clusters of berries hung in a mass of red beside the house next door. Behind the neighbour's house, a mysterious city of greenhouses and small sheds extended towards the encroaching forest. Green shrubs pressed against the hazy windows of the greenhouses, their reaching twigs entwined with disintegrating brown plants so that it was difficult to tell the living from the dead. The sheds had disordered roofs of grey corrugated iron and tall grass guarded the doors. Wooden boards painted yellow, green and sky-blue lay fallen, crushing the stems of the overgrown lawn. Loose paths, grey and pebbly, bowed aimlessly.

I walked to the edge of the yard, where there was a low, sagging wire fence dividing the *dacha* from the neighbour's property. As I moved closer to the ancient trees, they almost completely obscured the sky. The air was humid and heavy, full of mosquitoes.

A tall man stepped out of one of the greenhouses. At a guess he was aged in his seventies, with tousled grey hair and a wide wrinkled face, thick eyebrows. He held up one arm in a slow wave and walked over.

I wasn't sure I felt like talking, but he was approaching so I had to say something. Hello, I called out.

He squinted, nodded.

Pasha, I said. He shook my hand but didn't say his name.

You'd be a city boy, he said.

Yeah, Petersburg.

Same as us, he said, nodding to his unseen family in the house. Here with the wife and grandkids.

I'm in Primorsky, I said. Pretty quiet place.

We're on Vasilyevsky Island too. Not as far out. You're almost swimming out there—a grin cracked his face—nearly in the water.

I grinned too. Yeah, nearly swimming.

Come on over. He waved an arm again, then turned and walked towards a small shed.

I stepped over the fence. Twigs cracked under my feet. He went into the shed and I followed. Musty green, plants and dust. Lots of bottles lined up in a row. The neighbour was hunched over in one corner; jostling bottles released precise clinks and echoes.

My father's recipe, said the neighbour as he turned around and brushed off a stray leaf, a few dusty roots that clung like webs to the tall bottles. Home-brew, *samogon*. My father called it his secret *samogon*. Used to hide the bottles in the forest near our house when I was growing up. I'm not originally from the city. He'd bring one out every now and then, careful not to let the local committee know, if you see what I mean. The neighbour pointed his thumb to the air, meaning *them, up there*, wherever the authorities were. My mother and Oleg had always done the same and I felt a vague, old longing, thinking of them.

The neighbour held up a bottle at eye level, as if speaking to it. *Clear as a tear*, he said. That's what my father would say. You don't want it cloudy. They're some of the few memories I have of the man. Of my father. He'd walk in with a bottle, huge grin on his face. And now look at all these bottles here. They say it's legal now to make your own, but you never know. Seems I've inherited my father's secretive ways.

The neighbour winked. The wrinkles on his face deepened with his smile, his wheezy laugh. He held out the bottle; I smiled with him and took it.

Homemade, I said, feeling the cool, dusty glass. Haven't had any of this for a while. Sometimes my mother's friends brought over *samogon* when I was young.

He'd turned his back and I saw through the gloom that there was a little table in the shed. He was pouring us a drink each. We held up our glasses, nodded, threw back the drink. The shot released a wave of memory. I felt hollow and thought of my mother, dying alone in Moscow. Then I saw that afternoon as a twelve-year-old, sharing secret brandy with Dmitry. I had no idea what had happened to him. He'd moved suburbs before high school.

Dusty brown light filtered through the window in the shed. It was only morning and I wondered how I'd step outside and last the rest of the day. In the next moment, years from my previous thought, the neighbour moved out of the shed and I followed him.

Come for dinner tonight, Pasha, he said, and I heard myself say yes.

We parted ways in the humid air. The neighbour walked towards his house, holding against his chest two bottles of *samogon*—a liquid as invisible and incapable of freezing as memories. Beating away a few mosquitoes, carrying the bottle the neighbour had given me, I walked back between the leafy city of greenhouses, over the defeated fence, to lie down in the shade of the trees where the forest began.

In the afternoon, I took a long walk along the dusty road running in front of the house. Soon I reached the forest I had walked through the day before. I felt as though I'd arrived at the *dacha* a long time ago. Following the map I'd brought with me, I passed through thinner, scrubby trees and sandy dirt and eventually reached the water. I scanned my eyes from one end of the coast to the other, taking in the unending plane of sand and sea. The beach was empty. Where traces of tide left a watery glaze, the sand reflected a couple of clouds in the blue sky. The water, part of the Gulf of Finland, was the same that I could see through the bedroom window of my sixth-floor apartment in Primorsky. Looking out across the blue, I stood in awe of how close I was to another country. That the air, a life, a day, could be so different just over there, a sudden transformation at some point over the invisible border with Finland.

Yura's wife Piia was Finnish. He sometimes said he loved that she was from somewhere else; other times he wondered if the gap between their experiences was too vast. I said I didn't know if it was better to be with someone who had felt similar things. They seemed a good match, though.

Standing there at the water's edge, I was reminded of another ill-defined border between Finland and Russia, where the two countries met in the waters of Lake Ladoga. The lake wasn't far from where I was, in the north. I knew that it sometimes froze over, as if time stopped, and it became possible to cross the blurry threshold. This had happened in the war when the lake became the Road of Life. With Leningrad staggering in a German ring, each winter for two and a half years, Ladoga offered the only way out of the besieged city, like a frozen link between two worlds, or between death and life. And yet it wasn't solid, safe earth, but more of an imagined place. And so sometimes the false ground broke and trucks with Leningraders fleeing death or, driving the other way, with supplies bringing life were taken beneath the splitting ice. Lives stopped in the chasm, neither leaving nor arriving. It made me shiver, to think of that ice, and the wartime darkness of those night-time attempts to cross the tenuous, illusory land.

I took off my shoes and socks, setting one foot then the other onto the hard, damp sand. I walked a few paces into the water. The cold sand stirred. The water wasn't freezing, as I'd thought it would be; it must have been icy just a few months before. I decided I'd come back to the house in the winter sometime. The snow would fall as it liked, uninterrupted by buildings or cold commuters and schoolchildren trying to get through city streets. It would just fall, silent and violent and soft. Suddenly I craved winter, its consoling quiet.

Small waves rolled between my legs in the water. Old words, nearly forgotten, ebbed and drifted, coming close to my mind before rolling away, as though I'd lost the full moment as the water receded from my legs. I wondered if the waves on this shore were ever big enough to make a proper ocean roar. Sometimes in Moscow if you walked close by the multi-lane boulevards when it was raining, the roll of traffic on the enduring wet bitumen made the sound of waves.

I thought I should go back to the *dacha* and continue with my writing. I once spoke to an old writer, from my parents' generation, about how there were so few novels around about more recent events in the country, like the fall of the Soviet Union and even *glasnost* in the eighties. He said to me that we were not ready. A decade was a small measure when it came to history's shifting fault lines. It was too soon after the events. I wondered, standing in the water near Repino, if that immeasureable time was more effective than physical distance. I'd fled Moscow, but maybe time was the vital gap needed to view things as the past instead of feeling them as the present, such as it was.

For some reason I thought about the time I'd said to Anya that if she ever died, I'd move away, to the other end of the country. As far east as I could go: Vladivostok or Magadan or further, over the Bering Sea and beyond. Looking back, I was struck by how easy it was for me, as a young man, to throw words around like that, as though throwing them at fate. If fate existed. But in a way it had thrilled my young self, the starkness, the confessional feel of the words. She never said the same thing back to me, but then again she didn't like to say too much about what she felt, let alone about some imaginary future emotion. The future is forever not here.

I had a couple of hours before dinner at the neighbour's house, so I went back to the *produkti* and bought a few bottles of beer. At the *dacha* I sat on a seat outside the house, slowly drinking, watching nothing much at all. The clouds broke, giving way to an invisible evening of bright sun.

CHAPTER 9

I waited outside our apartment building, leaning against a wall with a smoke. It was a Saturday or Sunday—I didn't have to work that day—and families were out in the street, probably walking towards the Arbat, to weekend markets or the cool of city parks. I never really stood in the street anymore. When I was a boy I'd get bored after a while and walk around the building, or find Dmitry and Artyom to hang around with. Now I just rushed on; there was always somewhere to be. It was hot and muggy, the sky heavy with masses of grey and white.

There she was. Anya walked along the street, stepped quickly aside for an entwined couple walking the other way, and then spotted me. She smiled and held up one hand in an unhurried wave.

Though we were both children of the Freeze, Brezhnev's years, Anya wanted to hear my stories about what it was like to grow up a child of dissidents, of those who tried to break the ice. She wanted me to describe what the apartment looked like during my childhood when the underground meetings were held there. Although she was now standing in those very rooms, it was as though Anya saw two separate places, and the apartment of my childhood was an entirely different place, kept in a past she did not know but longed to. I told her about the adults standing around the table, my mother at the typewriter, the brandy-and-smoke air, the way I'd lie on the divan, listening to the radio and the murmurs beneath the yellow light from the kitchen.

It's like there's been two lines, I said, describing them in the air with my index fingers. One to follow outside, and one to live by at home. Easier not to confuse the two. Not to bring the outside in.

But now, she said. Now it's so different.

Yeah, now. *Glasnost* has been strange. I had a sort of inherited reality—the truth of the camps, the repressions under Stalin—and now it's *here*, in the world outside.

I looked at the bookshelves, which Anya was standing beside, browsing through. She moved to sit on the divan. Her presence there seemed to change the apartment for me, turn it into something else, some other place. She, my girl, in the apartment of my childhood, where I'd rarely had anyone from the outside visit.

Just as she now existed there, inside, the authors I'd read and loved now existed somewhere other than on those shelves, other than between the four walls we stood within. They were mentioned in newspapers, published in *Novy Mir* and *Ogonyok*. They weren't just confined to precious single copies handed from one underground meeting to another. Suddenly people were reading them, Shalamov and Platonov and Brodsky, on the metro and on park benches. Whenever I saw those writers, my writers, being read in public, I almost felt as though the reader had taken the book or journal from my own home.

We took a train to Izmaylovsky. Still overcast and humid, the day threatened rain. Anya had a scarf around her shoulders. I could hear the echo of voices from the Izmaylovsky Market, but we kept to the forested area. There were birch woods, dense with thin white trees, papery trunks with dark brown splits like slashed paper. The artificial ponds carved from the rivers hundreds of years ago were glassy, coolly inviting, and I could see Silver Island, where a cathedral stood.

I don't really need this, Anya said. My *babushka* scarf. She laughed and pulled it around her. We sat down under a big oak tree. Anya crossed her legs and she started telling me about her father and grandfather. Her grandfather was some tyrant for Stalin, she said, and had been one at home too, it seemed. He drank, had lots of affairs. And Anya's father, he hadn't been well for as long as Anya could remember.

He's just returned from the hospital again, she said. I have this idea that he needs to talk to someone separate from that system. He keeps going back to those psychiatric clinics, but I don't think they're helping him. He seems interested in the Memorial Society, the work they're doing with recording people's stories, oral interviews. I thought at first that I'd try to write about my grandfather, and my father, about their lives. But my mother doesn't like me bringing up anything about the past, especially not around my father. Maybe if someone else asks to speak with him, it would be different. You could write about my father.

I suggested that we could write together, and so that was what we decided to do. We'd write about both of our families. I told her how my own father had been arrested for his underground activity and was analysed in a psychiatric hospital in Moscow. I was so young when it happened, I remembered little. Or maybe the mind sends those sorts of memories somewhere deeper than we can readily perceive. I remembered things on the cusp of feelings, though they didn't feel like real emotions, just dull anxieties or unformed fears. I could recollect a handful of images, usually involving adults talking around our table and me hearing his name from the divan where I'd been sent to sleep; the fraught peal of the telephone and that yellow light thrown on the wall from the kitchen. A light with voices, it was, always accompanied by the radio or murmurs from the table. I could recall vitamin pills and how important they were, those orange pills, for his health, the way my mother sent them with a look of such fierce care, sent them to the prison ward, along with letters, or so I imagined, that I never got to read. He had never made it out of prison; he died in there when I was ten. He and some other prisoners went on a hunger strike.

Anya listened closely as I talked, watching me with those eyes faintly ringed with dark circles, blonde hair tucked behind her ears, her hands resting lightly together.

It's interesting that you haven't written about him before, she said.

Yeah, I said, feeling distantly that she was pressing at thoughts I hadn't myself touched. My writing so far had been surreal stories, inspired by Bulgakov and other writers who distorted reality in a disturbing way—I wrote a story about the Soviet bureaucracy operating in hell, for example, with applicants taking years to get there, hanging in limbo while the devil decided if he'd let them into the inferno.

Well, I said, sensing that we were forming the thing we wanted to write, well, maybe I will, now.

We took the metro back into the city. I walked with Anya to Frunzenskaya Embankment. I pointed to the other side of the river, the embankment running alongside Gorky Park, and told her how Oleg used to take me walking along there. I knew she liked to hear those stories.

It was while we were walking together along the embankment when I was a boy that Oleg told me about the Philosophers' Ships. Oleg often took me for walks. He must have sensed when home was too quiet for me, particularly after my father was taken and it was just my mother and me in the apartment. Over the long holidays, in the summer, we would buy birch tree juice somewhere near the Arbat; that glass of sugary liquid was all the more attached to my childhood as it became a far rarer thing to see in stores in later years. On one of those outings, we were watching a ferry edge its way up or down Moskva River; we could not see anybody on board and it looked just peaceful, gliding over the teal ripples of the water, reflecting away the strength of the August sun.

Pausing, staring out across the water with his arms crossed at his chest, Oleg said to me, It was about this time of year— early autumn, in fact—that the Philosophers' Ships set sail from a port in Petrograd, which was the name of Leningrad for some time, at the end of September in 1922. There were two ships, filled on Lenin's orders with the strongest intellectual minds of the time: the philosophers and the historians, the sociologists and the economists. The ships set sail on that autumn day, exiting through the Gulf of Finland, and the philosophers were sent away forever. Some argue that banishment was more humane than what came later for other such free thinkers, but I see it as just as destructive as any physical death. The ships went to Germany, so it is said, and from there the philosophers and scholars moved on, scattered across Western Europe and America. Yet I sometimes like to think that those ships did not set down in Germany that autumn and send forth our thinkers to new lives there, but rather that they never actually docked anywhere. I see them continuing their voyage over the oceans, never finding another place of their own, rocking over midnight-dark waves, passing unknown islands that emerge just above the surface like a slumbering ocean beast, easing the ships over calm dawn waters where lonely, pink, beautiful skies very nearly break their hearts each morning. And I sometimes have it in mind that they found their way back, so to speak, in more recent years, arriving unbeknown to us on a dark winter morning in Moscow or Leningrad, Perm or Murmansk, but were then lost in this Russia they did not know. At certain times, in those gruff, bearded drinkers you see out in the city on winter nights, their faces lit by flames in an old drum, in orange glow and shadows, rumbling seriously to each other, I almost see the image of them, the lost philosophers, roaming and adrift, wondering where their Russia has gone, without anymore having a place here.

The rippling blue of Moskva River, the water pulled along by a thin breeze. It was warm along the embankment, in the heat of the summer sun.

CHAPTER 10

I first went to Patriarch's Ponds, in Moscow's Tverskoy District, when I was eleven years old. I took a metro by myself after school, using a five-kopek metro coin I had in my schoolbag, then walked along Gorky Street and took a left turn onto one of the side streets to reach the ponds. There was only one pond that I saw, round and dark blue and still, surrounded by snowy lawns and lampposts. It would have been 1976.

I was there again in the summer of 1988. Ilya and I sat on one of the benches and I described that first visit. It was a location in my favourite book at the time, Bulgakov's *The Master and Margarita*. Oleg had handed me a copy a few weeks earlier, very worn, its cover wrapped in an old copy of *Pravda* newspaper. I'd read the book, I said to Ilya, and just wanted to see what it was like. I laughed. But it was February, four in the afternoon, winter dark. Ran home terrified.

Ilya laughed too and smoke tumbled from his mouth. For a while he had been talking of an odd group, some of them underground writers, some drunken bums, who were meeting in Bulgakov's old apartment building for readings, or just

68

for a place to go. The apartment was on Bolshaya Sadovaya Street, not far from Patriarch's Ponds, the infamous place where Berlioz, editor of a literary journal and board chairman of a Moscow literary association, is murdered in the opening pages of Bulgakov's novel. He meets a strange man, a very chatty 'foreigner', and within a few pages of that meeting Berlioz is hit and killed by a tram. It terrified me as a child: innocently Berlioz asks the foreigner Woland where he intends to stay while in Moscow, to which Woland replies with a smile, *Your house.*

What scared me was how subtle and almost benign the evil had appeared at first. Words, that was all, just words between poor Berlioz and a man sitting on a bench at Patriarch's Ponds; but it was a man who just happened to be Satan. Words became tinged with some unknowable madness, and Berlioz met his end.

Though it was summer as I sat on the bench with Ilya, I kept thinking of my winter trip there as an eleven-year-old. Being in the place of the crime, which seemed very real to me, was terrifying. The pond had sealed itself in ice and the trees were thin, sickly bodies. Thick fog stole the streetlamps and I may or may not have seen a man, dressed in a suit, on the other side of the water. I almost shivered again now at the memory. Somehow the warped Moscow given to me by Bulgakov in his novel amplified past horrors I'd not witnessed, and left a greater resonance than the Moscow that our dissident friends at home recalled late into the night, sipping tea after mentioning three disappeared friends in one breath. They spoke of *the repressions, the Terror,* and I could not really see or comprehend those things. But in Bulgakov's writing, it became starkly real. It was always books that told me life.

Come on, brother, Bulgakov's apartment—let's go, said Ilya, nudging me with an elbow. He had on his leather jacket, his black hair was heavy with gel, and he tapped his leg restlessly against the park bench. He was always like that before a night out. And always humming, as though he had a beat or melody permanently switched on in his mind.

Number ten, apartment fifty, Ilya recited, nodding as we walked, stepping in time with his nods. Off busy Bolshaya Sadovaya Street, awash with cars and heat, number ten began at a wide, low-ceilinged entranceway, the number marked just above head height. From there we went into a courtyard. High walls made a cool dim dusk away from the sunny street. Number fifty was on our left. Bulgakov's apartment was on the fourth floor but it was really the stairwell, not the apartment, that had become the meeting place of students, young dissident artists and writers, fans of Bulgakov, curious observers, lonely drinkers. I wasn't sure what Bulgakov's old rooms looked like, since we never actually went inside. Sukhanov and Lena were already there. Sukhanov pushed through a few people and came over to say hello. Lena followed slowly, taller than ever in thin-heeled boots, her lips painted pink. She kissed my cheek and then Ilya's, and asked me if Anya was coming. I briefly explained that she was busy with her family. Her mother had to go out, and Anya had to stay home with her father. A guy in a denim jacket, an artist friend of Sukhanov's, shook our hands enthusiastically, and a few others handed us each a can of beer.

This place is incredible—look at the artwork. Sukhanov gestured at the walls. His cheeks shone in the dim light. Anyone can write their own work there, or messages, quotes from Bulgakov's work, he said. But I say no more cat drawings. He laughed. There's enough bloody cats.

He took Lena's shoulders in his hands and announced, We're going to find that artist guy—I want to draw something on the walls. The two of them made their way over to a young guy talking in a small group. Ilya saw a poet friend and went over to speak to him. I went to look at the artwork.

The walls of the stairwell beside the stairs were covered in scattered scrawls, mostly in black ink, tilted left and right in long paragraphs. Over and around the words were strange drawings. There were many cats, as Sukhanov said—that weirdly human animal who accompanies the satanic whirlwind through Bulgakov's Moscow. Just as they were in the novel, the cats seemed unnerving, not entirely animal. Some sat on chairs, one leg crossed over the other; another stared almost derisively out at the gathering on the stairs, a careful paw at its spectacles; and one, sitting poised with feline grace and wearing a bow-tie, put one thick paw regally before it, while a gun dangled casually from the other.

I tried to imagine Bulgakov walking up those same stairs, turning the doorknob to enter his apartment, sitting down at his desk to begin another evening of writing, which I imagined he did after his wife had gone to bed, lamplight dim, the air close, slightly suffocating him in his study. I imagined him agonising over each word, every line, wondering what would get past the censors and what would be slashed like his heart. For me, Bulgakov had the same sort of presence as writers like Shalamov, as the voices from Radio Liberty who spoke to me from the mint-green radio on our kitchen table. Heard but not seen, felt but not touched.

I stood close to the wall outside Bulgakov's apartment, reached out and trailed a finger along one line of small, neat writing as if coursing a path on a map: *I am a historian. There will be a most interesting occurrence at Patriarch's Ponds this evening!*

I looked around. People sat in small, quiet circles stood alone reading the walls, or moved between groups. Ilya had joined a loud group with Sukhanov. Lena was talking to another girl with long black hair tied back. Nobody had to mention the author. We just wanted to be where he had been. Our presence acknowledged an unspoken respect, a kind of innate love for the dead writer.

I stood at the walls for a while, rereading passages I knew well. A young man, tall with light brown hair, black-framed glasses, olive skin and a gentle sort of face, stood quietly reading as well, and we were soon talking. Neither of us had been to the building before.

I'm Yura, he said.

He told me he had heard of the apartment from an acquaintance, a musician. Unlike others gathered in the stairwell, the many hand-waving students and poets, Yura was not full of idealism. He seemed thoughtful, a bit distant, as though he'd just paused partway through a long search for something. I asked whether he lived in Moscow, whether and where he was a student.

I'm trying to be an academic, he said, rubbing the back of his head. Science and the academy is all a joke here, though. Unless of course you have certain contacts.

A few young guys and two girls passed us on the stairs, one of the girls carrying a guitar.

I'm also trying to make my way out of here, said Yura, gazing for a moment at the group passing us. I want to move to the West.

I'm guessing that's pretty tough, I said.

Sure is, said Yura, raising his eyebrows once. Especially for a Jewish scientist.

You could write an article, I suggested. Getting some attention is a start. Me and Ilya—I waved an arm over at the group Ilya had joined—we've published a few things, we could help.

Maybe. Yura nodded. He gave a half-smile, as though grateful but unsure. I've never really done anything political before, he said. To be honest, I just feel the country is beyond change and I'd rather get out.

Think about it, though. A lot has changed since Brezhnev.

Yura shrugged and gave that uncertain smile again. You seem to know a lot about all of this, all the politics, he said.

I shrugged too, and said something about it running in the family.

My parents tried to emigrate in the seventies, said Yura. But no luck. He shook his head, as if something had bothered him for a long time. If only they had, I could be in New York right now, he continued. Your parents do one thing different, even your grandparents, and that's it for you.

A friend of mine has always wanted to live abroad, I told him, thinking of Anya. I don't think I ever really thought about it seriously until I spoke to her. But I'm sure things are going to change now, with Gorbachev.

Yura looked up at a large portrait of a cat with red eyes above us. I'm going to hope you're right, Pasha, he said.

I invited him over to where Ilya, Sukhanov and Lena stood. We sat against the old walls, drank beer and stayed for a few hours in the echoes of Bulgakov's presence, under the gaze of the malevolent cats and scrawls of *Manuscripts don't burn!*

CHAPTER 11

I left the *dacha*, not bothering to lock the door, walked under a burning sun into the next yard and knocked at the front door of the neighbour's house. No one answered, so I opened the door and entered a short, dim hallway. I entered the first room on my left, which was the kitchen. I heard oil spitting in a pan, and a radio, a woman's voice drifting at a low volume.

The neighbour's wife stood at the stove with her head covered in a white cloth, an apron over her dress while she stirred, one after the other, two or three pans and pots of different sizes. She turned to say hello, wiped her hands on her apron and with a warm smile pressed her palms to the sides of my arms. Her name was Vera Sergeyevna. The grandchildren were already at the table, playing with cutlery, the youngest kicking his legs beneath the table.

Pasha, boy, you're here, the neighbour said as he walked in. He moved about eagerly. Over a dinner of cutlets, potatoes and mushrooms in butter, and cucumber salad, he spoke constantly across scattered topics—*samogon* recipes, the prices of vodka and wood, Yeltsin's latest prime minister, the work needed on the *dacha* I was staying in. It was as though he had long been awaiting an audience other than the tired one of his wife and the naive one of his grandchildren.

Vera Sergeyevna listened patiently and gave me a knowing, weary smile every now and then as her husband's sentences grew longer and longer. She had something perceptive about her, in her eyes, so that I felt watched closely when she looked at me with her kind smile.

I was distracted, though. Too close to other, older thoughts. I came to some unfocused realisation that I couldn't really lose the desire to write, but what was once an excited longing had hardened into a kind of hopelessness. I'd stopped writing, had effectively stopped thinking, when I came to St Petersburg. I wondered whether my inner silence, the hours spent staring at the ceiling, the unhappiness that overwhelmed me at times, were the dying echoes of my old creative longings, the certainty that I would one day create something.

I repeated the thought to myself: the impulse to create art, when frustrated, doesn't disappear, but manifests itself in other ways. It was the first thought in a long time that I wanted to write down. That rare desire felt like Moscow to me.

I was half listening to the neighbour. He was talking about his father.

And when we went into the forest, he said, Papa would dig his boot into the ground, mark a line so we could find our way out.

Tak, Pasha, he said suddenly. Tell us about your friends, the ones who were here before you. He waved a piece of bread towards the house next door and then took a bite.

I wasn't sure what to say. Sergei Ivanovich was a member of the Memorial Society, and so I assumed that a few other members stayed at the house from time to time. The neighbour would have noticed different people coming and going. But I didn't know much about their current work. And most of all, I didn't know what it was safe to say. Not that the neighbours looked untrustworthy in any way; I just didn't want to burden them with things they weren't supposed to know. I knew the Memorial Society was still conducting investigations into suspected mass graves from the Stalin years. Oleg had told me as much. Since *glasnost*, ten years earlier, people had continued to come forward with information. For a few years, volunteers had been researching a suspected gravesite thirty kilometres from St Petersburg, near Toksovo.

I thought those things were probably reported in the press. There had been grave-digging expeditions going on for years. If anything, they would probably be ignored by the authorities. But I wasn't sure. I realised, with a pull of guilt or just unease, that I didn't even know what was safe or dangerous anymore.

They're part of a historical research society, I said carefully. The Memorial Society. I used to volunteer for them sometimes when I lived in Moscow. I've come here to write a sort of history, I continued, as if telling myself I still had a cause. I was in Moscow during *glasnost* and the start of the society, so I'd like to record those years somehow.

The neighbour nodded vigorously, murmuring *Da, da, konechno*, as I spoke. Vera Sergeyevna was silent and did not once nod her head. The children focused on their food, looking up now and then, neither interested nor bored. I wondered how much they understood or absorbed from the conversation.

I'd like to show you my own little research project, the neighbour said as we finished the meal. Especially since, as you say, you're writing about the past as well.

I took another drink and nodded.

Vera Sergeyevna scolded him, Oh, don't start on all that, you silly old man. He doesn't want to hear that. She looked away, turned her attention to the children. She seemed uncomfortable, as though she couldn't find enough mouths to wipe or glasses to refill.

The neighbour waved away her protest then beckoned me away from the table. He stood, tucked in the blue-and-green-checked shirt that had escaped his belt, blinked heavily underneath his thick eyebrows, and wandered out of the room. I thanked Vera Sergeyevna for the meal and followed the neighbour down the hallway. We reached a small room, similar to the one I used for writing in the *dacha* next door. The curtains were drawn and the room was dimly lit by two lamps.

Smotri, he said, look at this. I call them ghostless ghost towns.

He tapped his fingers on two maps and a few newspaper articles on the table. Resting in two puddles of lamplight, the papers looked yellow with age, though I gathered the neighbour had collected them relatively recently.

The children, who had crept into the room, looked on, innocently taking on the strange, eager mood of their *dedushka*, as though he held a secret that was either exciting or terrifying, they weren't sure, but in any case they wanted to know. I leant in as well, somehow also caught by the neighbour's voice, its fairytale tone, the shadows thrown across the room and the dormant silence of old papers.

This map here, said the neighbour. I took this map from a newspaper article about towns that were built during industrialisation and then, when the money ran out or workers were needed for other projects, were abandoned before a soul had ever lived there. Imagine it, Pasha, an entire city of new buildings left empty like that. A ghostless ghost town. And this here—see all the lines—is a map of the roads from Moscow to Leningrad that were never built, but were printed as real on the maps anyway.

He gave an uneven laugh. The madness of planning, he said, gave us maps that showed the future instead of the present, and entire cities created but never actually lived in!

While I had heard of abandoned Soviet cities, when whole populations fled overnight after the collapse of the Soviet Union, the power and life of the city cut off, pot plants left on windowsills, books on living room shelves, these towns without life to begin with—ghostless ghost towns—were new to me.

The children seemed mystified by the maps that showed things that did not really exist, and wanted to know what those areas looked like.

Well, as for the roads, there's only the one main highway from here to Moscow, said the neighbour. I have only ever taken the train, so I haven't got any idea what's out there. There's probably not much at all, maybe the remnants of where the roads were started but never finished. Maybe a house or two, or forests. But what I would like to see are the abandoned towns. The towns without ghosts.

He grinned. Perhaps one day I might make a trip out there. As he smiled, the skin at the corners of his eyes pulled together in tight wrinkles. With the dim light, the expectant quiet, it felt as though we were seconds away from the moment when old folk stories descend into inevitable darkness.

I thought of my recent trip to Chudovo, which was on the M10 highway to Moscow. Perhaps the town hadn't died because it was close to the highway, unlike abandoned cities across the old Soviet Union.

I heard the shuffle of slippers near the door, and Vera Sergeyevna entered the study. Her face looked firm in the attempt to get the children to bed. But I thought there was also a sadness that seemed to come and go from her expression, the sporadic shadow of a shifting cloud. She glanced once or twice at her husband before nudging the children out of the room. Their small calls of *goodnight, Pasha, goodnight, Dedushka,* tolled like faint bells from the hallway.

My wife, she's always worrying, said the neighbour. She thinks my little project here is going to bring trouble. He laughed, wheezing. She's terrified I will make a trip out there, to these towns, and find things I'm not supposed to find. He shook his head. She still thinks as though it's the days of closed cities and KGB towns. Although these days it's the mafia that terrifies her.

The neighbour frowned, then raised his eyebrows and held up his hands for a moment. She cannot fathom it, the investigations into the past. She cannot see anything other than dark consequences. Research of any kind is dangerous, so she says.

He put his hands down, resting the heel of each palm on the border of the papers before him. His fingers fell to the pages, neatening the layers.

And so, *i tak,* he said. These places that never really existed. They have something uncanny about them, I think. They tell us the history of a future that did not happen. But they're also a sort of relic of how things were. The way of thinking back then. They show how time is just a thing you make. In those years, the way time worked was changed—*they* changed it. The neighbour's thumb went to the air again, to them, *up there*.

We were living for the future, not the present, he continued. And you know, I think we almost lived *in* the future. If we didn't have something we needed, well, that was okay, because we shall have it when there is Communism, we shall have it tomorrow. That was what we were taught. The world, the *true* world, was not life in the present, in a cramped communal flat, or another day on the *kolkhoz* farm. No, the world was as it would *become* in the Communist future. The present felt like a grey halfway point.

My uncle, I said—meaning Oleg—my uncle tried to describe this to me too. How the ideas of *soon* and *now* were somehow confused.

Exactly, Pasha, the neighbour said, pleased or relieved that his words made sense to me. And that, he continued, that is how you had a map of Moscow in the present, and a map of how it was going to be in ten years' time. But the future map was already printed because that future was apparently just as real as the present.

As the neighbour went to get another bottle, I wondered about the effect of touching time as they did, causing it to change in strange ways. Those unlived towns, those maps of unreal roads. Most of us would never actually see the territories depicted on all the maps of the world. Like time, maps were something we created, a representation. And we had to trust the science of the cartographer.

I wondered about the tyranny of plans. About how much we let come to pass because we obscure the present with a future we think is real.

The neighbour returned with the *samogon* and some leftover salad. He sat back down, poured me another glass, then refilled his own. He was quiet for a while, looking over the map in front of us. Here and there with his right hand he traced the side of his smallest finger lightly over the page, over the roads and through the towns that never came to be.

In later years, he said, when things did not seem right, when the darkness, the troubles, began to touch my own family, the message from above still made a strong impression. You could never be sure where the source of the darkness really was.

I wondered how long the neighbour had been ruminating on these ideas. He'd mentioned over dinner that he had never been to university, but as though educated in other, deeper ways, he had something of the philosopher about him.

We returned to the kitchen, where Vera Sergeyevna was drying a glass with a cloth. She put them down to say goodbye. As the two walked me along the dim hallway, Vera Sergeyevna's palm at my shoulder, I had the image of the neighbour's maps in my mind. I saw the aborted roads to Moscow, cracked and decaying or maybe entirely overgrown with grass. The old rubble, now blended for good with the earth, would look just the same, I thought, as the roads that never left the paper. I thanked my hosts and, feeling tired, pressed a hand to the door, walking out into the late night where the sun was not yet ready for dusk.

CHAPTER 12

Anya's father, Mikhail Sergeyevich, looked older than I expected, older than the image I had formed of him in my head. Perhaps it was his hair, which was parted over his high forehead, grey with traces of brown. It seemed that he never moved from the wicker chair that was placed near the kitchen table but at an odd distance—just a bit removed, between the stove and a cupboard, away from the sink and the centre of the conversation. I noticed how the glow from the ceiling light was stronger by the wall, causing Mikhail Sergeyevich's shadow to appear more fully formed than ours.

He sat with one leg crossed over the other, thin legs in slack trousers. His arms cupped his elbows and he leant slightly forwards in a delicate sort of posture that matched his gentle rolling voice and attentive, slight smile.

I glanced beyond the kitchen as I walked in, saw the living room and the large painting above the divan that I'd seen there a few weeks before. It showed a man in official-looking dress, with a tie and pin, a moustache thick and black as a cockroach, and a slightly hostile look about him.

Even though I couldn't see the portrait from the kitchen, that glimpse stayed in my mind, perhaps because Anya had told me about her grandfather when we went to Izmaylovsky Market, and now his image loomed over the room, but maybe also because of its strikingly lifelike quality. I'd seen his face before, in a newspaper or a book somewhere, but the recognition failed to bring concrete details to mind. I recalled that he had been one of Stalin's ministers for a time, though I didn't know any other facts about his role in the Party, nor in the Terror, nor the circumstances of his death, if he was in fact no longer alive.

Anya's mother, Yevgenia Fyodorovna, had a plump elegance about her, with her coiffed brown hair and distinctive perfume, her clothes deep shades of magenta, plum and red. She had studied art history, Anya told me, and also performed in theatres in her younger years. But when I met her she worked as a singing teacher in a music school.

Mikhail Sergeyevich seemed eager to talk, though his voice was gentle. I'd later think of it as having the softness of ash.

Tak, Pasha, he said, Anya tells us you are a writer.

Not really, I said as Anya waved away my awkwardness. I had only one story published in a journal when I was at the Gorky Institute.

Well, that makes you a writer, he said. His smile, his wise and kindly manner, reminded me of Oleg, though his eyes were green-grey, unlike Oleg's bright blue.

We've got a few articles planned, I said. Anya has probably told you—articles for newspapers and journals.

Anya's mother's face took on a strange expression. Oh, she doesn't tell us about her research, Yevgenia Fyodorovna said loudly, her laugh undercut with something disapproving.

Mama, said Anya in a low voice, sighing.

I thought I must have kicked up the dust of old arguments. Mikhail Sergeyevich, I said, turning to him, Anya tells me you were a teacher.

Yes, yes, secondary school, he said. Thirty years. Though I've been retired for a few years now.

I have been thinking, actually, that I would write about your father, Anya said to Mikhail Sergeyevich. Pasha and I would like to write something together.

He raised his eyebrows, an unspoken question.

Anya, Yevgenia Fyodorovna snapped. That is your grandfather you are talking about. You do not write about your family.

Yes, I *should*. It's important for every story to be in the open now.

Ah yes, these *times*. Yevgenia Fyodorovna shook her head. You can go around embarrassing your family because of the *times*.

Anya had told me that her mother wasn't happy with Anya *becoming political*, as she called it. Yevgenia Fyodorovna didn't approve of Anya's volunteering for the Memorial Society or of what she called Moscow's obsession with the past during *glasnost*. But that was precisely why Anya had brought me to meet her father—to interview Mikhail Sergeyevich about his life. Anya had told me that her father was keen to talk, though I guessed his doing so might deepen longstanding fissures in the family, put pressure on their uneasy peace.

So, I said, as we sat at the kitchen table after the meal, I thought you could maybe start by talking about your childhood.

The idea with the interviews was that they would be formed of open-ended discussion, without direct questions. The environment was important: creating the right circumstances in which a person might feel able to talk freely. Some people preferred to be in their own homes, in a setting they knew and where they could be sure who was listening. Others wanted somewhere entirely different to their usual surroundings, as if being taken out of their normal environment helped them to talk about things they never usually mentioned. The Memorial Society offices were sometimes used for interviews. Some interviewees preferred to talk outdoors, as if our constructions—walls, conventions, boundaries, rooms—break down when we're outside.

My childhood, said Mikhail Sergeyevich. Yes. I was born in Moscow in 1934. My father worked for the Ministry of Internal Affairs, my mother stayed in the home. We lived in an apartment in Arbatskaya and moved here, to Frunzenskaya, when I was about ten. I went to school in the centre, close to the Lubyanka. And so I used to play right near that haunted building for hours when I was a boy.

That haunted building, as he called it, was in all of our collective knowledge, so Mikhail Sergeyevich didn't need to explain it. The Lubyanka was the home of the Committee for State Security, Komitet Gosudarstvennoy Bezopasnosti, the KGB. It was a large pre-revolutionary building, painted yellow, with seemingly endless rows of windows across multiple levels. At the very top, in the centre, was a white and blue circle that could have been a clock, though from a distance it looked like a single, wide, lashless eye.

And you know, continued Mikhail Sergeyevich, when the weather began to warm and the mud rivers dried from the streets, we'd all run around the streets during our breaks. There would be a soldier standing by each door of the

Lubyanka, in a *budenovka* hat, holding a rifle with a bayonet. We'd all heard rumours—talk from parents or from each other—about shootings down in the basement. It's strange how even as a child you know these things; they are your unquestioned reality.

As he spoke I was reminded of a joke told to me by one of the dissident uncles who visited our apartment when I was a boy. *The Lubyanka basement is the tallest building in Moscow: you can see all the way to Siberia from down there.* And somehow I always knew that *Siberia* meant exile, camp, disappeared people thousands of kilometres away in the frozen north.

Mikhail Sergeyevich had stopped for a moment. Yevgenia Fyodorovna was very quiet, watching her husband with a stern expression. Anya was listening carefully. I would not have thought so many words could rise from his soft, ashy voice and kept expecting him to run out of energy to speak.

My father helped with the planning and construction of the Moscow metro system, said Mikhail Sergeyevich. Kaganovich was in charge. The stations were supposed to be palace-like. Palaces for the people. The most ornate in the world, so it's said. And they are remarkable, even when we look at them now: chandeliers, mosaics, statues, pillars, marble, walls painted so many colours. And the lighting, bright as day down there, like another city with its own sun. We are so used to those stations now, I suppose, but when they were first built they were something to behold.

Maybe that explains my interest in the underground, he continued. I'm interested in the subway network, the rumours of a library beneath the city. A lot goes on underground that we don't even think about. We might even say it's the subconscious of the city.

Mikhail Sergeyevich looked utterly transfixed, sitting there next to the wall, next to his fully formed shadow. He was very still and there was something picturesque about his pose there in the wicker chair, gently holding his elbows. Despite his stillness, I thought he looked distressed.

Okay, that's enough, said Yevgenia Fyodorovna. And though Anya protested that her father had barely had the chance to say a word, we were ushered out with kisses and goodbyes, awkwardly putting on our shoes at the door, and then the door was closed behind us. I wasn't quite sure what had happened or what I'd missed. It was such a strange, abruptly aborted encounter.

In the elevator, which was old and wooden and screeched its way down, Anya buried her head into my collar. My mother, she said in a long, laughing drawl. It's difficult with her.

The elevator opened and we walked the ten minutes or so to the embankment. I said I liked them, her parents; liked listening to her father talk. Anya stood looking out over Moskva River, as though trying to see something on the other side.

It's all difficult, she said again. Families. At the same time, it's the first time I've really shared my family with anyone. She turned to me. Nobody has ever really known me like this. She was smiling distantly.

I put an arm around her shoulders and we stood facing the other side of the river, the inviting green wall of trees. The sun was still high and the water wore a tinted orange layer. We spoke about our plans for writing. Anya had clearly given it a lot of thought. She suggested we could write a history of psychiatry in the country—from the beginning—and show how the state had taken over the hospitals, used them for its own aims. Subverting language, manipulating psyches.

It would almost be like studying the whole country. I said I could ask the dissident aunts and uncles for information. She would go to the library. We would both start taking detailed notes. With our words we linked our creative futures to the pasts of our parents.

Yura called me a few days later. He had been keen to meet up after we met at Bulgakov's apartment, and had joined us at a concert and a poetry reading organised by Ilya.

You know, he said on the phone, I've been thinking about what you said, Pasha—about writing a story. Or an article, perhaps. Something to do with the bans on emigration. I was wondering if you could help me.

I said of course I would. I was sure my editor friend would want to publish something. We arranged to meet for a drink and work it out.

When I called the editor, Sasha Podrabinek, about Yura's story, he told me there was some space for me to write too.

I looked up to Sasha. He had been a political prisoner in the seventies and was adamant about exposing how, when most labour camps were closed in the 1980s, the barbed wire of the Gulag merely morphed into the locked white doors, the vicious injections, the patrolled corridors of the *psikhushka* asylums.

We each had our cause and we were running towards them. It was the time for everything to be open—the past, the state of our lives; everything that was wrong about our country was finally being confronted. The long days lent a haze, golden, to the city; a ringing gold, since to us noise was a promise, and the light promised clarity.

Meanwhile, our dissident hero and key voice in the Memorial Society, Andrei Sakharov, was preparing to go to parliament, and supporting rallies were organised across the Soviet Union. Sakharov had been in exile in Gorky—a closed city, no foreigners, riddled with KGB—since Brezhnev sent him there in 1980. He had been allowed to return in 1986, when *glasnost* began. An older man, grey-haired with glasses, Sakharov was a model for us during *glasnost*. He brought us ideas of a system of democracy that we could never quite picture, but which we knew resembled something we wanted.

When Sakharov spoke, I heard people comment on the purity of his Russian. When he wrote, his words had an honest clarity. He scorned the vague charges of *anti-Soviet agitation* or *anti-constitutional actions*—they were not precise terms, he argued. He wrote real words and described his dealings with councils and parliaments: *I spoke of the need to repeal the laws on demonstrations and on special troops, and of the flaws in the decrees of April 8, which were intended to replace articles 70 (anti-Soviet agitation) and 190-1 (slander of the Soviet system) of the Criminal Code. I repeated my main thesis, that it is unthinkable to allow criminal prosecution for opinion or for acts of conscience, provided there is no use or advocacy of violence.* Real words. From his sentences I had a sense of solidity I'd never felt before in the public world.

Ilya was pushing ahead with politics and music. It was always Ilya who would be charging into the room with tickets to or tip-offs about an underground concert, part of the *tusovka*

music scene from Leningrad, where there were spontaneous concerts anywhere, everywhere, in apartments and basements, old shopfronts—any place that was deserted—lit by lamplight or torchlight or no light at all. Always it was Ilya tapping the latest cassette against his palm. He joined a band, inspired by our idols Kino. The lead singer of Kino, Viktor Tsoi, stood for our dreams, he stood for *us*. His lyrics told of our boredom with everyday life—we lived for our art, not our day jobs.

We want change was Tsoi's rallying cry. We heard it all around us and we heard it within us.

We
Want
Change.

CHAPTER 13

The days seemed to float, merge in the heat of summer. Perhaps the only harness for time was the Nineteenth Party Conference. It had begun on 28 June 1988. We'd met at the Sukhanovs' apartment, the whole group, to watch. The Memorial Society had been campaigning heavily for the monument to Stalin's victims, and the petition—with the thousands of signatures collected on Moscow's streets, in cinema foyers, parks and at market stalls—was going to be presented at the conference. In the preceding days, some fifty thousand people in Lithuania had rallied, asking conference delegates to push for autonomy from Soviet rule.

Over four days we followed the coverage of the conference: me, Anya, Ilya, Sukhanov and Lena, Yura and other friends from university and the Memorial Society, all crowded into the tiny apartment, camped around the television, sitting on windowsills and on the floor. There was the tinkling of glasses, the smell of brandy and cigarettes, the indistinct rise and fall of murmurs and laughter, Ilya's music as loud as ever.

As part of the *glasnost* and *perestroika* reforms, Gorbachev had called for elections with multiple candidates and a two-term limit for government officers.

A clash between Yeltsin, who argued for political rehabilitation for Stalin's victims (which would mean compensation or at least certificates deeming past arrests were unfounded), and Ligachev, an old Party man, was broadcast only in the small hours of the morning, as if those above hoped to conceal by night such an important debate. Ligachev still spoke of *destructive forces*, of reformers *playing into the hands of our enemies* as if he was stuck in the past. Yet all of us in the Sukhanovs' crowded room, and likely most of Moscow, stayed up to watch the broadcast, alternating tea with brandy, snatching a moment of sleep here and there. Anya lay with her head in my lap, her shoulders moving softly beneath cotton as she clapped at something on the television.

Our cheers hit every wall of the tiny room when Gorbachev stood and announced that they would grant permission for a monument to Stalin's victims. The change felt so great as to be almost unbelievable; a change in attitude from all previous leaders and even from the present one, as it had taken years to get this far with Gorbachev. I was used to seeing nothing but reports of robust crops in the provinces and heroic factory output, not fiery debate and the uncertainty it entailed, nor concessions to public thought and petition.

Though Gorbachev didn't actually mention that the monument was a result of our petition, and nor did he refer to the Memorial Society, we felt it was our victory. That he neglected to speak of us, as though we didn't exist, seemed to me, as the son of dissidents, the way things had worked my whole life. For as long as I could remember, the media had spoken about sources of *anti-Soviet sentiment*, but never were those vague enemies actually named as the books or radio stations or imprisoned activists I had grown up knowing. As though, if they didn't mention those things, mention us, we wouldn't really be there. But on the first of July in 1988, the success of our campaign was proof enough of our existence.

When the broadcast was over we had left the apartment, wandering aimlessly, too elated to care where we were going. Anya walked beside me, her small white bag swinging from one arm, her other wound through mine. Eventually we decided on drinks in Izmaylovsky Park. We took a metro there. I always liked that station, since it was one of the few above ground; the carriage arrived into clouds of green leaves. It was such a warm night, we all lay on the grass, in the wooded urban forest, losing the night little by little, drinking beer and arguing happily.

We had a great group argument about the Russian soul. We couldn't decide if it was the same soul as it used to be, whether the essence of Pushkin, Dostoyevsky—the greats— had survived the twentieth century. Ilya stood in the middle of the circle, guitar in his arms. Sukhanov and Lena were entwined on the ground. Anya sat up, holding a glass of brandy, while I lay on the grass, facing the sky.

Of course it's there, said Sukhanov. Artists today don't work in a void. Neither did they in the sixties. You can't say we only begin with Soviet times; it's like saying our art only came because of Communism.

Ilya said the rock music movement was truer to our soul, nowadays. He and I both laughed, and I raised my drink to agree with him, but the others were serious.

But maybe, said Anya, maybe the better thing to ask is if it's possible to have a *collective* soul to begin with, and whether it can travel between people or generations. She took a sip of brandy and shrugged.

Right then I felt more whole than I ever had before: I had a girl and a cause. For the first time I felt a sense of equilibrium, of sureness. Moscow in 1988 was for me the promise of things to come, a future in which my life, once split into two lines, would join in a single clear path. The political and the personal were intertwined, each as promising as the other. On the grass in Izmaylovsky Park, Anya lay down next to me; I could feel her warm cheek on my chest, and a gentle hum from her voice when she murmured a few words. As the day began to darken slightly, Ilya, Anya and I rolled up our jeans to stand knee-deep in Lebedyansky Pond, which was gradually cooling with the long twilight.

I started carrying a notebook with me, and I was constantly scribbling in it, sure that my notes would one day form a coherent whole, a worthy piece of work. Writing our history of psychiatry, we could combine the stories of our two fathers—Anya's and mine—and by doing so write our own story of the country, write the truths censored from above. This would be my way to follow in the footsteps of the writers who came before me and to whom I felt as close as family. Our words could, I was sure, change the future by confronting the past. Before then, I hadn't known the power of being able to point at a thing and say you care so much about it.

My mother, when she heard about what we were planning to write, suggested I speak to Oleg. And so in the summer he and I went out for the day, walking through a small forest near Moscow we had visited since I was young. We used to go mushroom picking there, in humid autumns. The heavy green-and-pine air brought me to those young memories every time I went into a forest. Oleg spoke as we walked. His thin shoulders and slightly stooped posture concealed how fit he was; his voice remained steady and his feet stepped confidently along the uneven pathways.

My wife, Marya, left the Soviet Union at the end of May 1974, said Oleg. The same year as Solzhenitsyn, in fact. We were not really married by that time, however, just bound together by unspeakable things. She took a plane to Paris, via another city that I cannot remember—Frankfurt or Düsseldorf—and that is where the story of her, as far as I can tell it, finishes. But I'm running out of order here. It's difficult to start things at the beginning, so to speak, when you already know the end.

His wife. An image of Oleg from my childhood came to mind, of his blue eyes surrounded by cloudy red, his mouth straight, tense. I remembered that night; how his sadness frightened me, how I had hidden behind the divan, pretending to read, so as to avoid him.

We met through mutual friends who formed the dissident groups in Moscow in the sixties, said Oleg, groups so far underground, as the saying goes, who had to keep so quiet in their activities, that each scarcely knew any others were operating. In 1968, friends of ours started, anonymously, the *Chronicle of Current Events*, a true record of the state of things. It was the greatest crime against the state, sending those truths out into the world, across the borders.

Mostly our goal then was to disseminate information: helping truth to flow, writing the truth in journals and circulating true literature. Marya studied in Leningrad, and then came back to Moscow, her hometown, to work as a translator. She also wrote poetry.

We stopped to rest, sitting on a small slope of soft earth and pine needles. Oleg unlaced the thick cloth straps from the metal rings that bound his bag closed, reached into some precise place, as though in an oft-repeated gesture, and then handed me a photograph.

I had never met her, or at least I didn't remember seeing her at our apartment. The photograph, taken in the soft lighting of a studio, showed a woman with a defined nose and cheekbones, thick eyebrows and dark hair. Her skin looked smooth: white beads of light caught her chin, forehead, cheekbones, the way a pearl might take a lamp's glow. She looked away towards the right-hand edge of the photo. Alert eyes, an inner smile barely glimpsed by the camera.

She was pretty, I said.

Oleg took the photo from my hand and put it back in his bag. She is, he said.

What I should say, continued Oleg—it's funny how you forget the most basic facts sometimes—what I should say is that she was released from prison in 1973, after two years spent confined either in psychiatric hospitals or in regular prisons. We continued to live together right up until her departure, for the reason that there was nowhere else for either of us to live. It was very difficult to change apartments in Moscow. It was an awkward time. Once, some time after her return, Marya saw me looking at the photograph I just showed you. She seemed sad as she told me that she wished I could stop looking into that photograph as though the woman there was a lost love who I was still hoping would come home. *You look at her as though she is going to say something*, Marya said to me. She glanced only briefly at the photo and I had the impression that she didn't want to look at it any closer.

What I remember most vividly was that the boy in the room next to us—there were several families in the apartment, we could hear sounds next door almost better than those in the room with us—the boy suffered a string of ear infections. He was only three or four years old, and they must have been extremely painful. For weeks on end his cries could be heard all through the night. The woman next door, his mother, told us when we met her in the hallway that the infections would have to pass on their own, as so far no medications had worked.

It was pretty miserable in that crowded apartment. Lots of bickering, as so-and-so stole someone's sugar, someone-or-other broke the tap in the bathroom, the alcoholic down the hall stole the light globes again. It was made even more miserable by the crying of that little boy. With each night his cries became more tired and drawn out, until they took on something of an animal tone, a primitive wail. Marya and I still shared the same bed, as there was no room to sleep separately, and so every night for those last months before she left we were forced to lie side by side. I could not reach out and touch her, nor pull her to me, for she was no longer mine, though my body seemed to remember and long for her. So I just lay there listening to the heartsick moans of the child. On it went, as a bird cry might echo long after the call.

How darkly the imagination travels during a long night, Pasha. I saw—Oleg looked ahead as if in a trance, tapping two fingers roughly into his temple—I saw indistinctly in my mind some feeling creature, one of our ancestors, letting out that unending lament, and I was unsure whether it was sorry for what had been or for what was to come. Marya would put her pillow and then a towel over her head, and her sighs would sometimes wake me up or pull me out of strange half-dreams of crying half-humans. And we would, at some point, emerge into the morning, and the sound stopped with the sun. We would rise early, pour tea to drink, alone together in our room. We moved into another day, but we became increasingly fatigued as the long nights continued, and I felt less and less alert, which was all the more distressing because it seemed imperative that we remain ourselves, so to speak, for the last of our time together.

There was a slight flinch, almost unseen, when either of us recalled times from before our imprisonment. It was as though our experiences of incarceration, unknown to each other, set the course for who we were from that time on, rendering us mere traces of that young couple we had been. She took some small translation jobs, but rather than return to her dissident work in Moscow, Marya focused on making a pathway out, determined to bring about change from another shore. It was not that there was a sudden rupture, or any sense of ill feeling between us. But those years apart had damaged us, withered and changed us, leaving something entirely new and strange. Eventually we crossed a vague threshold, after which we were no longer husband and wife.

Oleg had been imprisoned years ago—I had somehow always known this, and I knew that it was when I was very young, though I couldn't remember him ever mentioning the experience to me. Time had blurred and I couldn't recall his long absence, a failure which always made me feel guilty. Surely that should have loomed as a memorable void in my early life. Even then, during our walk in the forest, he barely touched on it. A few words—*our experiences of incarceration*—were the tiny traces he left behind in his sentences, like drops of dye in a puddle of water; the dye was there, but some complex process of chemistry was needed to detect its presence, to understand what memories lived in the betraying lightness of a word.

You never really know what happens to another, Oleg continued, but I tried to understand what had happened to Marya. I read an article by one of our friends, published *samizdat* in an underground journal. It was about the use of psychiatric repression against political dissidents. The pseudo-diagnosis was *continuous sluggish schizophrenia*. It was ingenious, really, in its horrific logic. The diagnosis made political dissent a mental disease. The psychiatrists were trained—ordered, as it were—to diagnose this condition according to symptoms such as *delusional aspirations*, or a *heightened sense of self-empowerment*. By changing the meaning of medical words, of *disease* and *symptom*, they created a science of absurdity according to which dissidents must be mentally sick to act as they did, there being no other logical rationale for why one would oppose a system that was, apparently, the best in the world.

I read an anonymous report, he went on, about a woman, newly released, telling of the drugs given to political activists such as herself. The woman described the effects of the drugs: paralysis of the vocal capacities so that she was unable to unclench her teeth, to put food into her mouth, to speak the words she wanted to say. A certain haze, a mist in the mind—she couldn't see herself except as a shadow or, if such a thing were possible, as her former self, standing motionless before a mirror, her head turned away. *And I could not call her back*, said the woman.

I read it all, and as I did so I looked up now and then at Marya, who was sitting on the divan reading a book, her head tilted to the side while the tip of one finger moved slowly across the uppermost line of her lip. I watched her, I read, and the irrepressible notion came to me then that she, Marya, was the subject of that article. I was horrified.

Oleg took a deep breath. Although his voice was steady, it had grown quiet. For me, image overpowered speech, my mind awash in flashes of things I'd imagined as a boy as well as new images: Marya in hospital, her striking features drained of colour; an arm rising out of a white sheet; a waiting needle hanging in a white background. They wouldn't leave my head, and until they did I was sure I'd never say another word.

Oleg lit a cigarette. Science, he said, and cleared his throat, his voice louder as smoke rose in the air, science should need no authority but its own inviolable truths. And yet with those false diagnoses, the political authorities were changing truth itself. By creating false science, they redefined what it meant to be ill in the mind. Aside from the obvious outrage of the practice, it reinforced their whole philosophy, that it is delusional for the individual to see in themselves the capacity to change things. Yet it is about more than just the lie of the practice: it is about removing the individual. No one was permitted to have *other* thoughts, so to speak. And I worry about the next generation—the younger psychiatrists, who will not know how to diagnose, will not know a healthy dissenter from a real sufferer of illness. Once false science, false truths, are learnt—through no fault of our own—it can be very difficult to unlearn them.

What was strangest of all, Oleg continued, was that when I spent my first night alone in the room, after Marya left, I could not hear the cries of the neighbour's boy. It happened that, as she told me the next afternoon when I saw her in the stairwell, the boy's mother had taken him to her sister's for a night. And so the crying resumed, as long and slow as it had been on other nights. So it was a coincidence, that's all. But I never did know, said Oleg after a moment, what to make of that one night of silence that marked the threshold to our solitude.

He stubbed out his cigarette on the sole of his boot and we stood up, continued walking.

When Oleg told me those things I sensed that a parallel story was taking place, as if through the story of Marya he was telling me a million other truths. We took a train back into the city, and Oleg walked me through the dim foyer, up the stairs to the fifth floor, and stood at the door of the apartment where my mother and I lived. He smiled but his eyes looked troubled somehow. We said goodbye in the hallway. My mother wasn't home. I went into the living room, lay on the divan and thought I might be sick. I thought of my father and all the silent spaces in our apartment where he still lived, despite his death, where every day he still breathed.

CHAPTER 14

After dinner at the neighbour's, I went to bed and fell asleep straight away. But I woke in the night. I sat up, blinking at the glowing white room. I couldn't find my watch, but the silence outside, as if birds and wind no longer existed, told me it must have been very early in the morning. I seemed to wake up in the moment of that old conversation, in the company of Oleg, those trees, that forest in Moscow.

I went into the front room, which was next to the bedroom. Standing, I leafed through a few of the books on the tall narrow shelf. I read a few pages of Peter Kropotkin's *Memoirs of a Revolutionist*. I remembered Sergei Ivanovich saying at my mother's funeral that he was a great admirer of the writer, philosopher, adventurer, anarchist. I read about Kropotkin's early years in military school, camping at Peterhof, where the young men slept in tents and bathed in the sea. I turned over several years' worth of pages, and read about a fire in St Petersburg on 26 May 1862, and how the archives at the Ministry of the Interior were nearly lost. Clerks rushed out of the building carrying piles of documents in their arms. But the wind upset the piles; burning sheets flew over the streets, and tiny orange cinders mixed with floating traces of paper. Then he described his five years of exploration in Siberia. I read about his studies in geography and cartography, and his assertion that the then current maps of northern Asia, made by Europeans, included mountains that didn't exist or which were shown at the wrong latitude, representing an entirely false view of what was really there.

Yawning, I closed the book and went to make tea. I wished I had a map of Moscow. I wondered if I could draw one, or if I should just wait until I was back in Petersburg to buy one there. The Moscow in my mind was like several cities trying to make themselves seen, in their slight variations, all at once. Maybe from one summer to another the blue of Moskva River was slightly different, less vivid perhaps, or there were fewer people along its banks. The slightest shift and it would be like a photograph taken ten years earlier or later, though I had both images before me. What the neighbour said was true: time was just a thing we made, a construction of our thoughts. And so it was difficult to ignore the reality of the aftermath. That Anya had left Moscow, left Russia, that her father was gone, that I had left, too. I could only look at it all from above, like a horrible bird's-eye view of everything, all at once.

In my writing I was trying to see not my own Moscow, but the city of my parents and their dissident friends. I was a child of that disappeared city. When I left I'd resolved that it didn't matter whether I preserved it. Yet there were things I wantd to know now, and the need to learn what had happened to Mikhail Sergeyevich seemed connected to the sense I'd long felt of having lost all connection and meaning, all belief and understanding. Since leaving Moscow, I'd been living in a long autumn. A persistent twilight life. I needed to know that there was some point to *glasnost*, that some essence lasted despite my failure to preserve the truth of that time.

Kafka's hunger artist came to mind again. My father had starved to death, but to see that as art, to see death as art, was a troubling idea. To find some logical—let alone philosophical—cause for what he did seemed to put forward ill-conceived notions about something that was ultimately just death. Perhaps both murder and suicide. But maybe in a murderous system, such an act was all he could do to express what that system was—a suicide inflicted upon a people. Every 'enemy' created within the mind of every citizen came from the system that grew such enemies in those minds.

Maybe he was the ultimate artist, my father, at the moment he attained death by starvation. If art is free—something I didn't know for certain—then he chose what would happen to his incarcerated body and so was ultimately free. But he didn't choose the condition of that incarceration. It was an endless loop; I longed for clarity.

I didn't know what to do with such thoughts, however; my father's death was in no gallery or bookshelf. Nor did I know what I was writing. It was as if we all stood at a window—me, Anya, her father, my father, countless others who had shared their histories during *glasnost* and after—and our collective breath covered the glass in vapour. Ghosts of old hopes, words long said and dead. I didn't know what was through the window, if anything.

When it seemed like morning, I called Sonya. I imagined her standing by the kitchen window of her small apartment in Petersburg, standing by the stove where flower-patterned cloths were put to dry. I pictured her long eyelashes as she gazed out the window. Maybe she'd be drawing on a cigarette. I could hear her boys in the background, like gentle echoes. She told me she'd like to see me soon. I said that I was thinking of going to Moscow for a brief visit, but that I would come over before I left. After we hung up, I stood by the phone for a moment. I hadn't mentioned to Sonya that I was at the *dacha*. It was strange to think that for her, I wasn't here.

I was thinking of Sonya but also Anya. I seemed to have the same feeling when I thought of them both, of a gently pressing emptiness.

I spent the rest of the day trying to write. I needed to write both forwards and backwards: find somewhere to begin in the past and write running towards the future I already knew, as well as stand in the present and not run, exactly, but fall backwards into the past, feeling the inertia of knowing, and the despair of never really holding a moment that had passed.

I ate some bread, tomatoes, sour cream for dinner. For a few hours I lay outside the *dacha*, stretched out on a long seat in front of the house, taking a sip of beer now and then, dozing into an evening that never really arrived.

As if I hadn't moved, a few days later I was again stretched out on my back, now in the shade of the trees behind the *dacha*. With the intense heat, I had started spending a lot of time there. I lay as close to the forest as possible, where the air was coolest. The day wasn't sunny at all, but heavy cloud seemed to press down the humid air, so it was tiring to be anywhere but in the shade.

Sometimes I felt as though the *dacha* was a halfway point, balancing precariously between a past I was trying to recall and a present I was barely in. A place where memories came to gather and where present time, such as it was, didn't touch.

I heard light feet on grass, the breaking of thin wood, then saw the three children from next door. Two boys and a girl. The oldest, one of the boys, said they were going for a walk, and I could come too.

The sea is near here, said the boy.

They were quiet kids, and the thought of the sea appealed to me, so I joined them. We made our way along the dusty road in front of our houses, shaded by towering forests at either side. Eventually there wasn't a single *dacha* in the wild around us. It was still gloomy, cloudy overhead. With a warm breeze a few stray, cold drops hit my forehead, my arms. I brushed them away with my palm, and would've thought I'd imagined them if the children hadn't done the same, the younger boy looking back at me as though asking whether to keep going. I just grinned and raised my eyebrows, and we kept walking along the road towards the train station and the *produkti*.

Before we got there, the rain came. A sudden downpour, large drops of a deep cold as though from a lost winter. I knew there was a bus stop with a small shelter on the main road. We ran there laughing, streaked then saturated, my head blissfully cold, and we waited with the marching taps of rain on the shelter roof above us. The three children had the excited faces of those who have lost control of their surroundings, giggling and shivering; the rain, heavier and heavier, seemed to exhilarate and terrify them. A truck approached, two beacon headlights shining, its passage silent until it passed us with a thin hiss of wheels grasping the wet road.

Time seemed immeasurable in that wild loud rain, but after a while the rain eased and we stepped out again onto the road. I knew we were close to Penaty, the estate where Ilya Repin had lived at the end of his life, and that his former house was a museum. I had been to see Repin's paintings in St Petersburg. They were sad and beautiful, as if he was letting us peer into an everyday moment of struggle made poignant and stoic. Rough, bedraggled peasant faces on the Volga, cast in a pearly light; or Tolstoy, looking like history itself, lumpy nose and beard like a pine tree in snow. One showed a scene in St Petersburg during the 1905 revolution. A crowd in wavy, silent chaos, open-mouthed exclamations fixed in time forever. I remembered that there was a well-dressed woman holding a bunch of red flowers. What had struck me at the time was how they floated, those flowers, just above the crowd, as if risen like blood. There was a coil of chains somewhere too, if I remembered rightly; turning and curving like seaweed in the depths.

Come on, I said to the children, let's see if we can find the painter's house.

We left the main road, but approaching the entrance gate I saw a sign: CLOSED DUE TO TECHNICAL DIFFICULTIES. I was sure there would be nobody inside the property; possibly there never was and we were waiting outside a ghostly museum that operated on its own. We climbed the gate, helping the youngest boy over the crosshatched metal arms. We met a dense wall of russet tree trunks and vivid green leaves. Repin painted in the forest. Although fences enclosed it, there was something unrestrained about the place. I saw one wooden structure, a kind of outbuilding, brightly painted in white, blue, maroon. I thought of the mystical Russia of *skazki* fairytales, of the princess who never laughed, waiting for the one to marry her, of Father Frost who froze children to death.

Being in the forest reminded me of folk stories from my childhood, or at least the feeling of those stories; something about the way the air was heavy with fear of unknown things, and the scenes of stark beauty. I pictured the place in winter: crystalline ice shards hanging from trees, as if daring the wind to shake them.

A few drops of rain dashed my arms again, my forehead. I couldn't tell if it was light rainfall or just the echo of old rain dripping from the leaves.

Look up! I whispered to the children, and the three all craned their heads back. Above we saw a sky that looked scattered with green-leafed snowflakes, birch and aspen grew so thick that barely a spot of blue sky was visible.

Vera Sergeyevna had pinned a tiny gold bell to each child's shirt, as my mother had done for me whenever we went mushroom picking in the wide forests near Moscow, and so as they trotted here and there between the trunks of the trees, a faint ringing from the bells tinkled through the forest air. The little girl was humming, a sound bare and small like a fairy's song left in the air after the wolves have eaten the vampires, and the wolves themselves have run into the mouth of the mountains.

Soon there was sand at our feet, and the trees were thinning. Slowly easing our way down a subtle slope, the loose, sandy soil falling with our descent, we pressed through bushy undergrowth until the soil gave way entirely to sand. *The beach, the beach!* Their cries were long left behind as they ran from forest to sand.

The air by the gulf was still. There was nobody else. The water, metallic and reflecting, barely swayed. Where small currents pulled or sandbanks rose up, the watery sheet looked like a blanket unfolded, a bed unmade. At a distance, the drenched sand, scattered with stray branches and stones, was all that gave any sense of presence or sign of movement to the absent land.

Closer to me I saw the fast footprints of the children trailing them on the sand. One of the boys stood next to me and looked out at the water, squinting or smiling under the bright clouds. He asked whether the mass he could see in the distance was an island.

That's Kotlin Island, usually called Kronstadt, the naval base, I said. Where the sailors revolted against Lenin and the Bolsheviks a few years after the revolution. Lenin was brutal, though. Over a thousand died, maybe two. Lots were sent to the prison camps up north, the Solovetsky Islands.

The boy was silent, maybe taking in what I'd told him. I thought of the unburied dead, the perhaps thousands of skeletons unresting but gradually wasting away in the water. The other boy and the girl circled back, still running. They had not noticed Kronstadt floating so far from the shore.

On the way back we stopped at the *produkti* and I bought the children some sweets. The woman at the counter, her nails painted orange this time, asked me if we had been mushroom picking, and warned me to be careful of losing the children in the woods.

They're children of asphalt, she said, waving her hand, these kids of the city. In my childhood, we could tell where we were in the forest, and find our way out, by the way the light came down through the trees. Children can't see these things anymore. She shook her head, putting the sweets, my cigarettes and bread slowly into a bag. They get lost so easily, she said. They've forgotten the knowledge.

I took the bag and nodded my thanks. As we walked home, the little girl went on humming faint songs under her breath. The bells on the children's shirts tinkled. As we took the road back to the houses, they stopped here and there to tap their shoes over the surface of the large puddles that had formed in the grey dirt of the road.

And so I had begun my escape. I quickly came to love it. The mornings glowed early but were fresh thanks to the trees, which still knew what time it was and overnight took in the old air of the previous day. In the morning I would make tea, eat bread and jam, and write. Then I would lie outside next to the forest. I didn't have any music with me. The silence felt strange, because even though I'd stopped certain things I'd once loved—reading and writing—after I moved to St Petersburg, I still had my record player and radio.

Late summer rains, sometimes unbelievably heavy, sometimes just a sunlit sheet hanging in the air, continued for a few days. The wet weather sometimes kept me inside from one afternoon until the evening of the next day. When I didn't leave the *dacha*, there may as well have been no other houses, no neighbours, messy garden, dusty road, quiet dripping forest or overflowing rain-soaked sea out there beyond the walls. I hadn't brought many books with me. I sometimes read something from Sergei Ivanovich's collection; most books were by Kropotkin, and there were also a few uninteresting novels about small-town life on the steppe.

Late afternoon on one of those rain-soaked days, the neighbour came to visit while I was working at the desk in the front room. A grin cut deep wrinkles into his face, which seemed to have tanned darker over the past week. He held up a *samogon* bottle, a question. I beckoned him in, and went to get us glasses and a snack. We sat in the small front room.

The autumn rains are with us, he said, pouring and handing me a drink.

Though I was tired and liked my isolation there, talking with the neighbour wasn't like talking to other people—my boss, students, strangers. It wasn't an intrusion upon my solitude. His gruffness, his jokes, reminded me of the old dissident aunts and uncles of my childhood. Or maybe it was the place—the *dacha*, the forest, the timelessness of it all—that removed me from my usual self and helped cleave open something in me, just a fraction.

This air, said the neighbour, raising his arm, Vera tells me it smells like childhood to her. Mushroom weather. Vera's was one of those old peasant families. The seasons marked time—the rituals, their lives, you know.

I lit a cigarette, then passed one to the neighbour; he accepted with a nod.

She gets gloomy, though, he said. It's an old sadness. Her parents were believers. Celebrated Easter with all the traditions, the *paskha* cake, the vigil on Easter eve. It was very remote, where they lived. Relatives in the city, who couldn't go to church, would give them prayers written on paper so they could take them to their priest.

I'm interested in this kind of . . . *secret* knowledge, the neighbour said, stubbing out his cigarette and crossing his arms. I think you are too, Pasha.

I nodded. I felt worn out and intrigued at the same time. Bitov's ideal writing conditions involved a place with no time, no information, but here I was, stumbling on new stories after only a week.

It's hard to know, he said, how to tell the grandchildren and the children these kinds of things. Ten or so years ago, I read news about a famous old church. The old kremlin in Rostov Veliky right up north. The bells could be heard thirty kilometres away from town, so it's said. But in 1935 they were taken out when the church was shut down and turned into a stable or storehouse or something. And then there I am, an old man in Leningrad, and in the newspaper I read how because of *glasnost* the people in Rostov could go to the archives, find the old instruction manual and restore the bells. After fifty years they were ringing again. But the children, you know, they know what a bell sounds like. Of course. So it doesn't mean anything to them. You can't really say what fifty years of silence feels like.

The neighbour's face was very still, and without his smile the skin across his cheeks and forehead looked far smoother, just small cracks in sand.

I don't know if I'll ever go there, to those places on the maps and in the articles, he said. I just keep collecting things. Just keep collecting, the articles and the stories. I don't know what to do with them.

He rubbed a thumb harshly against his forehead. Vera hates it, he said. She hates it. My collecting, my maps. His voice was a bit drink-wavy. But you know, Pasha, it's only after a lifetime that you can start to understand the sort of country you are living in.

We didn't say anything more for a while, just had a couple more drinks and then spoke about other things; I said I'd help him with some work next door at his *dacha*, and then he went back home, leaving me once again to my seclusion, my silent walls and watchful windows.

I had a quiet few days. Time drifted. One evening I stood at the window in the bedroom, at the back of the *dacha*. I could see my yard, and the neighbour's greenhouses. There he was. He stood near the house, looking out to the forest. I sort of liked having the neighbours there. When I saw them outside I felt a lonely kind of company, in the way I imagined one in an isolated house in Siberia feels connected to the sight of a lone truck moving along a distant road.

There were strange reminders after I came to the *dacha* in the forest, when I thought I saw someone from my old life. When I was young there was an old woman who cleared snow from the streets at a quiet crossroads near our apartment in Moscow. She had the bundled, broad figure of *babushki* everywhere, and her rounded shoulders rolled with each low sway of her shovel. It was her eyes that were so distinct. Acute and Asiatic, beneath a straight fringe of slate-grey hair. Both severe and peaceful, the sort of eyes that knew and had seen all that it was possible, both good and ill, to see. Probably we never exchanged more than a low, wintertime murmur of greeting, yet she was there on the street, scraping the ground to raise up the snow, the dirt which had tarnished it to russet, a bruised sludge, on most days throughout winter in my childhood and teenage years. After that I no longer saw her, or was perhaps too distracted to notice her quiet presence.

And now, at a small stall near the train station at Repino, I thought I saw that woman from my childhood. I passed her some rubles in exchange for the three apples she held in one hand with uncommon dexterity. I watched her release the apples at once into a wind-whipped plastic bag, take the coins and hand the bag to me, her elbow stretched nearly straight as she sat on a stool so low and small I couldn't see it beneath her. Her eyes had the same watchful, ancient beauty of the Far East, beneath the same rim of dark grey hair. A barely perceptible difference in their features separated the two women. Perhaps it was that the lips of the Moscow *babushka* were thinner than those of the one in the forest town, or that the eyes of that woman from my childhood had clouded slightly, as though with age.

A day or so later, at the *produkti*, there was a woman who bore a resemblance to my mother. It was scarcely nameable, this likeness; some inner tone was similar. Perhaps it was the slight incline of her head as she waited in the queue, or the sense of patience, of solid, quiet confidence. The navy-blue coat she wore, and the hair coiled into a thick black bun, also reminded me of her. In a memory of one moment or many, I saw my small child's hand pulling at the edge of that coat. Come on, Pasha, my mother would say, we're going to Pushkin's. On the weekends we would go to Pushkin Square, taking a crowded trolleybus. They had a sense of lightness, those memories of our trips to Pushkin's. Maybe that was when my mother herself felt a little lighter, less plagued for a moment by the burdens of her life, heavy with risk and unresting fears for what her dissident activity might bring for the young boy beside her, and still ringing with new grief at the loss of my father. Maybe at Pushkin's she took comfort in seeing other children with mothers or aunts, running up to the ice-cream vendors that were there no matter the decade, beyond the violence that thrashed the city.

The woman in the *produkti* paid for her things and left, and for a moment I felt yet more alone, losing that graze of the past.

Back at the *dacha*, I started drawing a rough map of the Moscow streets I knew so well. The Arbat, I saw it paved and lined with streetlamps. Tverskoy Boulevard, wide and green, down to Pushkin Square. Red Square, a cold desert by the Kremlin. Broad Bolshaya Sadovaya Street leading to Bulgakov's apartment. Frunzenskaya Embankment and the bridge over to Gorky Park. It eased me, drawing it, imagining the images beneath the lines, as though I had finally found the photo of a loved one whose face I thought I'd forgotten.

Come on, Pasha, time to go to Pushkin's.

CHAPTER 15

Moscow in the autumn, every autumn, was a brief time. Just a twilight almost missed, gold light to grey. The parks always seemed full of couples, maybe clinging to the last days of walks without snow, without frost in the skin. Novopushkinskaya Park, lime trees letting go yellow leaves in the breeze, shuddering as though already cold. Tverskoy Boulevard, down to Pushkin Square, lined with colour from the trees. Couples hand in hand, palm to cheek, promises made. Our first autumn together, I saw the small changes that came with the season. The first time I saw Anya wearing the grey felt hat that pushed her blonde fringe out to the sides of her face. The first time she clung to me for warmth, walking down the Arbat, which was still streaming with people, on a day that felt as cold as winter. The first time she paused in walking to pull her white socks up over her leggings, or tie her shoelace, now that she was no longer wearing the brown summer shoes that showed the skin on the top of her feet.

Sometimes Anya stayed at our apartment. The two rooms of our *dvushka* were a bedroom and a living room. My mother had the bedroom and I still slept on a divan behind a screen, a sort of constructed room within a room. Anya explained that things were tense at home, especially since she'd said she wanted to write about her grandfather's life. She had the feeling that it was dividing her parents; Mikhail Sergeyevich supported her writing, Evgenia Fyodorovna was opposed to it. I thought of Mikhail Sergeyevich from time to time after that abruptly ended interview. Anya said she was determined to let him talk, and that we'd go back there soon to speak with him.

When she first slept there, and as she began to stay more often, I couldn't believe Anya was lying so close to me, couldn't believe I could be warm just from half her body lying on half of mine. She had become part of that apartment, that place. Cooking sometimes with my mother, or sitting talking with her into the night. I'd hear their quiet words first thing in the morning. My mother gave her books to read, and she would tell Anya about the lives of her dissident friends, the writers and musicians and artists who inspired us.

At night sometimes Anya would write. I liked to watch her as I lay in bed. I loved the small depression between her thigh and hip when, with bare legs, she sat up with the sheet a mess beneath her, an article or journal or notes resting on her knee, under the heel of the hand which held her cigarette.

In the morning I'd watch as she stood next to the bed pulling on her clothes, first her underwear, then stepping into her jeans, then slipping on her shirt, a cardigan. Watching her dress after we'd both been undressed for the night was somehow such an attractive thing. I'd ask her where she was going. It was never a question and we both knew that. Of course she was going to work. She'd just smile, roll her eyes, and continue to get ready. Where are you going, Anya, though it wasn't a question.

In the autumn I began to take a few walks with Anya's father. Anya said it would be better than continuing our interviews at the apartment. My mother, you know, she said.

And so Mikhail Sergeyevich and I would go to Gorky Park or Neskuchny Garden. Both were across the bridge from their apartment, on the other side of Frunzenskaya Embankment. The first time Mikhail Sergeyevich spoke about his time in a psychiatric hospital, we were in Gorky Park. Autumn was deepening then, the day sunny but cold. We walked a few minutes and then sat side by side on a bench. I took out a notebook, as I would do during all the conversations we had, so that I could preserve something of what he said to me.

I met a strange man here once, said Mikhail Sergeyevich. In this park. I came to think of him as the underground man. He was oddly dressed, in some sort of protective clothing, grey and shiny like armour, and his hair was tied in a long ponytail. He was bent over a manhole, opening the cover with a crowbar. I guess I was only going to pass by this man, but he started talking to me. He told me how he often went beneath the city. Perhaps his job had something to do with maintenance down there, perhaps he just explored of his own free will. Another whole world exists under the ground, said the man, and most of us rarely give it a thought. He described to me how instead of parks and railways, buildings, windows or clouds there was a maze of sewers, tunnels, underground rivers and metro lines. His father drove trains in the subway, and had taken him on rides as a boy.

As Mikhail Sergeyevich spoke, I imagined the underground from a view I hadn't before, looking ahead, into the darkness.

I saw, as if I was that underground man as a child in the driver's seat of a metro train, the sudden twists into dark, now into light, now again into darkness as the train rushed from one station to another. I saw countless branches sprouting from the tracks, the travels like a dark flight guided by the threads of a web, the silver underbelly of our city.

And so he still explored under there, said Mikhail Sergeyevich. He told me how he had a collection of relics he'd found over the years: coins from Tsarist times, a flask and gas mask, a telephone from the 1940s, a horseshoe, a mortar and pestle from who knows what time. He'd even found bones, unidentifiable limbs but also once a human skull. Didn't collect that, though. Didn't tell anyone until me, it would seem.

Mikhail Sergeyevich scratched his head absently, messing the grey and brown tufts. He looked younger, or lost, with his hair all askew like that.

I cannot explain to you why I found it all so interesting, he continued. But I kept on standing there, listening to this man speak. And I went back again the next day. He was there. Sitting on a bench smoking, as if waiting for me. We spoke again. He asked if I wanted to go down there one day, too.

Mikhail Sergeyevich bristled, a vague shiver. He smiled, but it seemed a falling defence, a frail wall soon down.

Oh no, I said to the underground man, no, thank you. Enclosed, dark spaces—no, thank you. But he told me what he saw, and I could almost feel as though I had made that terrifying trip myself. Down there it was cold but very, very still, he said. Though sometimes he came across rivers; real, flowing rivers that were lined with brick and white stone, their waters knee-deep, and a breeze would carry off them. The darkness pressing his eyes was the thickest he'd ever known; his torchlight could barely lighten even the smallest circle.

And I think it was during another conversation that he told me of the people down there. The true underground people, as it were—homeless, vagrants, what have you. Keeping out of the elements and away from anyone *up there*, I suppose you could say.

They *live* down there, Pasha, down in that reversed world, said Mikhail Sergeyevich. Almost as if they are people from the past who lost their way many years ago and can't live or die, they only keep on walking beneath Moscow.

Mikhail Sergeyevich coughed once, scratched again the back of his head, and apologised. I'm not here to talk about some old fascination, he said. I should tell you something useful. Of my father, perhaps.

He looked up at the sky, softly squinting, clearing his throat as if dissolving webs. The sun leached his face to grey.

Let me begin, he said, by saying I believe that how a country treats its ill tells us much about that country. It was my father who decided I needed treatment. When I was about fifteen he had me admitted to the Kashchenko Hospital here in the city—*the right environment to control your agitation*, as he put it.

Obviously this is something that's interested me for a time, said Mikhail Sergeyevich. And so I can tell you that the authorities above first involved themselves in treating the mentally ill back under Peter the Great, and before that it was the monasteries. After the revolution, Western ideas such as psychoanalysis were still allowed in, but all that changed with Stalin. Only a blend of Marxism and Soviet psychiatry was allowed. No longer was it simply a matter of science, or medicine. Pavlov's theories were chosen and made their way into medical textbooks from then on.

When my father died, he continued, I managed to reach a decision, and that was to abandon the treatment he, my father, had imposed. And you know, I felt finally detached from the system, Pasha. The system connected to him, to his work, and by extension to Stalin. That freedom of my mind was wonderfully liberating but also, in a way, quite terrifying.

He paused for a moment.

But I felt I'd *learnt* things in there, Pasha, he said. Learnt things about the way we talk about the mind, about the fact that, maybe after all this—he raised a light hand—all we have are our minds, not our bodies. But the way they get at your mind is through your body. So you have to find a way to protect yourself, to not let them in.

His face was grave. I crossed my arms at my chest, feeling uneasy in the face of the images in my mind, of hospital beds, the contours of white sheets encasing an immobile body still alive, the shiny corridor floors.

I told him how, in my research, I'd read that dissidents locked away in psychiatric hospitals feared that they actually would lose their minds in there.

Yes, Mikhail Sergeyevich said, nodding. When they have control of your body, you feel it encroaching upon your mind. The system was founded on total control. In that cold cell of a bed, I felt a war was being waged between my mind and my body. But it was a war begun by them, *up there*. They sought to control inner lives by control of external conditions. But I grew to feel there was something else—maybe it came from inside, from our bones and heart and thoughts—that works independently. But it struck me that perhaps our innerness has been damaged by our past. It's hard to know your direction when you are born into a system and then, suddenly, free of it. I wasn't sure how to proceed once I was released from the hospital. And I haven't been sure how to proceed since.

We continued to sit side by side in Gorky Park. The October breeze threw leaves around, and Mikhail Sergeyevich sat very still, his hands resting in loose fists on his knees.

This could be, I thought, a continuation of that afternoon several weeks ago with Oleg, when he told me about his wife's incarceration in a psychiatric hospital under Brezhnev. If each of us has our own inner chronology, for me those two moments were neighbouring pages of the story.

Mikhail Sergeyevich began speaking again, and rather than pulling me into the present I felt that he was joining me in that other conversation, a scene quite fixed in my mind, when Oleg sat next to me in the forest near Moscow and told me about Marya.

I have no doubt you'll write, Pasha, Anya's father said. As I grow older I'm more certain that what I've got to say is beyond my powers of expression. So it feels a good thing to pass it on, I guess.

Anya came over that evening, and we sat up talking on the divan after my mother had gone to bed. When Anya asked me how the meeting with her father had gone, I told her how we'd visited Gorky Park, and of our conversation there.

Or, actually, he spoke *around* the time he was in hospital. He didn't really describe it exactly, I said.

Anya nodded. Well, you can speak with him again. He seems to really like you, Pasha.

I'm not sure where it's all going, though, I said. What we'll be able to use or if we can write something from this.

I think it's just good for him, said Anya. And it shows my mother that talking isn't so bad after all. He seems fine. He seems to enjoy it.

In November the Memorial Society held a Week of Conscience in a Palace of Culture in Moscow. Survivors and relatives of victims of the Gulag and the repressions brought in hundreds of photographs. We displayed them on the walls of the Palace of Culture, along with the maps of camps and lists of names, which ran in long lines that seemed never-ending. Despite knowing of the volumes of testimony received by newspapers and by the Memorial Society, despite knowing the numbers, it was a staggering thing to see so many people gathered there. The pieces of paper, the stories and photos, seemed after generations of silence to be the first collective cry. The society received letter after letter during and beyond that week. The requests were simple: *My father was last seen on . . . His name is . . . I would like information on where he was taken.*

I have been told that my parents were put on trial on . . . sentenced and shot at . . . I would like to know where they are buried . . .

Some of the photographs on the wall had been sent along with those letters. Mostly they were black and white. There were austere family portraits, and young faces radiant beneath a professional portraitist's flash. Others were police shots, immediately gaunt and somehow suggesting a halfway point, as though some kind of torment had begun but wasn't yet over. No matter whether the photographs were of carefree young faces or haggard images taken by the police, they all seemed to hold the weight of what was to come. The perfect epitome of the fiction of time, all prior innocence lost, like memories they absorbed what was then and all that happened, even what came before them.

As people walked among those photographs on the walls of the Palace of Culture, a resonating hum seemed to accompany their murmured conversations. It was hard to tell if the people were speaking to each other or talking softly to the images as they walked up and looked at them closely. In fact, it almost seemed as if the sounds were released from the photographs themselves. Like a murmured symphony, a conversation between the living and the lost.

My mother and I walked slowly together around the large hall. She wore a navy-blue coat and a black scarf. The place, or the event, seemed to take a toll on her. She was very quiet, and looked shaken and distracted.

The last year or so has brought past time back to me, Pasha, she said. It feels like the years of the Thaw, after Khrushchev's speech thirty years ago. After that day, people wrote letters to the newspapers asking the meaning of Khrushchev's words, asking how he could possibly criticise Stalin. Some were relieved, some were angry. While now we say *Stalinism* and *Terror*, in those years it was *unjustified repressions* and *cult of personality*, those words that were suddenly delivered up, as the devil's name might be given to the church, as the excuse for everything, but which really in the end excuses nothing.

In that strange way the past has of coming back to us in patterns and faces, she continued, lately I've been seeing the same expressions, reading the same phrases. I see the wary relief on some faces, the anger on others. Or it's as if the angry letter sent by a woman after Khrushchev's speech, defending all that Stalin did to *bring us up in the world*, is then echoed word for word by her granddaughter thirty years later as she angrily watches a Memorial Society protest. As if the sad letter written by a middle-aged man, about the pain of his return from the Gulag and how he no longer feels he exists in the world, has been posted through time and re-sent by his great-nephew, newly released from Brezhnev's camps.

My mother's face was sombre and she took my arm as we left the hall.

The emergence of memory seemed to me like a warped wound, with a welt or bruise that had arrived inexplicably late. As if the visible evidence of the injury had suddenly sprung up now, though the blow itself had occurred years before. I wondered what might be the consequences of that delayed bruise, the cost of long-unseen blood that finally rises up under the skin; an injury not treated soon after the impact.

I wrote a rough draft of a short story about a town of people covered in bruises that were the sudden, overnight manifestation of every knock and fall that had happened during their lives. But the story turned into a mess as I tried to list the multiple injuries, attribute each mark to its inflictor, discern between that which might have been caused by a childhood fall or by a beating by a parent, or by something that nobody could remember. The narrative became twisted and confused when I tried to account for the more vague maladies, such as the days plagued by anxiety, or widespread aches. Both allegory and realism escaped me; maybe I wasn't meant to be a writer after all.

After the Week of Conscience, the Memorial Society received numerous letters of protest. Memory was raw and angry, never old, never over.

Stalin defended the socialist course adopted by the Party, and he advanced a culturally and economically backward country . . . Don't destroy with Stalin all that was accomplished by the people. You must not dishonour and insult all that is great in Russia.

The conversations with Mikhail Sergeyevich in the park and with Oleg in the forest near Moscow had brought back something—not so much memories as the feeling of my childhood, of uneasiness and a nebulous sense of confusion. The only research I enjoyed was talking to Mikhail Sergeyevich, which felt more like a conversation with an old relative than anything I might one day write about or the books I had read.

It got me thinking about the roots of knowledge, and made me wonder how I knew the things I did about my country, about the meaning of words and concepts used without a second thought.

At some point as a boy I grew old enough to understand the meaning behind the words used by the dissident aunts and uncles in the apartment of my childhood. There was a shift in my perception, after which I understood meanings, or could appreciate, if not explain, a difference between *Gulag* and *repression* and *psikhushka*.

The word *Gulag* I associated with older stories, of the kind told in Solzhenitsyn's *The Gulag Archipelago*. I understood that the word didn't refer to one camp in particular, but to an administration system. I learnt that so much could stagger under the weight of a single word, that there were hundreds upon hundreds of camps in enormous networks across the Soviet Union, where prisoners—criminal and political alike—mined gold in Kolyma, built canals in the north and even, as Solzhenitsyn himself did, constructed tower blocks in Moscow. And I gradually came to know (it was strange to me that I could never recall the first moment of that realisation) that the people who sometimes disappeared from the kitchen table meetings had been sent to those camps, or had once been in one. The woman who made the delicious *kotleti*, the young man with black hair who left his cap behind on a chair in our kitchen, who both disappeared in my childhood—them I associated with *Gulag*.

The word *repression* was often said along with *execution, shot, false charge, show trial, the Terror, the Purges, the Lubyanka, the KGB, interrogation.*

The likelihood of a person returning from the fate either word suggested—*Gulag* or *repression*—seemed to be equal. To me both words went to the same place of disappearance and silence. Twenty years in a labour camp sounded like forever, and the indefinable place of repression never meant certain death, as paper could not be trusted and sometimes people thought to have been shot did come home.

The *psikhushka* was different. This I associated less with words than with indistinct utterings, as if emerging from underwater, spoken by Oleg or my mother. Thinking of the word now I felt a certain tone of memory, a sense of disquiet and inner pain. Though I knew that the word was connected to my father and his death, such an association began at a time when I didn't have the information to make the right connection between word and event. It was only when I was older that I understood enough to be able to picture the place of my father's incarceration, to join word and image.

We had, in the apartment, an official document, a charge sheet, dated 8 May 1973, which cited a crime under Article 190-1 of the Criminal Code of *circulation of fabrications known to be false which defame the Soviet state and social system.*

My father was taken first to Butyrka Prison, from there to the Serbsky Institute on Kropotkin Lane in Moscow for one year; and from there to Oryol Prison, two hundred miles south-west of Moscow, from where his body was retrieved in the autumn of 1974 after he succumbed to the effects of a prolonged hunger strike.

Strangely, I couldn't recall the first time I saw the charge sheet. But reading it must have made me able to connect my father with specific places, with psychiatric hospitals and prisons. I looked at it, sometimes, as a teenager. But as I got older I didn't; I had essentially memorised it, anyway. My mother and I never spoke about the charge sheet or the circumstances of my father's death, and rarely about him at all. There was nothing to say beyond the things we already knew, and so we left him as a silent presence, a fully formed absence, inside our apartment.

But at any time, a word could have an association without my knowing what it really meant, such as Anya talking often about *over there*, about wanting to leave. The threat of her absence always had its own form and I felt it lodged somewhere, even though I didn't know what her absence would look like or when it would happen. Yura had still had no luck getting an exit visa, and often the talk among our group would turn to the idea of leaving the Soviet Union. At the Sukhanovs' for dinner one night in the winter, Yura told us the story of a Jewish scientist who had obtained an exit visa and gone to the United States, and who had then returned for a short visit to Moscow. Yura seemed in awe of the man.

The scientist's friends said it was like he had disappeared for good, said Yura. So when he came back for a conference, people looked at him as though he'd returned from the dead. No one could *see*, they couldn't even imagine, where he might have gone.

Yes, said Anya. The West or anywhere abroad, *over there*, always seemed to be a place that didn't quite exist. A made-up place.

But now, said Yura, now things are different. There are more openings, people can see footage and photographs of places, there's more contact with other countries.

Exactly, said Anya. And we should all be allowed to see those places for ourselves.

I didn't say anything. I had grown up wishing that I didn't have to have a secret life, a hidden history, and now that a life without secrets had arrived I had no desire to leave my city, my country. The question of Anya leaving was a mostly unspoken but noticeable presence between us, like a small stone carried around. It gave an uneasy edge to our relationship. I felt a sort of veil between us, sometimes—I could still see her, she was still with me, and at times I could push it aside and she'd seem content. Other times I sensed that she had pulled it down again and saw a world on her side of the veil that did not include me.

CHAPTER 16

Each night at the *dacha* a glowing orange sun and a weak pearly moon hung together in the sky. I spent a week of ageless evenings on the long seat in front of the *dacha*, although Vera Sergeyevna next door warned me, with her *babushki* superstitions, not to leave the chair out overnight. Careful, she said, you should know that moonlight destroys furniture. But still I lay listening to the summer sounds of insects, tree shivers, creaking wood. I was so tired by the end of each day, but it was the kind of fatigue that brought only difficult, disturbed sleep.

My routine began in the morning, brewing tea and eating bread, usually standing at the front window, as if the trees and sky gave me some regularity. At least I knew the beginning of each day. I would write a bit, drink more tea, stand again at the window, then go back to the desk. The phone never rang. The windows rattled if it was windy.

Oblivious to whether they wanted me there, I kept returning to the neighbours' house. Vera Sergeyevna would make tea and we'd sit in her kitchen snacking on fruit or sunflower seeds.

Sometimes she asked how my writing was going. She always had the radio turned on in the kitchen and I once mentioned something about seeing Popov's grave in St Petersburg, and how he had invented the radio.

Ah yes, Popov, we know him well, she said, smiling. I was just a girl when the radio arrived in the countryside. Like a voice from heaven! But there was something terrifying about it.

I nodded, drank my tea. I knew that a nationwide radio network had been installed under Stalin. The Ministry of Ideology was behind it—their goal to enter the home, mind and heart of every person, so it was said. Even the radio, like my city, seemed tarnished by old violence.

The neighbour would come in after a morning outside, short of breath, his checked shirt coming untucked from his trousers. We would chat about nothing in particular—the weather or the city or the children. The slow, easy conversation had something warm about it, like summer, green and softly breezy.

I had a theory that the neighbour knew more about those dead roads than he let on. Perhaps he'd already been there but didn't want Vera Sergeyevna to know. An image formed in my mind, like a still frame from a movie, of the neighbour standing on the concrete edge of an unfinished road, holding a bottle of *samogon*. It was nearly dark, and he was just standing because there didn't seem to be anything more to do after arriving at such a place. My head was full of those kinds of still images which never went anywhere.

I talked more than usual when I was with the neighbour. It was something about his manner; as though he belonged to another place, a time separate from my present life, so that

I somehow knew anything I said wouldn't leave the *dacha* boundaries.

Early one afternoon the neighbour and I went walking in the forest. For some reason I hadn't ventured in there yet; I'd kept to the road to the beach, the *produkti* and the station, or the yard bordered by the wall of trees.

A bit further, a bit further, said the neighbour.

The trees huddled closer together the deeper we went. The air cooled.

We had a conversation about Moscow. He'd been there once. When he started talking about it I felt not so much longing as a pained admiration for the city. The neighbour mentioned the main sites, well known to anyone. Dzerzhinsky Square. Detsky Mir toyshop. GUM department store. Red Square. The Arbat. We stayed pretty late, sitting on a fallen log until early evening, nearing the end of the bottle. At some point the neighbour asked me what I was writing about, or maybe he asked me who I was writing about. And so I told him about Anya and her father, and more or less what had taken place in Moscow. I couldn't decide if the slow process of remembering and writing down felt less taxing than to suddenly, upon being questioned, state so briefly the things that had happened.

So they're both gone now, he said. The girl and her father.

Yeah, I said, taking a shot, then eating some pickles the neighbour had brought with him. Both gone. But it's hard, when you go to write about something like this. There's no *before* when you know what happened. Time is just there, all at once. Linearity is a lie.

Just write it, my boy, said the neighbour. Start anywhere and just tell what happened.

We went to the forest again the next day, and the day after that. It became a strange memory place, that green around us, the clear air; almost a city, almost Moscow. We were bringing back so many past moments, the neighbour and me, with our *samogon* and our words.

But really, Moscow was always with me, in fragments that were difficult to put in order. I wondered how or whether we decide what to remember. In the sun of those evenings in 1999, I was bathed in the heat of 1988. Probably it is unavoidable, our tendency to recall past seasons as the same sun watches over another summer, then autumn, and then the cold returns again. As if doing so might provide an essential marker: what was before, what had since come.

Just start anywhere, the neighbour had told me. Just tell what happened. The memory of an event takes on the shadow of its aftermath, like a second skin. Skins of memory: I felt those layers over me, over the apartment near Arbatskaya where I grew up, over the city. In the apartment I couldn't only see Anya in the mornings, getting dressed as I lay on the divan, relaxed, murmuring to her. The scenes could never fully play out in my mind; they broke down partway through as later events demanded their own time on show, as did the half-hopes of what might have happened instead.

In 1990, Anya was there again, in our apartment, through nights that felt completely different. Her father was very unwell then, and Anya wasn't speaking to her mother. Looking back now, I wondered how her face might have looked in the dark.

Draped over us were the thin sheets I had slept beneath for years. We would have spoken softly, so as not to wake my mother. I wondered how many conversations I'd forgotten. I tried to bring back what we said, how her voice sounded, recall my hand resting on her side just beneath her breast. I wondered if she had been able to sleep at all.

The night after Anya left, in 1992, I lay alone on the bed behind the screen in the living room. It no longer felt like my bed but the one I'd once shared with Anya. I'd forgotten to turn off the light above the kitchen table, and the yellow square thrown onto the ceiling above me, that old childhood comfort, was now something I blamed for keeping me awake. I was imagining the next time I might see her. I couldn't precisely picture the situation, how such a reunion might happen; it never did, anyway.

Every scene played at once, as in dreams, when all sorts of strange impossibilities are possible. Some days at the *dacha*, by evening I would be annoyed with myself, horrified even, that I couldn't really say what I'd done for so many hours. I kept letting the present disappear or get away from me. And it annoyed me because I didn't really want her anymore. She didn't exist to want, that girl with a burning heart in 1988. I had no idea who she was in 1999. She was a place in time, a time in me. I wrote in my notebook: *You don't exist to want.*

But then it all ended, too soon. A new set of classes was about to begin at the language school. I couldn't afford to miss any more work, and I knew I had to leave the *dacha*. Two days before I was supposed to return to Petersburg, I stood with the neighbour at the edge of his yard, close to the forest.

The voices of Vera Sergeyevna and the grandchildren drifted with the wind from a short distance away. Four chairs from the kitchen had been moved outside. Vera Sergeyevna sat on one; the other two were empty as the children played on the ground near her feet. They were all going back to the city that afternoon, the neighbour had told me; he wanted to secure the doors of the greenhouses and sheds before the winter came, and pack a few bottles to take back to the city. Heavy dew saturated the grass. The greenhouse windows were foggy and traced with lines from the plants' reaching branches.

You're a good man, Pasha, talking to an old man like this. Vera, you know, he said, his head knocking the air towards the house, she doesn't like me talking about anything like that. You mention politics and she starts banging pots. I try to tell her; I say, Vera, it's so different now, you have to understand it's different now. But no, she says, it's none of our business, not our place to talk about it. And then she repeats her mother's saying: *The further from the Tsar, the longer for your life.* He waved a thick finger in the air.

I saw a lot of that hesitation back in Moscow, I said. We recorded interviews at the Memorial Society with survivors of the repressions, the Gulag. But sometimes even people who came by choice to speak found that they couldn't. They would sit there looking horrified, as though they'd stumbled in by mistake.

The neighbour nodded vigorously, and I wondered what he knew, what stories he could not quite tell me. It's good for you young ones to see that, he said. He crossed his arms at his chest. That fear in the eyes—it's an old fear, Pasha. Always wondering who is listening, who will tell. It's how we grew up. Hard habits to break.

The neighbour looked over at Vera Sergeyevna. The way the voice lowers, he said, when she wants to complain about the food at the markets or the cost of certain things. An old fear.

The neighbour motioned to one of the greenhouses. I followed him over and helped him tape some old newspaper over a window that had a deep crack running its length.

We learnt when we were growing up to be careful with words, he said, using his forefinger to smooth the tape over the paper with great care. We were raised with those warnings from our mothers: *You'll get in trouble for your tongue. You know you can't speak about that. The walls have ears!* That kind of thing. And so it really was a surprise when Vera turned to me one day, after thirty-odd years of marriage, and told me about the other half of her childhood.

I told you, he said, that Vera is from an old farming family. The committees, or their loyal followers, came in 1931 to turn over the farms to state control. Vera was eight. With her mother and siblings, she was deported to the Altai region, in Siberia. Her cousins fled, an aunt and uncle were killed. She never saw her grandparents again. They were put in one of those special settlements for *kulak* families, so-called 'rich' peasants said to have exploited the poor. A wooden barracks beside a river. She has said very little about it other than to mention the cold and hunger.

We walked into another of the greenhouses. Inside, it felt cool.

A different kind of air in here, the neighbour said. As though we're not entirely outside or in.

I looked through the window and saw Vera with the grandchildren. She leant forwards, slightly regal in her chair;

there was something of a sad queen about her as she spoke words I couldn't hear.

One of the grandchildren, the little girl, stood for a moment beside Vera Sergeyevna, touched her face with a palm and used the other hand to trace lipstick onto her grandmother's pursed lips. She then returned to her doll on the ground, whose face she had been decorating from a make-up kit. The wind lifted her hair.

As he passed me two bottles, the neighbour remarked that his and Vera Sergeyevna's children had never known what their grandparents looked like. When my father was taken, my mother destroyed all our photos, he said. I've wondered if I should try to draw them, the faces of my parents, to try to pass something on to the children and grandchildren.

It was the first time the neighbour had hinted at his father's fate. Certain words had telling connotations when loaded with meaning from the past: *taken*—my father was *taken*, he had said. *They're inside. They're lost. Disappeared. They've had troubles.* It reminded me of the people who disappeared during my childhood and turned into names or just a word—*Gulag, the charge*—which held so much within it. I said that I could help him write something, or perhaps use his story as part of the larger work that I was writing. He nodded but didn't answer straight away.

After a long moment the neighbour went on to speak of how, in recent years, things had gone fairly well for his children, and his son whose children were here for the summer, had purchased the *dacha* the previous year. Their daughter had taken a job with a foreign company in St Petersburg, which paid in dollars not rubles, and so they had all survived the fearful inflation of the past decade.

So perhaps breaking with the past has been good, he said, though his expression was still sombre. Yet these days, it seems that things are worse for most people. I sometimes wonder whether it was better before, with the USSR. Back then, you didn't see old *babushki* begging at corners in Leningrad like you do now. You didn't hear stories from neighbours who can't afford a funeral bus to take their families and the coffin to the cemetery on the day of a funeral, travelling together like the old ways.

He stood watching Vera and the children. But yes, he said. Yes, I think I'll come visit you in Petersburg, Pasha. Write the story down.

I gave the neighbour my phone number and he said he'd call me to arrange a meeting in the city. At the end of the day, the neighbour and Vera Sergeyevna packed the car and I waved goodbye to the family as they drove out along the dusty road into Repino and back to Petersburg. Again I was alone.

My thoughts shifted to the city. I felt uneasy about returning, though I wasn't exactly sure why. I liked the *dacha*. If I could, I'd just remain there. I'd found my timeless place. In fact, I wasn't even sure of the time. I had misplaced my watch somewhere along the way from St Petersburg to the *dacha*.

I lay on the seat in front of the *dacha*, drinking the remainder of the beer I had bought at the *produkti*, and fell asleep for a few moments, wishing on the edge of sleep for the warmth of a girl next to me, the weight of her on my chest. The garden sweated, the white night hummed.

CHAPTER 17

As winter thickened, the walls of the Sukhanovs' place seemed to close in. Perhaps more people were coming at that time of year—the snow had arrived as if for good—craving the alcohol, heat, inspiration of the tiny confines of the apartment. There was a strong sense of need and energy buzzing through the rooms.

Yura's story on Jewish exit visa restrictions had been published, and he'd received a good response: letters of thanks from others in the same position, and he was quoted in news articles about *refuseniks*, those unable to leave the Soviet Union or attain decent academic positions within it. When I'd first met him, in the stairwell of Bulgakov's apartment back in the summer, Yura had been quite despondent, feeling hopeless about his situation. Since his article had appeared, he seemed a man transformed. His mood lighter, he joined us often for drinks and was eager to talk about politics. And he seemed less intent on leaving Russia. He kept thanking me for suggesting he write a story in the first place, and though I didn't feel I had done much to help him, his excitement fuelled my own support and hopes for *glasnost*.

Meanwhile, Ilya was still all about the music, and his band was gathering a strong following in Moscow, holding concerts in clubs or apartments. He organised a semi-regular night at the Sukhanovs' apartment to play new songs to a small group there.

Not everyone believed in *glasnost*—some thought Gorbachev weak, too scared to really bring Stalin's name down once and for all, or just as power hungry as every other leader we had known, wary of giving the Memorial Society too much leeway.

When a Memorial Society member, Dima Yurasov, was arrested, the doubt could be felt drifting through the room at the Sukhanovs'. The KGB were waiting at the airport, we heard, when Dima returned from the north after giving lectures on the Stalinist repressions. From the kitchen I heard someone yell, *Glasnost* is a joke, and the sound of a glass shattering, though I didn't know if the two were related.

My own writing wasn't going very well. I worked full time at the library, and at night, if I wasn't distracted by concerts, Sukhanov's weekend gatherings, or spending time with Anya, I would try to work.

In me was a whole history that I longed to convey, but there was a strange halting, as if time had gathered, become confused, causing a blockage, a sense of inertia. I couldn't really explain the nebulous space between my boyhood horror, that edge-of-knowing awareness, the heavy silence, and my present understanding of the facts in the press, in the open now.

It was similar to the feeling I had when I tried to describe for Anya the apartment of my childhood. Physically, it was the same as it appeared now, but in other ways it was so different. Back then that apartment reflected my internal reality: just like me, it held the secrets unspoken outside. But by 1988 that reality was out in the streets, out there in Moscow. And it was so difficult to convey what that shift meant, or what really happened with that change. It made me feel unsteady, uncertain, because I couldn't write about what was so important to me.

I grew dissatisfied, easily irritated. I started walking by myself, ridiculously long distances. One day I thought about going to the Serbsky Institute of Forensic Psychiatry, where my father had been taken. But instead I found myself suddenly diverting, following some other course through the city.

I had read in one of Viktor Nekipelov's books, *Institute of Fools*, of his encounters with others in Serbsky who were, like him, clearly of a sound mind but who had feigned madness because confinement in the psychiatric ward was thought to be better than imprisonment in a Gulag camp.

Although it had been constantly in my mind, I was never sure if I'd actually been inside the Serbsky Institute. It was true that I had memories of being inside an asylum, though the memories didn't extend to the building's exterior, so I could never be sure which hospital it was. All I could remember was the ward where my mother and I went to see my father. I wanted him to stop smiling, because his face scared me; the creases around his eyes looked unnatural, so many wrinkles, and his mouth contorted as though grimacing. Only as a grown man did I understand that it was probably the combination of fatigue, medications and horror that had made him seem much older than the thirty-something he would have been then.

It occurred to me that going to the actual place where he, my father, had been held for a time—for two months of psychiatric evaluation in the seventies—was unlikely to help me in my writing. It seemed the more I came into contact with knowledge, with information, with tangible experience, such as standing on the very road the truck or car he was put in would have driven down, the less close I felt to him. Perhaps keeping him in the space of my childhood memory, where I didn't know many details but had intense bursts of feeling, was more real than the facts and figures I could find through research, or even the understanding I gained by talking to Mikhail Sergeyevich about what it was really like inside.

Anya and I still spoke about our plans to write something together, but in the meantime we were working on separate things. I had one story published in early 1989, which felt like a tiny salvation after months of nothing. And so I decided to stick with writing short stories for the time being. Anya had grown close to Lena, Sukhanov's wife, and became interested in working on film and TV editing. In early 1989 she got a part-time position at the TV station where Lena still worked as a sound technician.

Lena was sometimes able to get hold of films that weren't screened at the usual cinemas. Some filmmaker friends of hers in Leningrad were compiling newsreel footage, unedited, of parades on Revolution Day in the Brezhnev years.

Anya said she wanted to go to Leningrad to meet the film-makers and work with them. It's brilliant, she said, using *their* footage, the state propaganda, for their own work.

One afternoon we sat down with tea, crammed into the Sukhanovs' one small room, watching some of the film. Cheering crowds stood in the rain, smiling even as the ice showers from the skies ran down their faces, waving flags and shouting *Long live the Party!* like some scene of collective madness. The old Communist leaders watched on, raising an arm regally, nodding slowly, as if the reel had slowed down or they were eerie windup toys slackening with age.

Watching those scenes now is important, Lena said. We can show how what seemed normal then—what was reality—was just a construction of the system. Perspective is everything; change the conditions of perception and you see things in a completely different way. Make people *think* about what to do with the information we have.

It's true, Anya agreed. You can only understand our situation now by appreciating *that*—she pointed at the screen—as once being real life.

Another film which Anya said really changed things for her, made her think this was the form she wanted to work with, was called *Protsess* (*The Trial*). We all watched it together at the Sukhanovs'. On the screen for the first time, as if delivered up from nightmares, was footage of Stalin's show trials in the 1930s. The prosecutor, Andrei Vyshinsky, a stocky figure in a suit, was delivering a tirade at the trial of Bukharin. His arm rose and fell as he denounced the deviants, saboteurs, spies who were plotting to bring down the Soviet system. The shadow of his arm moved on the curtain behind him. His voice was glazed with that antiquated, slightly surreal waver of old movie footage.

The men and women in the audience looked odd, unnerving to me. They shifted with the strange tics of footage running at an increased speed, hands flitting to their glasses, blinking, scribbling notes, sharply turning their necks to look around them. The flickers and occasional spots in the images all created the impression that they were either very nervous or possessed by some fervent impatience. At times, a voiceover stated facts and numbers about the show trials and repressions.

The thing is, said Anya, pointing energetically with her cigarette at the screen, the voiceover is from someone *today*.

I watched, impressed by the creation, but also envious, perhaps jealous of Anya's admiration for these Leningrad filmmakers I'd never met. Although she continued to ask me how my work was going, I felt increasingly that the difficulties I was having with my writing weren't interesting to Anya anymore; that in her eyes I was no longer suffering the pains of burgeoning art but wrestling with inability.

That winter I finished a short story but couldn't get it published anywhere. It described a network of psychiatric hospitals, grown so large through the designs of the authorities that it formed a territory of asylums. Sane dissidents were locked away, tied to beds arranged in rows in rooms where lamps glowed light green and dark yellow for days and nights on end. As those in power tightened their control over the populace, and more and more dissidents were locked away, the number of asylums for the so-called insane grew. Eventually the asylums covered the land, overtaking the territory of the so-called sane, where the rulers were the only ones left. I called the story 'Territory of Fools'. I guessed that something was lacking and I left it alone.

I felt a distance growing between what we hoped to do and what we were doing, perhaps a young man's first realisation that you do not always grasp the great things in your mind.

Anya went to Leningrad in the winter of 1989. She suggested we have some time apart to *follow our own paths*, as she put it.

I probably didn't fight for her then, because I knew she was right, that I hadn't done what I was hoping to do and I wasn't the best company; I was frustrated all the time, as if constantly engaged in an internal argument, and sometimes Anya got caught up in it. It was as though I could feel what I wanted to create but not see it. I knew what the words sounded like but couldn't write them.

While Anya was away, I alternated between seeking company and desperately wanting to be alone. Sometimes I threw myself into messy nights out with Ilya, at concerts or drinking in the park. Billy Bragg toured, bringing the West to us. I saw Bragg's photo in a newspaper, a KGB minder at his side, the singer wearing an *ushanka*, the sides of the hat pinned up. Ilya and I went to the concert, held in the old weightlifting hall from the 1980 Olympics. We walked around aimlessly afterwards, and as I went to a *tabak* to buy cigarettes he loped past me to a Pepsi stand up ahead. He came back with two cans, yelling, Gorbachev's juice! Keeping Soviets sober! in his most comradely and patriotic voice. The tired morning light was somehow relaxing. Our stupid mood transcended the mist and we laughed, held high our Pepsi cans, walked and drank and smoked through the freezing morning.

Going out became addictive, the apartment painfully quiet and boring. One night I went to a music festival. Live bands, people everywhere. Inside, every face seemed lit from within, somehow bright in the red-tinged, smoky darkness. There was a girl, a friend of Ilya's girlfriend at the time, who talked and stood close to me, and in the wisp of a moment took one step, rising slightly as though a dancer poised, and kissed me. The girl pulled away and I realised I'd kissed her back. I looked at her and then around me, saw Ilya looking over, grinning.

Though I put my arm around the girl, I was thinking of another moment, a few years before, at the Yolka Festival with Ilya, and that girl in the darkness who had walked over and kissed me before leaving, trailing her arms in the air. A great distance seemed to separate those two moments.

In the morning we walked through the city. We hadn't slept. The wintry sky was barely distinguishable from the night just over. Moskva River blew icy air over our faces. Ilya stepped as though avoiding cracks in the pavement, tired chuckles lifted his shoulders, his leather jacket in place as ever. At some point I said I had to get home, get some sleep. The girl waved and smiled, I held up my hand to the group and then went the other way.

When I returned home, the apartment was quiet; my mother's bedroom door was closed. My mouth was heavy with beer and my head was starting to hurt already.

To me, Ilya stood for the now, the present, and only the closest future. We rarely spoke about things from the past, though one night that winter, when leaving the Sukhanovs' apartment we sat down, with the sudden logic of the intoxicated, to have a conversation in the dirty stairwell.

So they just rehabilitated my grandfather, Ilya said. Rehabilitated! They say *the crimes have not been proven*. Ilya spat out a laugh. It's bureaucracy gone mad, he said. Bureau*crazy*. So according to them, there *was* a crime, they just haven't got enough *evidence*. Neither of us spoke for a moment. His beer bottle broke the silence as he scraped it along the walls. The concrete looked ripped and the grating sound echoed.

Ilya told me that his grandfather had been arrested in the forties, after being found at the factory where he worked with a leaflet of apparently unpatriotic thoughts. He was given a ten-year labour camp sentence. And so his son, Ilya's father, was labelled a relative of an *enemy of the people*. He was marked, as the saying went; certain jobs and courses of study were barred to him. Ilya's father was now a labourer at an electrical plant, his grandfather a pensioner.

It is a joke, Pasha. It's absurd. The papers—this so-called *rehabilitation certificate*—should say he is rehabilitated because of the *absence* of a crime in the first place. But no, they must have their crime; they have to pretend there was a threat. Even now, after all that time, they've got to create their fucking enemies.

March arrived. One day, when Anya was still away, I went to Red Square to take some photographs for the *Express Chronicle*, the paper my friend Sasha edited. It was the anniversary of Stalin's death, 5 March. The group called Pamyat were laying a memorial wreath at the necropolis by the Kremlin wall. The square had a sense of desolation at that point of the year, when it seemed that time was stuck forever in a continuous moment of winter. Beside the red walls of the Kremlin, from beneath the still, grey concrete, spruce trees and statues of former leaders rose up like a malformed forest.

An elderly woman in a navy-blue hat stood with three flowers, one red and two white, in her gloved hand. Another woman and two men wore old army uniforms. On their chests were golden medallions pinned side by side, the one nudging the other to form a golden patch like glowing dragon's scales. I looked through the lens and captured the scene from a distance, thinking that perhaps it would be better to do away with any kind of anniversary, when such things can be used to remember in all sorts of ways, for good or ill.

Anya came back just before her birthday in March. We had a night at the Sukhanovs' apartment, drinking and listening to music, arguing happily like always. After her return, Anya had a new sense of composure about her. I thought it was maybe the peace of those who have glimpsed what they want; for her, a way out. Confined to Moscow for her whole life, under her mother's anxious cloud, in Leningrad she had stood for a while out of the shadow of that cloud.

Behind that composure was a new kind of inner urgency, a focused determination to leave the Soviet Union. She spoke more practically, about exit visas and potential jobs abroad. At the time I didn't really take it seriously. To me, people didn't leave because they wanted to, only when they were taken. Yura couldn't get out. I couldn't see how Anya would be able to get a visa—and, more than that, I didn't believe she was really unhappy enough to want to go.

CHAPTER 18

Early in the new year, 1989, Oleg asked me to visit him at his apartment. I'd never been there before. It was not far from Chkalov Street, part of the Garden Ring. The streetscape around me would have looked as it always did. Every winter was the same. Thin snow like loosely woven gauze, almost transparent, over the footpaths and tree branches; cars speeding by in a bright winter sun. As I walked to Oleg's, a man walked past me holding flowers wrapped in newspaper, a copy of *Pravda*, carried high in the air. Up ahead, on a building bleached gravel-grey in the sun, a banner proclaimed glory to labour in red letters on a snow-white surface. Beneath the words were stars on one side, a hammer and sickle on the other.

Oleg met me at the entrance to the building and we took the elevator to the sixth floor. Walking along the hallway, we passed the kitchen. A young woman around my age stood in jeans and a long t-shirt, cooking at the stove. When she looked up, something hissed inside a pan on the hotplate. She said hello, turned back to the pan, shook it once or twice by the handle.

Oleg had two rooms in the apartment. The door opened into a living room, neat but crowded with books and ceiling-high piles of paper, like a replica of those in our apartment. Apart from the books and papers, there were only a few objects: a radio, an empty vase, both on a small square table on a piece of brown carpet. A small framed picture of a lake, and at least four hats, each hung in place on a wooden spoke near the front door.

For quite some time, I have been working on a sort of project of documentation, Oleg said. And it occurred to me recently that I should show you, or somebody, because otherwise—Oleg tapped three fingers to his temple—it does not really leave here.

We passed through the living room to the second of his rooms, which I had thought would be the bedroom. Yet it looked more like a study, with a large desk taking up most of the space apart from a couch that must have doubled as a bed. Oleg turned on the light. The desk was covered with papers and so were the walls. A great mass of black lines, letters and stars covered the sheets of white paper. I realised they were all maps.

The Gulag. *Vot.* There it is, Oleg said.

He nodded in answer to my hesitant step into the room. As I came closer, I saw names that were familiar to me in a distant way, as the names of childhood books or old relatives remain at once forgotten and known: Perm, Murmansk, Kem, Kolyma, Arkhangelsk, Vorkuta, Dudinka, Norilsk, Igarka, Tobolsk, Omsk, Novosibirsk, Karaganda, Mointy, Frunze, Samarkand, Krasnovodsk, Magnitogorsk, Chelyabinsk, Berezniki, Molotovsk, Kotlas, Totma, Yaroslavl, Kargopol, Tambov, Kharkov, Monchegorsk, and, far above the White Sea, the Solovetsky Islands.

Clustered in some areas, dispersed in others, were neatly drawn stars in black ink. Each star is a camp, Oleg explained. Or was.

Although the Gulag years were spoken of during *glasnost* as they never had been before, it was hard to truly see the past. One could not know if the old faces on the street were survivors or shoppers. They could be traumatised or they could just be tired of waiting in long queues for things bought only so they would not starve. Harder still to see in Moscow, metropolis of new concrete and renamed streets, of buildings that housed the sons and grandsons of the very system that endured throughout. I touched one area of smooth paper and thought, then, how invisible the past was in the city in which I lived.

We made a plan that night. We would go to the old camps in early May. I wanted to witness the remains myself, and it would help the historical research division of the Memorial Society to make a record of those sites of memory. It was important for Oleg, too. We stood together in front of the maps.

I need to see it, Pasha, he said.

I looked from the walls to Oleg standing next to me. He was reaching out with one arm. His wide, crinkled hand made a star on the map closest to him. It was a small star on the expanse of paper. It seemed to me that blindness was as powerful and terrible as silence, sight as important as speech. Stone and ground told as much as any words.

Oleg traced invisible lines across the maps. We will go from here to here, and all the way up to Solovetsky, Pasha. To see it. I am glad you're coming. Oleg's expression, as he looked at the maps, was never mine to describe.

I met with Mikhail Sergeyevich one more time before I left. We hadn't met at all during the winter, perhaps because it was too cold to sit in the snowy parks, or because Anya was away. But it was spring now, and the city was recovering its green. He began talking almost straight away about the psychiatric history he thought might interest me. He seemed eager to talk, more lucid than when we spoke before the winter. I wondered whether he was feeling better than he had the previous time we spoke, or if it was just that he'd had more time to think about what he wanted to say. In any case, he spoke directly about the asylums.

I've got some information for you, he said as we walked slowly along the embankment that ran along Gorky Park and then to Neskuchny Garden. He began by telling me how, in the early nineteenth century, an asylum called All-Mourners had opened in St Petersburg.

Such an odd name, he said. I can't work out why it was called that. The first proper study of the state of asylums in Russia was by Pavel Yakobi in Moscow in the late nineteenth century. Yakobi argued that the structures of society directly influenced the treatment of and attitudes towards the mentally ill. Which, as I'm sure you'll understand, is very interesting to me, given the control I saw both within the psychiatric ward and outside it, exercised by my father and other officials. Yakobi warned of a widespread fear of an abstract madman and saw the proliferation of asylums across Russia as a symptom of society's constructed fear of those deemed to be threatening, rather than as the proper treatment of ailments of the mind.

We left the embankment and walked into Neskuchny Garden. It was Moscow's oldest park. Old summer pavilions and residences were scattered over hectares of green; you could see them in the traces of yellow and white and blue that dashed the grass. We walked around a few of the ponds, over the stone bridges. Mikhail Sergeyevich moved slowly.

There were different classifications of mental illnesses over the years, he continued. Some sound, nowadays, very dated or more like philosophical ailments than medical or scientific— conditions like *over-intellectualisation* or *metaphysic intoxication*. These were, perhaps, less physiologically provable instances of illness, and maybe more symptoms of dissatisfaction with the person's condition—their role in life and society, their contribution, perhaps.

In the 1950s, continued Mikhail Sergeyevich, it seems the entire industry of psychological study had become a facade, a travesty of academia. In many ways it was a microcosm of the larger designs of the political establishment. It was common practice then for psychiatrists to gain positions of power by virtue of their political loyalties, and the outlets for true academic exchange of ideas were effectively shut down. Only one academic journal remained, espousing the official view, enabling the powers of the day to dictate the sharing and withholding of scientific thought.

I guess that time is interesting for me to study because it was when my father was working, and when I was receiving treatment. It's the world I was treated by, so to speak. In the early fifties, a hearing was held and supposedly reactionary or idealistic psychiatrists were condemned and forced to publicly acknowledge their mistakes. Basically, it shut down the exchange of thought in the Soviet world of psychiatric research. And it meant the parameters of madness and sanity, as it were, could be dictated by the government from their offices in Moscow.

And then there's the question of suicide, he said abruptly. Under the Soviet dogma, to take one's own life was portrayed as weak-willed, a betrayal of the collective in favour of the self—privileging *I* over *we*. Those committing such an act were lacking proper faith in the Party; a person didn't belong so wholly to themselves that they could decide whether to live or die. No, they were to put collective interests first. Killing oneself was the height of individualism, so they said, and it undermined their whole idea that labouring together—becoming *we*—could help prevent such inclinations. And maybe there's some truth in the notion that being part of a common cause is good for you. But in this case it was the cause of a system born of theories taken to an extreme, theories that should never have left the books in which they were written. I think that common cause should be far less tangible—the pursuit of art, or some similar idea.

And so, although there were some early Soviet studies of suicide, they ceased by the end of the 1920s as the official stigma took hold. By the 1930s, suicide vanished, in a manner of speaking, as official statistics were no longer released.

Mikhail Sergeyevich went quiet, and seemed to have run to the end of his thoughts for the time being. We sat for a while before parting ways.

The next time she came to our apartment, I asked Anya about her father, what she remembered of his illness from when she was a girl. She was standing by the window, sipping tea. I couldn't see what she was looking at outside, if she was in fact looking at anything beyond the other concrete towers.

I was very young when it all happened, she said, so I'm not sure if I really remember going to see him in hospital as a girl or whether, because I know he went to the hospital, I *feel* like I remember. Mama, even now, doesn't like to discuss it. There was such a stigma around it. It's like with the stories now, with *glasnost*. She's worried, she's got this fear of information, about things *getting out of hand*—I don't know whether she means his illness or what people will think. Probably both.

But in some way it's tied to his father, my grandfather. *He* was the one who wanted my father to go into hospital in the first place. He had absolute faith in the system, of course. Stalin and Brezhnev apparently sent their sons to asylums. They believed the right conditions for the body would fix the mind. Work therapy, that sort of thing.

Anya gestured towards the city beyond the window. I just hated it, she said. I never felt that I had proper friends, because they'd never know this thing about me, this secret that my mother convinced me was something to be ashamed of. And the official walls went up, bureaucratic walls, when it was known someone had psychiatric treatment on their file. It was hard for him to keep working.

Anya said that he was prone to outbursts, when he couldn't articulate what it was that so hurt him on the inside, but everything in a physical sense, be it touch, food or noise, was unbearable for him at those times.

One day I went out and stayed at my friend's house, Anya said, lighting a cigarette and resting one elbow on her hip. My father wasn't working then, he was spending a lot of time sleeping, or disappearing for long walks. Those walks of his made me so anxious. The apartment was just so quiet. I couldn't tell if anyone was home or if he'd gone out wandering again. I felt like something was about to break, a glass was about to shatter. I needed air. So I stayed at a girl's house, a girl from school I didn't even know that well, since I'd never let myself get close to anyone. When I came home the next morning, my father had taken a bad turn. Mama was packing his things. Folding his shirts, pressing socks into a large black bag. She told me he was going to spend a few days in a clinic. It had happened before. This time, though, Mama blamed me. Look what you've done! See, your father is sick with worry about you! She even hit my cheek. And I truly believed I was the cause. I was horrified. I never argued after that. I just drifted along silently with whatever she wanted. Until now, until *glasnost*. And now she hates that she can't control it. I'm older now, I'm making my own decisions.

She exhaled, smoke making a thin barrier between her and the window.

Let's talk about something else, she said. Your trip—you're going soon. Tell me what Oleg has planned.

She gave a fractured sort of smile, her eyes ringed with those neat circles. She said it was good I was going; it would be such an experience, she said.

But inexplicably, or maybe for many reasons, I was uneasy about leaving Moscow. Maybe because I'd never travelled so long or far before—or perhaps on account of what I was leaving behind.

PART II

A good thing they taught us how to read, for you can imagine some illiterate needing to be led by the hand and told, The tomb is here.

José Saramago, *The Year of the Death of Ricardo Reis*

CHAPTER 19

We took a Red Arrow sleeper train from Moscow to Leningrad. It left Leningrad station in Moscow at five minutes to midnight and we arrived the next morning, after dawn. It was the end of May 1989.

I had never been to Leningrad before. We stayed with Oleg's friends Ivan and Susanna. I understood, without being told, that they were *zeki*, former prisoners, although I didn't know their stories or what camps they had sat in. Ivan's thick hair poured back in dark grey streams from his forehead. His shirt, navy blue, was buttoned neatly at the wrists and collar. His wife Susanna was a tall, statuesque woman with full lips and thin, fading hair. With a warm smile, she said many times how glad she was that we had come. She seated us at the kitchen table, from which I could see the living room, a site of unfettered creation: partly completed artworks, canvases, jars of translucent coloured water, curls of paper, paintbrushes, rags.

Ivan is something of a celebrity nowadays, Oleg said as we sat down to vodka and snacks. He nodded towards the unfinished artworks in the next room. Today's generation prize Ivan and his work.

I wondered if Sukhanov would know of him.

Ivan waved away Oleg's words. Fame, he quoted, is just the summary of all misunderstandings that crystallise about a new name. Rilke, he said with a nod.

Oh, think of your own words, said Susanna with a laugh both curt and fond.

Ivan put his hands together, as if in prayer. She has spoken, he said, winking at me.

There was a firmness to Ivan, as if some strong force—pain or art or something—emanated from him.

Oleg told me that Ivan's paintings were well known for being in the notorious Manezh Exhibition that was shut down by Khrushchev in the early 1960s. The art was slammed for being too *nonconformist*.

They just drove us underground! Ivan hit the table almost gleefully. Ah, the times we had!

When Oleg and Ivan began to reminisce about Moscow under Khrushchev and Brezhnev in the sixties, I thought of Ilya, how he would've loved to hear the stories that mirrored our own. The underground concerts, tickets for four rubles each, made from small postcards with stamps of animals, scrawled with the address of the concert—the only way such events could be advertised.

Remember poor Yuri Ayzenshpis, said Ivan, raising then knocking back a drink. All those concerts he organised for us, and then he got eighteen years.

His words reminded me of the kitchen table gatherings in our apartment when I was young, when disappeared people became a name attached to a measure of time sentenced to a camp. And I had another feeling from childhood: the sense of a lesser knowledge, of not quite seeing what it was they knew. It was as if their experiences made those dissident uncles and aunts, the *zeki*, the native speakers of a language that I had only learnt through years of study. I was watching the witnesses, in a way, trying to learn things I hadn't seen. And as they spoke that language, I missed the nuances, the barely perceptible cadences never truly captured in words.

Later, as we drank tea, Oleg brought out a couple of maps. Running his thumb over the paper, he described our proposed trip. I watched them, Oleg, Ivan and Susanna, as they pointed and murmured, noting certain places and names. I wondered about the territories they saw, places somehow beyond the paper and beneath the printed lines.

The next morning, I took a walk alone in the city, leaving Oleg to pay visits to a few old friends he was quietly keen to see. The Neva River drew me towards it. I crossed a bridge from Vasilyevsky Island and reached the Winter Palace. I was content to look at the exteriors of those grand buildings, feeling some aversion to the organised history inside them. The pastel-coloured facades, mint green, white, yellow, made me think of settled, dry, dead stories of crinolines and tsars and large gilt-framed portraits. Of names and dates printed in a white square and affixed at the bottom-right of the image. If only all histories could be so sure. I walked through the palace square, where two white horses were harnessed to an ornate carriage, their necks bowed, sleepy and majestic.

I passed the entrance to the Hermitage Museum and was reminded of a story about the months leading up to the Leningrad Blockade in 1941. With the certain threat of a German invasion or air attack, the Hermitage curator tried to get as many artworks as possible out of the city. He began to collect supplies—cardboard, bedsheets—anything in which he could cushion or wrap the paintings and sculptures. Then he sent them, thus packaged, to safety on the final trains to leave the city before the siege began. I imagined the curator's care as he wrapped and taped the artworks. I thought he must have been heartsick at the station, at the terrible uncertainty of that farewell.

Most of the frames, except those of the most fragile paintings, were left behind in the museum. I pictured the cavernous interiors of the Hermitage, utterly dark, echoing like an abandoned cathedral, with row upon row of blank frames hanging on the walls, their past occupants gone. It must have resembled a graveyard, I thought, the frames and labels like cemetery fences and etched headstones.

But then, according to memoirs and accounts of the time, the curator and his colleagues continued to run tours of the museum. Gesturing to the absent works, they spoke to groups about the former contents of those empty frames, naming the lost images as though the paintings were still there in some way, in the remains.

I walked by a side entrance, where towering giant statues appeared to hold up a portico, almost as if they actually were the walls. The weight of the roof on their shoulders, like Atlas bearing the weight of the world, though really the effect was an illusion created by an architect long dead.

I went back towards the river. A light wind grabbed the smoke from my cigarette, threw it away like dust, as I crossed the bridge back to Vasilyevsky Island.

The embankment was nothing like Frunzenskaya Embankment in Moscow, where Anya and I sometimes walked near her family's apartment, where the parks opposite formed a wall of green. In Leningrad the embankment was grey, concrete and water alike. There was no green. The spire at Peter and Paul Fortress stood out, sharply gold in the distance, looking as though it could have cut the clouds, sent them raggedly drifting on.

I wasn't sure where Anya had stayed when she was in Leningrad, but the city hinted of her. Knowing she had been there before me, I saw the place as if through her eyes; I saw the statues of the sphinxes on University Embankment and the star-strewn blue dome of Trinity Cathedral and I knew she'd seen them first. The subway stations, she'd travelled through them only months earlier. I thought of Mikhail Sergeyevich and our conversations. The underground could be the unconscious of the city, he had said. I considered calling Anya, but didn't know what I would say.

When I got back to Ivan and Susanna's, Oleg told me he had met with some Memorial Society volunteers conducting mass-grave investigations. The founder of the Leningrad Memorial Society, Veniamin Ioffe, was studying suspected mass gravesites near the city dating from Stalin's Terror years in the late 1930s. He and another well-known Memorial member, Irina Flige, used old maps and aerial photographs to find indications of grave locations. They also made visits to these sites. The soil gave its own clues, softer where it had been turned over some fifty years earlier. Ioffe and Flige were dissidents from the generation before my own. Tireless and

163

pale, they had already made many trips to windy, desolate places of grass and forest, paddock and road, armed with shovels to begin their searches.

The KGB had released a small amount of information, recognising the existence of one burial site. Yet the Memorial Society suspected many others were out there, unacknowledged and lost for the time being. Two and a half miles out of Leningrad was a village called Levashovo, and nearby, it was said, there was a burial site that had once serviced the Rzhevsky firing range.

In most cases, the whereabouts of mass graves had only recently been disclosed by terrified or wary locals, who had seen the guards at the end of a long road near home or had grown up avoiding certain areas, warned by their parents to keep away. And now, after decades of silence, they had released those details from themselves. As the press began to carry reports of mass murder in the Stalin years, they felt safe enough to speak. It was also thought that there were mass graves beneath Moscow and Leningrad, among other places, where Soviet officials who themselves became victims, as so often they did, might have been buried. But the more remote graves, which formed the majority of the sites, held the workers and peasants, the homemakers and teachers, the priests and musicians, the soldiers and ballerinas, the pensioners and beggars.

Despite knowing some specific locations, the Memorial Society searchers could never identify who it was they found, since the remains were too jumbled, numerous and decayed. Finding a mass site at least gave a measure of certainty, however. A defined forest, a few mounds of grass, was a place at which to stand and mourn; a veritable pinpoint compared to the endless silence of the Russian expanse.

I wondered about the consequences of inadequate mourning. I wondered whether the dead found other ways to remind us of their presence. Plagued by the uncertainty of loss, the lack of a gravestone, perhaps there would be a sense of disquiet, nauseas of the mind, deep depressions—all as manifestations in the living of the mute presence of the dead, the knocking without hands, the calls without mouths.

We stayed a few nights in Leningrad. On our last night, Susanna cooked a large meal and the four of us sat at the table, sharing one of the bottles Oleg had brought with us, smoking and talking long into the night. The conversation turned to art and the consequences of controlling it.

Some kinds of art come before language, said Ivan. We begin, in our earliest years, with images in our mind before words form in our mouth. And so to command imagery is to have power over the very beginnings of our understanding. To control art is to control all. As we grow older we rely more and more on words. The height of our thinking, so we are told, is when we can understand only with words—abstract thought. Yet even the naming of something as *abstract* is our attempt to control that which we cannot grasp. I think of certain words—*justice, freedom*—we can name without needing an image. Yet they are the hardest to grasp, the easiest to lose.

He reached out to touch Susanna's face, his palm over her hair, his thumb on her cheek. It is both the beauty and tyranny of words, he continued. How beautiful, when we cannot say what it is that moves us most, though we try.

Susanna smiled, took his hand from her face and held it in her lap.

A tender moment becomes the crispness of air, said Ivan, the diffusion of light, a look between two people.

He kissed Susanna's hand and then rested his own on the kitchen table, forming a small arch with his fingers.

A lost moment of childhood becomes the scent of polished wood, he went on, the eyes of a rocking horse, the feel of crawling over floorboards.

Ivan crossed his arms. Oleg did the same; he was nodding slowly.

And yet, continued Ivan, the dictatorship of words works in the same way. *Enemy. Other. Madness.* To control such labels, or their apparent meaning, is to command fearful hearts, to dictate the worst in our nature. Even now, we use *their* words—Ivan pointed a thumb to the air—we use *the repressions*, when really we should say *the murders*. Abstraction becomes dangerous. When we cannot see the enemies among us, we see them everywhere.

I looked across the room, where several of Ivan's paintings hung on the walls or were stacked among the clutter of art supplies and blank canvases. Most of Ivan's works depicted people in murky locations, dwarfed by tall buildings or lost among trees bare or dead. On each of the painted faces there was an expression of searching, longing or sadness. An embracing couple, beneath a purplish cloud, could not seem to meet each other's eyes. A long line of people snaked away from a building, waiting for something the viewer couldn't see. They all felt uncannily quiet. I could feel the cold concrete, the windless air, the tiredness in the immobile figures.

It seemed to me that art had a peculiar importance under tyranny. Art should tell us of life, but in a place where the outward perception of reality has been so manufactured by the state, in some ways art is the only thing that is real. Art represented the truth of our inner lives, which was not real according to the official word. Oleg had told me that Ivan's works were despised by the state, condemned for their *severe style*, their *unrealistic depressive quality*, which ran counter to the acceptable way of doing things—set down by Stalin as socialist in content and realist in form, all thick-armed heroic workers and senselessly happy peasants in the *kolkhoz*.

We sat in a comfortable silence, the four of us. Susanna served more tea and biscuits. At some point past midnight, Oleg suggested we get some sleep.

We were travelling north from Leningrad to Kem with Lake Ladoga and Finland to the left, Lake Onega at the right. The word *Arktika*, plastered on the side of the train, made me think of an icy rush leaving its mark on the carriage, telling where it had been and where we would arrive after a journey of around twenty hours.

We travelled in a four-berth carriage, though the other two bed-seats were empty. Wood-grain panels covered the interior walls. Thin curtains, pink or brown depending on the light through the window, shifted with the carriage's sway. It became my unofficial duty to get tea from a samovar at the end of the carriage. Often I stood for a long moment at the window. I saw an old man walking on a grey road, weighed down by a bag in each hand. Two children in a green field ran and ran alongside the train, their pounding steps and excited calls muted by the glass. I liked to see how the view had changed once I went back to my seat, as if time had sped up or a moment had been missed; the children had disappeared from view, the old man could now be seen up close to the window.

Oleg slept a lot for the first few hours. I tried to read but couldn't concentrate. The train rocked with gentle clattering noises. A few people stood talking in the corridor outside, and the attendant bustled past them. On the spare seat next to Oleg were his maps. I stood up, took them lightly off the seat, and sat back down opposite Oleg. He dozed, seemingly peaceful.

Next to neatly printed names, a symbol appeared over and over on the maps: a triangle sitting on two wide rectangles, which then sat on two more rectangles, long and narrow. Sort of like an arrow, sort of like a tower. I didn't count the symbols myself, and couldn't decide whether Oleg would surely have done so, or would surely have not.

The arrangement reminded me of a cemetery: the jagged, haphazard layout of graves, how in some areas the head-stones are clustered together, while in other parts there are blank expanses. It was as though the grassy walkways in a cemetery found their counterpart in the vast Russian plains on those maps.

I was sure that, now I'd seen Oleg's maps, any time I looked at a map without camp markings, the absence would be shocking. As if the map's creator had made such a grievous error as forgetting to include the capital cities or neglecting to mark an entire country. Names referring to a camp but missing the symbol would hide what was truly there. Safe behind a word, the label could conceal the reality on the ground: Kem, Arkhangelsk, Vorkuta, Magadan, Kolyma, Krasnodar. In the absence of those small markings symbolising a camp, I likened it to an entire metropolis or the depths of an ocean disappearing by the omission of the cartographer's hand.

I put the maps back on the seat next to Oleg, then sat back in my own seat, watching the view.

After six hours we had a twenty-minute stop at Petrozavodsk. Travellers emerged from the carriages, stretching their legs, chatting and smoking. A couple of food stalls were open. It was late afternoon and the sun was high. Being suddenly thrown outside, into the open air, I was struck by the loneliness of unfamiliar surroundings. We'd travelled far beyond any place known to me.

From Petrozavodsk the train continued past Lake Onega and on to the north, to Kem and its port on the White Sea. Oleg was quiet for a while, looking out of the window, his eyes ticking from side to side as he watched the view from his seat moving backwards. I faced the other way, looking forwards. Curved expanses of water emerged over the flat, green rushing view. Oleg mentioned Kizhi, pointing it out on one of his maps as the train's path slithered close to the island. He said that he had never been to see the collection of churches on Kizhi Island, but that one day he would like to go, look up at the Church of the Transfiguration with its twenty-two domes, and see the ancient wooden Church of the Resurrection of Lazarus, built in the fourteenth century without a single nail.

Next there was Medvezhyegorsk, some three hours and one hundred and fifty kilometres from Petrozavodsk. Again we emerged onto the platform for a cigarette, and bought pastries from a woman selling food. A wide sky stretched silently above us. It was evening time but not dark. Lake Onega had accompanied the train north, and Medvezhyegorsk stood on its northern bank.

This is where the White Sea–Baltic Canal begins, said Oleg.

The canal connected the White Sea to Lake Onega, which then flowed into the Baltic Sea via Svir River, Lake Ladoga and Neva River.

Prison labour, said Oleg. Worked them at a ridiculous pace under a Five-Year Plan, determined to defy time. Stalin, with his mania for complete control, even legislated on the granite to be used on the river embankments in Moscow. Frunzenskaya. Prechistenskaya. He gave the engineers a box of grey stones sent from here, from the canal. He made laws on all matters like that, Oleg continued—city planning and so on. He mandated a six-floor minimum for apartment buildings, and prowled the city by night, flanked by bodyguards, making orders for the watering of lime trees and the banning of double-decker trams, paranoid as he was that they would tip over.

Back on the train, we folded out the seats into beds for the night. The sun was very low, glowing orange as it fell slowly towards the horizon. I sat up watching the light change, the precise shifts impossible to really grasp, until the sky was awash in orange-gold. It looked as though invisible fires were reflecting their burning light upon the walls of wooden houses in the distance.

Eventually I pulled the curtains across the window, covering the shifting view and the long dusk, then lay down. Such silence. Only the rock of the carriage and gentle ticks. I missed Moscow's music. I wished I'd asked to borrow Ilya's Walkman.

After a while, Oleg started speaking into the dark. I was just thinking about the writer Platonov. His son was imprisoned under Stalin. The boy was only fifteen. I cannot remember where he was taken, but I know that he returned from prison and when he did, he had tuberculosis. And so Platonov cared for his sick son. Maybe it was easier for him to care for that physical ailment; those symptoms, the fevers and sweats and night terrors, the hallucinations and insomnia, would all have been something of a veil to obscure whatever other horrors the boy had brought home with him. But then poor Platonov himself caught the disease, and it killed him. Nothing can immunise us from all things.

I lay there looking up at the grey ceiling of the carriage. I recited one of Platonov's lines: *The cricket lived under the porch many a summer and sang there at eventide; perhaps it was the same cricket that sang the year before last, perhaps his grandson . . .*

Oleg gave a soft laugh. That's the one, he said.

I heard him roll over and we went quiet.

I slept a little, and then we arrived at Kem. It was a strange sensation to arrive at the station with the sun, at five o'clock in the morning. We'd left the night somewhere along the tracks behind us.

Kem was the gateway to the Solovetsky Islands. It was a silent place. We stood at the harbour, where the White Sea pooled in through Kem River. I could see a few wooden boats hovering on the water. A mass of logs lined the waterside in rows; others extended out across the water like an unstable pier. A few stood upright, resembling stakes in the ground or the trees they were once.

Beyond the river I saw buildings, brick and wooden, that looked haggard from a distance but still had something uniform about them, in the way they all faced the water, and in the symmetry of the multiple chimneys on each of their roofs. From one or two chimneys rose a grey feather of smoke, ebbing almost imperceptibly towards the sky. After walking a few minutes in silence broken only by stones at our feet and the breeze at our ears, Oleg began to speak about Kem's past. The wooden cathedral, he told me, had been built some two hundred years before. Its three octagonal towers, like sorcerers' tall hats, were called tent towers. I imagined the transient dwellings of some nomadic race of the steppe, camped on a grey barren earth. Now the logging industry sustained the town, Oleg told me as he pointed out a sawmill. The Solovetsky Monastery nearby had mostly retained control of Kem throughout its long history, but Kem was once also known as a transit camp on the way to the Solovetsky Gulag.

A man walked along the embankment, close to the water, so slowly he looked almost still from a distance. There were two shadows next to the man, one stretched to an unnatural length in front of him; the other, which I realised was actually the shadow of a nearby tree, looked like it was following him. His hands were clasped behind his back.

The sight of him reminded me of a photograph in the Sukhanovs' apartment back in Moscow. They had a lot of movie and music posters, paintings, and black-and-white photos pinned to the walls. One of those was a copy of a photograph from the sixties, taken by the Lithuanian photographer Antanas Sutkus. It showed Jean-Paul Sartre walking in a mass of white, bent forwards like the man I could see at the water. There were two shadows on the white: Sartre's own and one of a figure behind him. The second shadow looked to be attached to him, but it wasn't his. I thought the tree's shadow on the embankment, immobile and still as the sea appeared to be in the light, looked just the same. The photo was called *I Exist*.

We were not sure where to stay for the night. On a pale, dusty road we approached a local woman who sat mending a pair of shoes. She directed us with a silent gesture of her hand to another local, a man with a very round figure and thick, arthritic hands. Boris, his name was, said we could stay at the house of his sister.

He took us to the house, which was away from the town but close to the water. After telling us that most of the lights didn't have working bulbs and that it was possible a rat colony lived beneath the house, he ambled away, disappearing around a corner of grey road. We never saw him again, nor did the sister ever appear in the house. But it was close to the harbour, from where we'd take a boat the next day to Bolshoy Solovetsky Island, the largest of the Solovetsky archipelago.

We moved the only working lamp into the front room, where a couch sagged, a broken clock was stuck on twelve fifteen, and some plastic toys lay, their colours dulled by a layer of dust. There were a few photos on a low table. A young couple stood on an open stretch of grass, squinting without smiling at a past sun, perhaps late afternoon, which threw their faces into half-shadow. Another, the same man from the first photo. He wore an army uniform that could have been brown—one of the older Soviet uniforms of the Great Patriotic War. He had the cruelly sterile and calm look of young soldiers in new uniforms, somehow already carrying their bloody futures. Next to that was a more recent photo of two young soldiers in Soviet *Afghanka* uniforms, guns slung casually at their sides. They stood in a foreign street and there was a feel of the desert in the quality of light, the dust on the ground. I felt like an intruder as I stared at their faces and they looked back at me.

The room stayed gloomy; the midnight glow couldn't find its way inside. The smoke from our cigarettes met the orange lamplight, mingled with the dust in the air. We could have been by a weak campfire on the endless landscape of the steppe. A moth flitted around the lamp and another lay dead nearby, though when the first moth rested from its desperate flutters neither looked alive. Before going to bed I went to the bathroom, but couldn't use the shower because the taps had rusted tight. When a little water did come out, it pooled in a clogged drain. A copper cloud of water spread and a metallic smell rose up. I turned off the tap but the water stayed in its silent pool. I gave up and went back to the living room, where Oleg lay quiet. The moths were still.

From the harbour at Kem it took three hours by boat to reach Bolshoy Solovetsky Island. Kem had been a mere transit land, a place where prisoners waited for transportation to the islands beyond, and as the boat rose and fell on the waves it felt as though we had crossed a threshold, an unseen border into the past. I thought of how Bulgakov mentioned Solovetsky in *The Master and Margarita*. Ivan the poet declares that Kant should be sent there as punishment for writing his own 'proof' as to the existence of God. I wondered if a person visiting the island would feel as I did upon approaching it, feel haunted, if they didn't already know the history of the place. Maybe, I thought, some things are absorbed in a landscape and left there for those who come after. Perhaps we were in a place where one could comprehend, as far as one could, all that was unknown about the past. Some things had to remain a mystery in order to be understood. It was as if there was a truth accessible only through certain means: by walking over places of memory or staring for as long as we could bear it, into the eyes of unknown faces in old black-and-white photos or in the most heartbreaking works of art.

From a distance the monastery buildings, surrounded by eight towers and seven gates, appeared to float just above the water and just below the clouds. As we got closer to the land, the monastery looked down on us, rising up into the sky. In the sunlit waters around our boat, onion-domed towers and fortress walls moved in their rippled reflection. Sparks of sunlight hit the sea. The reflected buildings were lifelike as though the true settlement was down there beneath us. I imagined the citizens of such a place to be submerged statues, flesh grey and wasting.

Thick walls protected the monastery, and for a strange minute I thought we would be denied entrance, although by whom I wasn't sure. Oleg told me that until 1965 it had not been possible to visit Bolshoy Solovetsky Island. A museum was here now, he said, with a settlement village of just over a thousand people. The monastery was in the uncertain, grey hands of neither the navy, who took over the old camp in 1939, nor the Church, who no doubt wanted it returned to Orthodox control.

We reached land. Beyond the walls of the monastery I could see multiple navy-blue domes squatting on white towers. Tufts of green grass covered the land around the monastery. Further away I could see a small group of cows, heads bowed to the ground. Blue flowers scattered the grass, the sun shone, and a bird made miserable retching noises far above us. We began walking inland. Forests of spruce and pine hovered close and I felt their cooling green breeze.

There were wooden cottages, marked by red-brick chimneys, fallen wire fences, and here and there a larger building that might have been a former barracks. It was hard to tell what anything had been once. The dusty roads seemed no longer useful, just lonely, pale snakes twisting through a ghost town that held only the subtlest evidence of past occupants.

Oleg's pace slowed as we approached the monastery and its small settlement of church buildings.

Up close I could see that the enormous thick watchtowers, hundreds of years old, were made of large round stones. Like eternal barricades, greying thickset walls connected the towers.

An eerie breeze swept over from the water and I wondered why such a stronghold was necessary at the end of the earth. Probably it was the atmosphere that caused me to think that the strength of those walls stood for protection from some ancient threat, a threat in the air, of spiritual violence rather than physical.

There were cracked facades, peeling paint, forgotten pathways, loose stones, holes in the walls. Oleg said that work had begun on reconstructing the buildings, restoring them to their former state, before the camp was there. It seemed to me impossible that there had once been thousands there when on that afternoon we were the only ones.

I started to think that maybe many such buildings were troubled vessels, full of an unknown substance. Even when abandoned they aren't empty, but we don't know exactly what gives them their heavy presence. But in some cases we did know the sources of such auras: I remembered how Mikhail Sergeyevich had called the Lubyanka a haunted building. And it was true that it still housed the sons and grandsons of the KGB, just as the roads we walked over in Moscow were once pathways for the Black Maria trucks bound for shooting ranges, and from the hallways of communal apartments footsteps in the middle of the night had once struck terror into the chests of millions. I'd grown up among all of those places too, of course, just like Anya and our friends. As children of the Freeze, we had walked the same streets in the same years.

And the act of taking a stone all the way from Solovetsky to Moscow, to make the monument we had petitioned for, was surely a sign that we give things and objects and matter a little of our own minds—we give them the pasts that they carry. The memorial stone would first travel by boat, Oleg had told me, from the island to Arkhangelsk, and from there journey by train all the long way back to the city.

Back to the city. It was as if Oleg was calling the stone's arrival there, in Moscow, its return. It was going back, back to Moscow, he had said. And in a way I understood that its presence would be a kind of return for those who did not, that somehow the stone had already been there, in Moscow. I wondered at its vast weight, surely immeasurable, and whether the stone would in fact be even heavier than most would think, as I sometimes thought the piles of paper in an archive might be far heavier than the historian would ever have anticipated.

CHAPTER 20

I returned to St Petersburg from the *dacha* at the end of August. I took the *elektrichka* train as I had a few weeks before. It felt as though a lot of time had passed. The neighbours had left only two days before me, but that also seemed a far longer absence. From the window of the train the scenes going back looked completely different; I recognised nothing.

From Finland station I entered the metro. The dusty metallic heat pressed all kinds of city memory forcefully back over me, a heavy and oppressive feeling. I rode the train to Primorskaya. It was early evening, warm. I could hear music, a cawing electric guitar, coming from the bar near the intersection. I took the bus to Korablestroiteley Street. It was quiet as I walked between the tall apartment towers. Families would still be at their summerhouses for the holidays, or maybe at home together for their evening meal.

I rummaged in my bags for a while before I found my keys to the apartment building. On the tiled floor of the foyer a discarded newspaper lifted a page in the gust from the door.

Light flickered in the small elevator. After slowing, straining, the elevator stopped between floors with a clink and echo. I waited a minute. It didn't move, so I called the operator. *Thirty minutes*, said the voice from the silver speaker. He sounded bored. I said thanks, probably sounding just as bored. Though I should have told him that, without a watch, I had no way of measuring thirty minutes, hanging there between two floors.

A while later I was released into the hallway. My apartment felt unchanged, though stuffy from the summer heat, the lack of air. I stood at the window and smoked. I felt restless. I missed the peace of the *dacha*, the walks with the neighbours' grandchildren, the warm evenings lying on the chair at the front or in the shady cool of the trees behind the house.

I went to see Sonya that night. I told her that my mother had died. It had been weeks since the funeral. Her death didn't feel so much like raw experience as something that had happened some time ago, a thing now to be told. But I didn't say how her death seemed to bring me closer to my own; how my mother's passing was like the falling of a wall between me and repressed thoughts about death. I hadn't really confronted those yet myself. Or perhaps it was the same thought rendered in two different forms: a longing to cease living and a desire to find a reason for being alive.

I told Sonya how I'd been to stay at the *dacha*. I described the small house, how the yard at the back extended right to the forest wall, and how the neighbour and I would sit either in the forest or in his yard that was like a city of greenhouses, and that we would drink and talk.

I thought you seemed tired, she said as we lay in bed. And your face has had lots of sun. She smiled her gentle, languid smile.

I told her about the walks with the grandchildren, how they loved to run along the empty beach, how it looked to me as though they were running in a liberated way that was impossible in the city. I said that maybe her boys would also like such a place. I had not met Sonya's two young boys. She didn't answer me directly but rather, after remaining quiet for a while, told me about an acquaintance of hers, a woman of the same age, who had also lost her husband. She had two children, a girl and a boy. The woman had remarried, and her children had a great fondness for the new husband. This pleased the woman, or she felt it should. But the day they first called him Papa very nearly destroyed her, said the woman.

Sonya reached to the low bedside table next to her, lit a cigarette and lay back, looking up at the ceiling. I rested the back of my hand on my forehead, closed my eyes, tasted the welcome drifts of smoke.

Sometimes, she said, I don't want too much to change. When you lose someone, every week you live after that day takes you further away from them. If things stay the same, you can pretend—

Sonya held up one hand as she tried to find the words, but then lowered her arm and drew on her cigarette.

I would like to see this place, she said a long moment later. It's strange that you didn't say you were there. The tone of her voice wasn't accusing; rather it seemed like a detached observation.

I was trying to write there, I said. At the *dacha*.

I didn't know you were a writer.

I'm not. I used to try to be.

She stubbed out her cigarette and turned onto her left side, listening.

I rolled onto my right side, put a hand to her face. She had one hand holding the sheets at her waist, the other arm tucked under her naked ribs. Her hair touched her breasts.

Stupid youth, I said.

She smiled and kissed me. I left soon after, exiting the drab apartment building and the brief place that was time with Sonya, feeling that perhaps I didn't want to leave so soon. Back at my apartment, I struggled to sleep. My mind was plagued by toxic, naked-body flickers. Glimpses long gone: Anya was sitting up on the bed, maybe talking to me, maybe silent. One bare leg bent up on the bed, the other splayed out next to her, down to the floor where her toes would have grazed the carpet. The image didn't move; I couldn't remember anything else around it. There was also a phantom recollection—maybe the memory of a photograph, black and white—of a woman crouched down beside a bed, naked, as if she was about to pick up something from the floor. The blankets on the bed next to her were disturbed but it didn't look as though anyone else was in the room with her. Maybe one of the Sukhanovs' friends had taken the photo and I saw it at their place.

A day or so later, the neighbour from the *dacha* called me. He suggested we meet at a bistro, a good and quiet place, he said, on one of the narrow streets near Dom Knigi bookshop on Nevsky Prospekt. He said he would like to tell me more things, more about the past, if I was still willing to write those things down for him. I assured him I was, and we arranged to meet two days later, very early in the morning.

On the appointed morning, I found the bistro easily enough. It was in a large old building painted bright blue, the windows trimmed with white, with large yellow signs just above them. A man in a business suit was leaving with a paper bag and a coffee cup, and when I went inside I was the only customer there. I ordered a coffee. The neighbour walked in a few minutes later. He looked different. His grey hair, usually a bit wild, was combed, either wet or held in place with cream or gel. He wore a light blue shirt, buttoned at the collar, and a dark green jacket of a thin material, maybe cotton. And instead of his dirty overalls and brown boots he wore black trousers and black lace-up shoes. I didn't know if that was how he always looked in the city or whether he had dressed that way for this occasion. He ordered tea, I another coffee. I had my notebook on the table.

The feeling of quiet and expectation that came over me then, as if my mind was clearing itself and I didn't want to speak but only hear what was to come, reminded me of the times I had sat in similar situations with Mikhail Sergeyevich. But I felt changed in some ways since those years; a man heavier with the passing of time.

I wanted to start with the day Vera and I first spoke about these things, said the neighbour. About our pasts. It was because of all the newspapers. The late eighties, with *glasnost*. Every new copy of *Moscow News* or *Novy Mir* or *Ogonyok* had something in it about the past. One day I just told Vera. I told her: when I was a boy, my father was arrested, and I never saw him again. It was 1935.

I could describe to Vera—he held up one hand as if to grasp that brief moment as it flared up in his mind—I could describe the feeling of that time, the Terror years, as they call them. Every person around me had a look about them as though they were capable of anything. I was a boy of ten years. Even the old *babushka* who sat in the hallway and lived in one of the rooms in the apartment upstairs changed from a sad, withered woman to a thing of dread, like a witch from a folk tale, with the power to tell *them*, them *up there*, that we had done wrong, that we were enemies of the people. It was a suspicious feeling, a metallic fear in the air. And there were shocks before then, before my father's arrest. Neighbours and friends and even the most harmless of shopkeepers disappearing overnight. Not them, you'd think, surely not them, who seemed protected from all that. To me as a boy they were like the good characters in a book, the ones who stay safe. Such a shock, each time, hearing the news of who was taken in the night. We would hear the next morning, *They've had problems next door* or *He's not working today*, and we'd know, Pasha, what those words meant. Some mornings you'd see a piece of paper pasted on a neighbour's door with the secret police seal stamped on it, marking who had been arrested. There was a feeling that something incomprehensible was happening, that we were living according to rules I didn't understand, that terrible things happened because of them—and the worst thing was that the adults didn't seem to know how the rules worked either. That's what scared me the most.

The neighbour accepted the cigarette I offered, finished his tea, and went on. I've heard, since those *glasnost* years, that there are lists of those executed. I've wondered if my father's name is on them. I'm not sure if I want to see a list like that.

I haven't suggested this to Vera. And you can never be sure if a list is trustworthy.

He looked up at me as if asking a question.

It's true, I said. Sometimes the lists were wrong.

I remembered how back in Moscow, at the Memorial Society, there were stories of people whose names had appeared on a list of those executed, but who then turned up at their old homes years later. They might have been twenty years in a camp. And that usually meant the person killed was murdered under the wrong name. There were quotas to be met: a certain number of enemies to be found. They were like enforced predictions—deaths marked in ink so that they were bound to happen.

Identity didn't matter to them, *up there*, I said. It was just about the numbers.

Yes, yes, said the neighbour. And you imagine them dying in so many different ways, when you don't really know. You lived in fear of hearing the creaking ascent of the elevators at two in the morning, but I've never been sure if I actually heard that sound on the night they came for my father. He was gone in the morning. We never saw a grave.

I'd like to try to help, I said. A lot of archives are open now. There might be something recorded.

The neighbour nodded, rubbing his thumbs one over the other. He accepted another cigarette. It's a funny thing, he said. You don't expect the young ones to be all about the past, like you, Pasha. It's a good thing. It's good for the kids to know.

I've just remembered what Nadezhda Mandelstam wrote, I said, about a rule among her friends. The rule was that you could never ask why—you couldn't ask what a person was arrested for. In their circle of poets and dissidents, they actually forbade the question. Because if you ask it, she said, if you ask that question, then you are granting a dignity to the system that it does not deserve. Questions fed the Stalinist system. Asking why or what for suggested there might be some kind of logic to it, some higher order and truth behind the persecutions. But there wasn't. There was only fear, a kind of persecution mania.

The neighbour nodded and stubbed out his cigarette in the ashtray. Senseless, he said.

I was suddenly struck with the image of Mikhail Sergeyevich—or, more precisely, the setting: a man sitting next to me, drawing on a cigarette, talking about his father, something both grey and shattered about him, his voice. I wanted to help the neighbour as I hadn't been able to help Mikhail Sergeyevich.

Look, I said, feeling uneasy, so averse to my old faith in information, in the ability of words to find answers. Look, there are no certainties, but we can try.

Yes, he said slowly, yes. I think I would like to see what you can do.

We stood up and left the bistro. He thanked me, shaking my hand with his left, his right palm pressed on my forearm.

Let's meet again soon, Pasha, he said.

That evening, wary of sleeping badly yet again, I took a long walk through the city. It was late in the summer, so the white nights were waning. A thin darkness tinted the city in the early hours. The streetlights were only needed as guides for the shortest time. The lights glowed on Nevsky, along Griboyedov Canal, and then petered out to rare orange beacons on the more deserted streets and beside the silent, thin canals.

I went to a bar for an hour or so, drank beer, then left again. I saw the usual groups of people who seemed to exist at no other time of year than summer. The laugh of one girl peaked high in the humid air like a lone dusk bird. Others then joined her as if in echo. On the sandy embankment by Peter and Paul Fortress there were a few white-night drinkers. Their words were muted by distance as they splashed, seemingly silent in the steely Neva water.

I walked past queues at nightclubs, caught glimpses of girls with winking gold jewellery, heads turning with smiles, men looking identical, all dressed in black. I heard the hum of words, the perceptive beep of metal detectors, and the haze of music as the crowds waited for their drinks and dance and lights and pills. I walked away from those queues but inevitably found others.

I kept moving beneath Petersburg's pressing sky, aware of some encroaching eventuality that if I stopped, I would look too closely at the smiles, which seemed somehow malicious, and see that they had forgotten, or didn't know, all that had happened and the weight of the past. Despair would win, a weight of loneliness would bear down, as would a deep repulsion from the facade, the apparently clean slate that seemed to be made by that girl's laugh, which had long drifted into the warm heights of the air.

At about two in the morning, the glowing grey sky turned briefly dusky and I saw the bridges rise. It was that time of night when the bridges of Petersburg split in two and open to allow the steamers, ferries and ships to pass through the canals before closing again at the end of the night. Once the bridges had risen, they stood out due to the bright orbs of orange and red that lit the ends of the bridges and rose with them.

Only at certain angles could I see the black silhouettes of the structures themselves, standing upright like eerie corpses, inert bodies suddenly struck with life. As the bridges stood cracked in half for those few hours, I couldn't escape the impression that time itself had been suspended by the great arms reaching up, as if calling to a halt all that was progressing relentlessly with the hours.

I thought of those stories from years before my own, how after the revolution those who remained from the old, extinguished aristocracy were called *former people*. I didn't know if the term was used for more recent history, attached to the names of former camp guards, prisoners, executioners.

On my way home, when I saw a figure walking here and there in the night, unspeakable questions formed in my mind. I wondered who they were back then, what they had done which had then been forgotten. I wondered what former people hid inside them.

Even in the *glasnost* years we had all heard of Lazar Kaganovich, the last of Stalin's closest circle. Mikhail Sergeyevich had mentioned that his father had worked for him. Kaganovich still lived on Frunzenskaya Embankment and stories were told of how he answered the phone only after a coded number of rings, and played dead when American journalists came knocking on his door. A ghost who still woke every day, still washed his hands and face, blood still moving through his limbs and organs, just like the system of which he had been an administrator. Kaganovich and Communism survived long after Stalin. It was a system that thrived on its ghosts, the power of memory, the tyranny of words and silence. Perhaps Anya's grandfather, even in a grave, was as alive as old Kaganovich on the embankment. Memories did not settle, the children breathed in the dust. Nor were we separate from the dead, for the horror was surely greater than time.

It was dark when I reached Primorsky, feeling uneasy and alone. Near the stray dogs on the way to my apartment, I saw on a prefabricated wall the words *Death to Yid!* painted in red beneath a streetlight. A swastika was enclosed within the arch of the final letter and I wondered at how real the red paint looked, like blood or tears—perhaps more convincing than real blood or tears would have looked.

A week went by and I didn't hear from the neighbour. It unnerved me a little. I didn't have his phone number. Perhaps he felt that he'd said too much, associated me too closely with the things he'd spoken about, and so was happy to leave me behind. Or maybe something had happened to him; he might have been unwell. Every connection was utterly fragile. I would wait. Surely we were now in a time when people no longer disappeared.

Another week, then two more. My thirty-fifth birthday passed. I went to work, I travelled the metro, tunnelling through the city. I went home again, ate the same food every night, smoked and stared out the windows. It was autumn soon enough. Each day gave a little more darkness to the sky. At night I could no longer see the gulf; the windows hit back with the image of my own apartment, my own yellow-lit face. I went to Sonya's two or three times. We didn't talk again about the *dacha*, nor about her husband or children, but I sometimes thought about our earlier conversation while

I was at her apartment. I thought that maybe we were a little similar, Sonya and I, living in the presence of those lost—for Sonya her husband, while for me it was not just Anya but Moscow itself, and my dead who were there.

I wondered if my writing about Moscow was bringing back to me the feel of the place, the memory-feeling, fraught departure from the city. I might have been slowly turning back into the twenty-something-year-old man who had everything to say, every hope, and no idea how to say it.

One morning, glancing through a newspaper, I read an article that reminded me of the neighbour. It was about the Salekhard–Igarka Railway, also known as the Dead Road. An expedition group had been out there to take photos. Its construction ordered by Stalin, the railway was supposed to span more than one thousand kilometres, to creep and weave over the vast, desolate northern parts of Siberia, and between the prison camps dotted across those lands. When Stalin died, the project was abandoned, but some seven hundred kilometres of track, leading to nowhere, were left behind. Like his maps of roads to nowhere, the neighbour might've liked to keep the article. I would hold on to it for him.

That night I had a dream about the Philosophers' Ships, which Oleg had told me about when we stood by Moskva River one autumn, a story I'd repeated to Anya when we too were by the embankment. I was alone in a room on one of the ships. The floor was panelled with dark wood, and beneath it I imagined the ocean floor holding the remains of old wrecks in its shifting sand: remnants of ships, wood, algae, seaweed, bones and belt buckles, while schools of fish, thick comets of silver, streaked through the debris as though they couldn't bear to look at it all. I never left that room, in my dream, but

I heard the sound of voices and murmurs and laughs from outside, up on the decks of the Philosophers' Ship. One of them sounded like the neighbour's wheezy grey laugh.

In my dream (or perhaps I'd woken by then and had begun to imagine such scenes), as I heard the neighbour's laugh I thought about his father, lost perhaps to a firing squad or the Gulag. But then I imagined that he'd escaped somehow and was traversing the barren, camp-riddled lands of Siberia, trying to come home, or living as a fugitive in a Moscow criminal gang, biding his time. I wondered whether I would recognise him, should I one day stumble across my father—for now it was he as well as the neighbour's father who I saw or sensed was lost in our vast Russia. I wondered if I'd know it was him, if he was there in the streets around the Arbat, or the crimson-brick desert of Pushkin Square, or in St Petersburg passing the statue of the Bronze Horseman, or walking beside the canals off Nevsky Prospekt. It was a comfort, of a sort, to see my father camping a windy night by a fire on the Russian steppe, or waking to a summer sky, beneath an old blue coat, sheltered below the arch of a bridge somewhere in Moscow.

In the morning I seemed to take a very long time to wake up. As I sat with my second coffee, staring towards the television in my kitchen, more annoyed than anything by its sounds, I went back over my dream thoughts several times, knowing that soon enough they would likely be gone from my memory.

Soviet psychology abhorred dreams. Something so internal and individual ran counter to the ideology. There were to be no uncontrolled, unreadable inside selves.

In one of Dostoyevsky's short stories, the narrator describes a dream about his dead brother. The brother was part of his life, he said, was with him each day and had a role in his affairs, but all the while he knew his brother wasn't alive anymore. Yet because it was a dream, it was possible for both states to exist together, for the dead to be fully present.

I swear to you gentlemen, he wrote, *that to be overly conscious is a sickness, a real, thorough sickness.*

CHAPTER 21

The sky above Solovetsky was a yawning blue, unending. Though I was a child of tower block apartments and loud Moscow, I grew used to the new quiet.

Oleg had arranged for us to stay with a man named Vasily, who lived in a cold wooden house on the island. His father had been imprisoned on Solovetsky in the early 1930s and the family had lived there ever since. I had heard of such Gulag families; a people deported, a course of life uprooted and forced to start again in a new, wild environment. They might have been dying out by then, Vasily's family almost the last of their kind.

It rained heavily in the night. By morning, mosquitoes travelled in thick masses, unrelenting even in the strong wind that had gathered while we slept.

We walked again over the roads of grey stone and grey dust to the Solovetsky cemetery to see the new monument to victims of the Gulag. It had been erected that month, June 1989, by members of the Leningrad Memorial Society.

With gentle, silent movements, Oleg took from his pocket three photographs, two of young men and one of a young woman, three red silky ribbons, and one dried, pressed flower. They were from friends who couldn't come themselves, he told me. He placed the tokens on the ground at the foot of the memorial, covering the edges of the photos with stones, tying the ribbons and flower to a stray branch lying on the ground. When the photos shuddered in the wind, as though longing to take flight, Oleg secured them each one with another stone. The ribbons danced.

In the afternoon, Vasily arranged for us to borrow bikes from a friend, and the three of us rode the ten or so kilometres north to Sekirnaya Gora, Hatchet Hill. Oleg and I followed Vasily along a dirt track carving its way, an adder through grass, across the forest floor. Our path was obstructed sometimes by fallen logs, dense clumps of pine needles, and roots crawling out of the ground and over the earth. Once or twice a rabbit stopped suddenly to stare at us, apparently horrified, before disappearing into the trees. I passed close by the hanging branches of a pine and saw, up close, the remnants of the night's rain clinging in droplets. And in the weight of that forest air I felt strangely moved, as if those drops had run down a face that I knew.

When we stopped for a rest, sitting on a few fallen logs with cigarettes, and tea from a thermos, Vasily told us about the winters on Solovetsky.

The way to recognise the truly cold days, he said, is when you see a bright, shining mist that completely fills the air. And when a person walks through it, their body forms a corridor in the thick whiteness, like a passageway. It holds the shape of their body in silhouette. After they have passed, the corridor remains and the silhouette of the vanished person is still present in the mist. You know, I remember looking out the window of our house as a boy, and I watched the town walk around without ever seeing a person. You could tell by the shapes in the mist whether a child, or a tall person, or two adults, had not long ago passed by.

Meanwhile, Vasily continued, those wooden cottages, just as you are staying in here, gradually they blacken a bit more each year. The wet wood is never able to dry. Each season those houses are victims of more rot and decay. And when the winds are thick, draughts of deathly cold come in through every gap in every windowsill, no matter how many layers of cotton wool, felt, rags you try to press into the edges.

And when the spring comes, said Vasily, his features crumpling as if in disgust, the earth moves as it warms and the permafrost in the earth releases its frozen pressure. The earth sags and the houses, my house, slide into the ground. Gradually they're taken downwards, while the roads and yards wilt into the mud.

We took up our bikes again and rode for another twenty minutes or so, eventually slowing as we reached Ascension Skete at the top of the mountain. Long grass rose to our knees, forcing us to perform a disconcerting walk, goosestepping like soldiers. A small white church clung to the summit. It was crumbling from inside. Fresco faces clung in patches to the domed ceilings, as if disintegrating before our eyes. But if I focused on the scattered remains of paint, I could sometimes make out the side of a face, an eye or cheek, and then it seemed as though they were becoming more clearly defined, the faces emerging one after the other over the walls as if reappearing from oblivion, responding to our presence.

Behind the church, a tall flight of steps stretched up through the trees, seemingly infinite. It was called the Torturer's Stair, Vasily told us without further comment. I looked up at that forest staircase and my gaze wavered with a strange feeling of vertigo as I tried to count the steps, one then another, losing track of the number and then beginning again, which caused them to jar out of focus, as if toppling out of control down towards us.

The mountain, Hatchet Hill, gazed over the waters and islands surrounding Solovetsky. I looked out across the green tops of the trees. Lakes cut patches in the forest like blue sky breaking through teal clouds. The ocean was faintly visible below us. In the streaks of grey water, I pictured the beluga whales with their doughy white skin. I imagined them turning over in their cool fluid world, both heavy and weightless, rolling their bodies and pushing forwards through the water. I knew they arrived in early summer, the belugi; they could have arrived already, or perhaps we'd just missed them. They were said to have a birdlike, twittering call, but we couldn't hear it from where we were, up on the heights. Their sounds were said to travel faster than our human ears could catch; their call hitting objects in the water and then returning as echoes that only other belugi could understand.

We stood, three diminutive figures in the high landscape, water and forest appearing like a map below us. The environment was at times overwhelming, almost as if I truly was nothing without this presence, the absolute clarity of watery lake sheets and shifting winds and quiet soil.

And in that brief clarity I saw my confused mind as being like the layers underground. We must have as our perception a palimpsest—must be conscious of the space beyond the one we're in, and pasts beyond the time we experience. Somehow, surely, we don't forget everything.

Solovetsky seemed to bring out Oleg's memories for him and he sometimes spoke about his father. Oleg told me for the first time that his father had been imprisoned when Oleg was a boy. We had been on the island a few days and were sitting outside, near a woodpile at the back of Vasily's house. There was no fence bordering his property, so the rocky ground stretched on as if to the sea.

To see it all, Pasha. It's good to finally see it, said Oleg.

He looked out over the ground, perhaps gazing all the way to the water.

I feel I've been walking towards this place for a long while, said Oleg. Since 1956, in fact. The year of Khrushchev's famous Secret Speech. I suppose I would be what they now call a *detya dvatsatovo syezda*, a child of the Twentieth Party Congress, when Khrushchev made that speech condemning Stalin. That was the year I learnt there was something behind the silence around my own father's imprisonment. The speech made me understand that the leader, not my father, was to blame and that it was not right for me to feel ashamed. They called those years the Thaw.

My parents, I think, had long settled into silence. I doubt it entered their minds to test the consequences of the Thaw. To them, any suggestion of public discussion about what they'd been through must have seemed both sudden and uncertain. In the silence of ice, to go with the metaphor, that frozen space felt safe for them, I suppose. It was all they knew. A thaw suggests uncertain ground, and nasty hidden cracks, sharp jagged things that might or might not be visible to the eye.

Whereas I was captivated by it all. I was just a young man. I read ravenously the discussion in the papers on the cult of Stalin, the letters about suffering. Letters from people feeling suddenly betrayed because of all they did not know; what had been done in the name of the system to which they had given their whole lives. And that was before we really knew the scale of death—it was nothing quite like *glasnost*. I brought the newspapers into the house but, almost as if they were stuck in a lake of ice themselves, they never moved from where I placed them on the table or the floor. My parents wouldn't touch them. My mother once said, *It was the time*, and shrugged. It was the time. But she didn't say any more.

I was so struck by the revelations, I think, because it opened the possibility of another life for me, one that meant I did not have to find a story to explain my father's absence or his inability to work when he returned from the Gulag, or why my parents were so reclusive. For me it was connected to my need to live more truthfully.

I knew of others who, as far as I could see, denied the true identity of their parents for their whole lives. I had a friend at university whose father was in a camp, and if he ever had to fill out a form or submit anything official, he wrote that his father had died in 1942; an easy year in which to hide him, amid so much death.

After he returned, said Oleg, I often tried to picture what it was like for my father in the camp. I'm not sure where one gets a first impression of these things, these places. It's as though information is heard or absorbed somehow, especially when we're young. In my mind I saw a flat land beset by grey skies and hard rain. That image grew to something resembling a camp, a place of long buildings with few working lights, fences of sharp wire and towers inhabited by eyes that saw all, and still the rain and the grey sky.

So many flat, grey, dirty days; the close, dark air of the mines in which the prisoners toiled beneath the ground; the fact that time could well not be moving at all, for one day mirrored each and every other. Some old prisoners tell me they would have preferred a single bullet in Moscow to a lifetime out in the camps. That a life suddenly extinguished would have held more value, instead of being reduced to an ignored life in the camps, lost in a mass like cattle. Men and women and babies dying all around them. Children in orphanages or camps themselves.

Because there, in the camps, death was usually incidental rather than pursued, said Oleg. And to have that knowledge, to know that one is disregarded, seen as no more than a working mass, there only for the industrialisation of the country, as machines to do all that the actual cogs and wheels cannot, must have been very nearly unbearable.

Oleg looked over the desolate island. A light wind travelled around us, almost gently, and the day was warm.

I've tried to picture him, my father, when he was locked up, I said to Oleg.

I had never mentioned that to anyone and it felt strange to say it out loud.

Of course you have, said Oleg. If you love, you imagine.

We were quiet for a moment.

I could not quite picture my father there, Oleg said. I think instead I visualised things as though it was *me* in the camp, looking perhaps from the perspective of my father. Sometimes it was reassuring to be able to see what I thought he might have seen. It put him somewhere, I suppose you could say. He existed. Other times it was awful, picturing the worst, but then also being gripped by the conviction that I was utterly wrong in what I was assuming—wrong about where I was putting him, so to speak, with my thoughts.

And when he came back, said Oleg, it was as though I knew, in some internal, visceral way, what had happened. The damp dirt scent that seemed never to leave my father's clothes very nearly reminded my nine-year-old self of the camp. His agitation, his look of horror, if lunch was to be an hour later than usual, almost reminded *me* of the regimented meagre meals in the Gulag, the only certain moment of each day. I would go so far as to say that if those memories could have spoken, I would have understood them even before I understood the Russian language.

As Oleg spoke I felt a horrible, heavy feeling in my chest. I felt weighed down by the sky at Solovetsky and by events that I hadn't experienced. The place gave me a renewed need to create, to make, to do something to preserve all of the silenced voices and murdered people. It was less of the heady, excited rush I felt within the walls of the Sukhanovs' apartment, more of a hardened, grey need.

Not long after we arrived at Solovetsky, we visited Zayatsky Island, home to the infamous dancing birch trees. Years of forceful winds had battered the papery white trunks as they grew, eternally freezing them in poses of arthritic stillness, both artistic and horrific.

Large grey boulders made a scattered path towards a wooden church, Andreyevsky Monastery. It was small, intricately constructed from many panes of wood turned grey by past wind and winter. Two small stone houses stood nearby, close to the rocky edge of the island.

You come somewhere like here, said Oleg, and you realise how far we've come from treating our dead in the right way.

We walked over a vast stretch of grass, around mounds of stone that sometimes obstructed our way. Masses of small red flowers spilled over the green.

Mourning was a process back then, said Oleg. Back in the days of religion, I mean. Not that I'm a religious man. But it does make you think. In an Orthodox burial, before the body was put into the ground there were three days of ritualised grief: mourners would weep and moan and wring their hands. During those hours and days, the dead were very much with the living, still in the room. Weeping women would kiss the newly departed on the mouth.

For the funeral service at the church, the coffin would be opened, and near the head of the deceased were placed a bowl of *koliva*, a dish of boiled wheat with honey, and a burning candle, to symbolise the cyclical nature of life and the sweetness of heaven. Candles were given to all those present at the service, their wicks alight in a constant flame, just as the mourners were to remain standing, like wavering flames themselves, for the duration of the service. Then, memorial services would be held on the third, ninth, twentieth and fortieth days after the death, those being the stages, so the custom goes, of the parting of the soul from the body. And it was the custom not to touch the dead person's belongings until that fortieth day. What is quite striking about all this, it has always seemed to me, is the ease of being close to the dead. It is an ongoing relationship, so to speak, a connection maintained. The consequences of insufficient mourning were not to be incurred.

It's been said, continued Oleg, that there are many Old Believers in the remotest corners of Russia—the Arkhangelsk region, the Altai mountains, in Tuva, across Siberia. And from times even earlier than Orthodoxy, there are stone burial circles covering the islands here. It seems to me that thoughts and beliefs rise and fall with the years. I like to think that all that is suppressed remains known somewhere.

As Oleg spoke we returned to the edge of the island. We waited for Vasily to take us back to Solovetsky.

This all now reminds me of Shalamov's *Kolyma Tales*, which you'd remember me showing you some years ago, Pasha. We had it underground in the seventies, but it was officially published only recently, in 1986. After nearly a decade labouring in the land of the white death, as they sometimes call Kolyma, Shalamov had been reduced to a *dokhodyaga*, a 'goner' in Gulag-speak, one of the soon-to-be-dead, emaciated as he was and on the verge of succumbing to typhus. It was only after a fellow inmate, a doctor, secured a new position for him in a hospital that Shalamov recovered some of his physical strength. I wondered if my father was a *dokhodyaga* himself, or how many of those men haunted him long after his release. They had loose, dry skin, deep hollows beneath the eyes. They stopped taking care of themselves, lost even the ability to control their bowels. Any mention of food sent them wild. I see one image, one man, covered in excrement, holding his thin arms up in the air, his mouth open in a silent wail. I've never even seen the man, nor do I know who he is. But he is the *dokhodyagi* in my mind, and in a strange way I feel that I know him.

And I was always of the mind that once one is a *dokhodyaga*, 'one who is walking towards the ultimate end', as they have been called, one never truly leaves that state of precariousness, of near-existence and near-death. As if they instead are doomed to continue walking towards that ultimate end. I think perhaps that is the state in which I saw my father persisting when he returned from the camp, as though he never quite lost sight of that place at the end of things, a place he had once, and hence always, walked towards. Stuck in an endless loop of time, the same convoluted, repeated moment.

I'd read Shalamov often since Oleg gave me a copy of *Kolyma Tales* when I was a teenager. And I was always haunted by the *dokhodyagi*, the soon-to-be-dead. The things we call certainties, life and death, blurred. Death became an uncertain concept because the *dokhodyagi* seemed to be both. I thought of the stories I'd heard during *glasnost*, of men and women, fathers and mothers, daughters and sons, who were sentenced to the Gulag with no right of correspondence for decades. Their families couldn't know if it was ridiculous to hope for their return. The whole notion of loss was warped, altered to a permanent state of uncertainty. I could only liken it to the way psychologists say an infant's mind works: when a child is very young, they don't understand that when a person leaves their sight, for even the smallest period of time, that person will return. They don't have the notion of constancy, the ability to recognise that although they cannot see them, their parent is still 'there', maybe even in the room but out of their line of vision, and that they are safe. And so they cry for them as though they are gone forever.

It was as though the Soviet state had damaged our sense of constancy, of whether or not a short absence meant forever.

A result, no doubt, which gave even more power to the rulers of the day, who became holders of the knowledge needed to ascertain if the loss was true or not—whether the person would ever return.

We did not know where they were, who was buried with whom. And yet we lived among them, the unfound dead. As though those lost were all in the room, just outside our range of sight.

A figure appeared on the water, waking me out of my thoughts.

Ah, here they are, our guide and our boat, said Oleg after a long moment. Vasily's figure swayed with the water's rhythm, his features creased, wrinkled against the wind and glare, as if he had emerged through a night of storms. The birch trees, pushed about in the breeze, danced with their peculiar rigid wave.

We stayed on the island for three weeks. Oleg said it was unheard of for visitors to stay so long on Solovetsky. But Vasily agreed to have us if we laid low. Our presence there wasn't exactly illegal, but since we weren't part of any organised tourist visit or religious pilgrimage, our position was a little uncertain.

I'd never been so removed from a city before. Aside from mushroom-picking trips and forest picnics near Moscow, I didn't have a regular connection to such quiet, deserted places.

Every morning I walked alone. I loved the strangeness of the weather, how the heat could bend to sudden freezing winds, summer forever laced with winter. I loved the clarity of noise, the wind's shuddering hands at my ears, the graze of rock scrapes on footpaths. I loved the green, salty breeze, the sun filtered by scattered-feather clouds. At night the sun would dip slightly and coat everything in amber.

We did things I'd never done before: we fished, and ate the fish fried in butter, chased with vodka. Sometimes we'd head out with Vasily in his small white truck, sitting on the back tray while he went around doing odd jobs. We picked mushrooms and berries and ate them in the evenings. We chopped and stacked wood—summer was barely a day long, so Vasily told us with his rare, enormous laugh. I swam in the sea. I walked more and more, sweated lots, felt something vital in sensing the salty beads rising from me, dampening my shirt then evaporating in the sun, dissolving back into me.

I went to the nearby islands a couple of times and walked in the heavy silence of the small churches there. The odd bird rested to watch me, but it was otherwise quiet. I carried my camera, took photos. More than anything I wanted to capture the faces of the painted frescoes before they vanished for good. And I wanted to preserve those traces of brick, wire, wood, steel. Sometimes I put my hand on something, a fence or wall, while photographing it, or aimed the camera at my shoes on the stones, as if also seeking evidence of my own presence there, to record my witnessing of those places.

Vasily would sometimes light small bonfires near the water— Just a match and a few shots! he'd yell, triumphant, throwing on vodka and wood. Every sound soared in echo. Oleg would tend the fire, throwing on some smaller kindling, chatting to Vasily. I'd stand by the water, just watching. The sea grabbed at the firelight, sending it back to the shore in burnished waves, rolling blue, amber, blue. Sometimes I had my notebook out and wrote a few impressions of the place.

Vasily was calling me. His face glowed orange from the fire or the falling sun.

Enough with the vodka poetry, Pasha boy, come and eat.

We would sit around talking, drinking, long into the night.

A few times, Vasily told us about his family, his life there on Solovetsky. Almost every resident there was descended from either prisoner or guard, all now living together.

You probably wonder why I stay out here, in nowhere, he said. This is real, out here. Close to nature, close to animals. We are more animal than you think. Books and smarts and cities, *civilisation*, they're just clothes—he pulled roughly at his checked shirt—you can strip 'em off a man or woman in a moment. None of this human-spirit stuff—don't give me none of that. This place knows—he swept an arm over the island—you can build over your cities and forget, but these stones, they know.

He poured us all another shot.

I think I'm talking shit, said Vasily, throwing back his drink, laughing once. Let's go.

We left, Oleg and Vasily walking in front of me, the sun gold.

On our final night on Solovetsky, the skies remained low and cloudy. Oleg and I took a last walk, then made our way back to Vasily's through the island's small township. A faint night-time presence touched the light, a sudden change from the bright sun of other evenings. The wind picked up, causing drifts of mist to gather speed with a sudden, unnatural pace like grey, spectral traces flying through the air. The Solovetsky settlement, made up of large wooden buildings painted blue, seemed almost always empty. It was almost as though nobody lived there at all. Three goats nuzzled the ground, then turned their heads, their thick horns tilted upwards in the gathering breeze.

A little way ahead, a procession of cloaked figures left one of the pale blue buildings. Monks, dressed from head to foot in black garments, which made them appear uncannily tall. With bowed heads they moved with slow grace up a small hill. We paused to watch them. I heard or imagined a Gregorian chant travelling to us on the wind. After a long moment, when the monks had disappeared from view, Oleg said they were likely visiting the island to secure their return to Solovetsky and the resurrection of the monastery their forebears had established centuries before.

We went back to Vasily's and had a simple meal there. We were both pretty exhausted. We shuffled things around in our bags for a while, folding maps and finding pages long crushed, extracting stray cigarettes. I found the lens cap for my camera and a hat I'd forgotten was there. I was glad to be going back to Moscow, to Anya. I had so many things I wanted to say and write. I felt like I needed to be near her infectious inner drive, a reminder of desire, of what I wanted to create.

Oleg sat at the end of the bed and leafed through a book. I sat down beside him.

Shalamov, said Oleg. As I was saying the other day, Shalamov was an answer to my need to know what had happened to my father. My father sat in a Kolyma camp, just as Shalamov did. When I moved to Moscow as a young man, I became fixated on the camps, on learning as much about Kolyma as possible. It was at this same time that I met others investigating the past, and when I met Marya. Friends were working to expose hidden information about those still in camps. It was an exhilarating period. I felt we were all working to break knowledge itself out of cell and chain.

I found a map of the camp archipelago, said Oleg, saw Kolyma located in the far east. I soon learnt that, in truth, the name Kolyma stood for something in the range of one hundred and sixty camps. One name for all that trembled and suffered beneath it. When one word is supposed to mean so much, there's no real understanding of what it means.

Like Shklovsky's philosophy, I said. He criticises lazy perception, when someone uses a word or phrase without question, and so they no longer really *see* what it is they are talking about. *We don't comprehend the object, merely its silhouette.*

Exactly, said Oleg. It's just as Shklovsky says. And as I'm sure you know, Pasha, dear Shklovsky had to flee the country after he let loose those heretic thoughts. Oleg smiled, his wrinkles deepened.

He became an enemy of the people, I said. Another label that doesn't say much.

Everything and nothing, he agreed, nodding. The beauty and terror of a word. If it becomes powerful enough, we unquestioningly accept labels at the expense of being guided by deeds—which of course requires greater efforts of perception.

As we sat quietly for a moment, I contemplated the dead writers and banned books, the forbidden thoughts, and I wondered why I had such a love for, or faith in, words. Shklovsky said art has the ability to shake us from those lazy habits of perception, to recover the sensation of life and things as they *are*, not as they have been branded with words. I felt a great need to find what it was that made words art. I knew that Shklovsky had come back to Russia after his exile but was forced to denounce his old ways of thinking—though for him they remained his true life, existing between the official lines, and so in a way he was spiritually exiled.

And so here is Shalamov, Oleg went on, holding up the book in his hand. You could say that his writings taught me my father. In his *Kolyma Tales* I read how the train journey from Moscow to Vladivostok took weeks, and that often the prisoners were made to stand the entire way. There was a final trip north by ship, through the Sea of Okhotsk to Magadan, which I imagined to be a treacherous voyage, the boats moving through eerie, dark blue waters, broken sheets of ice glinting in moonlight. The air cold in any season. The prisoners certain they were descending from the known world and into some kind of Arctic underworld, to the heart of a darkness never known to them before.

I believed, quoted Oleg, *I believed a person could consider himself a human being as long as he felt totally prepared to kill himself, to interfere in his own biography. It was this awareness that provided the will to live. I checked myself—frequently—and felt I had the strength to die, and thus remained alive.* I sometimes imagined that my father was the one who wrote those words spoken by Shalamov's narrator, who was possibly the author himself. I even heard a certain voice, not actually my father's but one that seemed all the more real to me because the things he said sounded so true. In this imagined voice my father described to me his mundane days in the camp, and his return from Kolyma. It was as if I could use Shalamov's words as a kind of foil, to look through them and see the essence of my father, as though in the reflection of a dark mirror.

Oleg handed me the book and I read a few lines to myself while he silently smoked. I had the feeling somehow that the lines were going through Oleg's head, learnt by heart, at the same time as I read them.

> I saw what a forcible argument a simple slap could be for an intellectual.
>
> I saw an isolation cell carved out in rock, and spent one night in it myself.
>
> I learnt to 'plan' one day ahead, no further.
>
> I learnt that passing from a prisoner condition to civilian is very hard, and nearly impossible without a long adaptation period.
>
> That a writer must be a stranger in the subjects he describes. And if he knows the matter well, he will write in such a way that no one would understand him.

But you know, said Oleg after a while, a lot of men met their best friends there, in the camps. They laughed in there, Pasha. They had the odd day that wasn't so bad. They heard and read and wrote poems in there. For some it was the only place that was real. The true state of things—they could see it there. In the cities, in the supposedly free places, the appearance of things belied the reality they knew.

Thinking of all those physicists mining coal in Magadan, the poets and teachers digging canals, the engineers, doctors, young parents buried in unknown, unmarked mass graves with a single, neat, horrific hole in their skulls, you wonder what might have been. You wonder what today could have been, and at certain times you imagine in some fantastical way that it is actually occurring, our other Russia, somewhere else. As though that essence lives on elsewhere, away from us.

I read Shalamov so much, said Oleg, that I began to lose the sense of the words. As if they could not speak anymore. Rather than see my father there, I had the sense that I was returning to the same story, with a character that never changes and scenes that remain static. I have bought countless copies of *Kolyma Tales* over the years, since I threw the book away so many times: thrown into Moskva River, onto railway lines, left at bus stops, at the foot of trees in Alexander Garden. Poor Shalamov, he's strewn all over the city. But I needed desperately to be separated from words. They had given me all that they could.

Perhaps you needed to write your own, I said.

I think that's true, Pasha. Though I'm no writer, not like you. I think of my maps as my books. They are my biography, and my father's.

Oleg and I returned to Moscow at the end of June. As the train took us closer and closer to the city, I was thinking of Oleg, of his father and my own father. It was hard to take in the scale of things—all those statistics and articles that came out with the freedom of *glasnost*. All the memory that returned. I could see why Oleg would need to throw the Shalamov book away at times, when words could only take him so far. But then he'd buy a copy again and again. Perhaps we return to words because a human needs their experience reflected somewhere. We return to art because it reflects our incompleteness; true art is full of gaps, and so we need it again and again, because that is how we live and remember.

I remembered a conversation with Anya, more like an argument—one of those you revel in having, passionate, as though it's taking you somewhere, making you a better person— about how to adequately represent the scale of mass murder committed in the name of the Soviet Union. She maintained that there weren't enough statistics being published. I said numbers destroyed faces. She said people should be confronted with those numbers, made to count them until nauseous. I said to recite numbers was like asking questions about the meaning of it all—those things can't be done because they attempt to impose order on the incomprehensible. Maybe it was true that numbers and questions were both the essence of the past and its blinder. I agreed with the poets in the thirties who banned questions among their group—you can't grant the system the dignity of attempted explanations. There was no logic to it. I swore to her that if I ever wrote a book about it all, I'd make a point of there being not a single question mark in the entire work.

CHAPTER 22

In St Petersburg I was still drifting in that sort of halfway place, living in a city different to the one my mind walked through so often. In the parks the oak and lime branches shuddered, red hearts and gold coins, in a breeze that whispered winter. A few fell. By October the ground was covered.

I met up with Sonya early one morning in the city. She was holding a bunch of flowers. We went to a cafe and then I walked her to the stairs of a church nearby. A few women in headscarves passed us on their way inside. Sonya was on her way to her mother's, she said, holding the flowers up as if to show me. But she wanted to make a quick visit to the church first.

Her blonde hair reminded me of Anya—or Anya as I knew her, because I didn't know what she looked like anymore.

I looked at Sonya for a long moment, until she asked me if everything was all right. She said I seemed preoccupied. I looked at this woman as she tucked her blonde hair under a headscarf, looked at her slightly glassy eyes fringed with thick lashes. I wondered whether I hadn't let Sonya be her own woman in my mind. As though I'd only seen her as someone who wasn't Anya.

I was always one who let memory plague a present moment. I wondered whether I was just repeating old feelings of hopelessness, revisiting prior loss. A lack of peace. It was as though there was a building where we once lived together, Anya and I, and that building was a tower still standing, even though we weren't in it. And I was walking by it every day, throwing glances at it, in my mind taking Sonya into it, too. Most of us can only draw a city based on the structures we've seen before.

I said to Sonya that I needed to go to Moscow for a while. I wasn't sure how long I'd be there.

Sometimes, I said, sometimes I look at a clock and time means nothing to me. And it's the same with a word, such as a station sign on the walls of the subway. There's a moment, I'm not sure how long, one of those never-ending seconds, and whichever hour it is or whatever station I'm in, the words and numbers have no meaning. Then I think of somewhere I'm supposed to be or the next thing I have to do. I cling to those things, and I find myself again. But lately I feel less and less that there are those things to do or places to be.

You'll find them, she said, reaching out to tuck strands of hair behind my ear. You've maybe just forgotten where you are. We sometimes forget why we're doing things or what we care about. You won't disappear just yet. And when you come back from Moscow, we'll go to the *dacha*.

I nodded. Her words had a simple strength, something very real about them. I waited outside while Sonya was in the church.

Then she emerged, and we parted ways with a kiss. As I stood watching her go, she turned and smiled and held up the flowers, as if to show me again. I watched her, Sonya in her belted blue dress, cream stockings and white tennis shoes, walk away from me, wait at the traffic lights, cross the street and go down the escalator to the metro. As I turned and left I heard airy choir voices call out behind me, faint as dissolving smoke, high in the air.

I was finding it hard to stop thinking about things that couldn't happen anymore, all those futures not possible, and of the things I still didn't know about the past. Maybe, I thought, I was one of those *former people*, and in the world here, the present, I was not really a person at all.

That afternoon I bought a ticket for the overnight sleeper train leaving for Moscow the following evening. A journey of five hours, though in other measures it was a trip to a place very distant, years away from me. I'd heard it said that you should never go to the places in the most beautiful of paintings, or in the books you knew well, for it would destroy with the real the effect of the art. Moscow had for me become a kind of loved painting, a set piece, a handful of photographs. But I was never at peace and could not stop sifting through those photographs.

I went home late in the afternoon. I checked the answering machine but there was only a message from my boss; nothing from the neighbour. I sat writing at my desk, writing down the neighbour's story and then returning to the Moscow years again. By evening I'd had more beers than I could remember. It was the kind of drinking that turns you inwards, that amplifies loneliness. When thoughts seem acute but then the world seems blurry.

The next evening, I was ready. The train was due to leave at five to midnight. Buses to the metro were few at night, so I walked through the dark to the station. Even the dogs were quiet. I lit a cigarette.

Nobody else boarded the metro at Primorskaya station. I took out the notebook in which I'd been recording the trip I'd taken with Oleg. Past expectation seemed to blend with present.

In 1989, Oleg and I had taken the Red Arrow train. I'd never been to St Petersburg before, but it was called Leningrad then anyway. Names were false certainties, just markers made.

In 1989, the camps had awaited me, too, up in the islands of the north.

And on my return, Anya was waiting for me back in Moscow, in a future I didn't yet know.

Ten years later, and I was again taking the Red Arrow. Only Moscow was waiting. But for a minute a phantom feeling, one of those ghostly birds that pass the cheek, convinced me that someone, Anya or my mother, was waiting too.

Leafing through my notebook in the lonely fluorescent glow of the metro, my attempt at re-creating those moments, the 1989 trip, the weeks on Solovetsky, as if I didn't know what came next, seemed absurd to me.

The train arrived at Mayakovsky station. There were no direct metros so I walked for twenty minutes to Moscow station, where trains left for that city; a station so sure of the future.

PART III

Perhaps all this world and all these men are myself alone.

Fyodor Dostoyevsky, 'The Dream of a Ridiculous Man'

CHAPTER 23

Perhaps, at the height of creativity, one is also verging on a total abandonment of art. And maybe, when a political system seems strong, it is a step away from fallen. And when the conditions around love change, that is also maybe the start of its loss.

June 1989, spring broke over into summer. Seeing Anya was like we were beginning again. Summer again, love again. Rather than a different year, the season felt like a return to the old. The Arbat continued to contain an ever-shifting crowd, the punks and dancers, the families and ice-cream vendors. The parks were bright green again.

I returned to work at the library. Anya was studying for her candidate's dissertation in philosophy. Yura got a job at Moscow State University, not a proper academic position but something like a tutor or assistant. He was warier now about writing for journals or newspapers, as he'd likely lose his job if he did. Sukhanov held an exhibition of his paintings in a small gallery, a second-floor room of an old *kommunalka* apartment in Tverskoy District. We still went to see him and Lena every weekend. We went to concerts held in apartments and basements. We went to movies. Ilya had a girlfriend, briefly, who played bass in a punk band; she was from Leningrad but squatted in a friend's apartment because on her internal passport she wasn't registered to live in Moscow. Ilya still worked for the stock delivery driver, but it bored him.

When I went to the Frunzenskaya apartment, Yevgenia Fyodorovna seemed to avoid eye contact with Anya, who showed an equal coldness to her mother. But I was struck not by the distance between Anya and her mother—I knew they'd long argued—so much as the transformation in her father. Mikhail Sergeyevich looked far older than when I'd left in the spring. I knew there had been family disagreements about Anya's writing, her ventures into activism. But more than anything, Yevgenia Fyodorovna looked very wary. Anya had told me about what she saw as the sometimes-strange behaviour of her parents. How any time they stayed away from home, her mother insisted that Anya sleep in the room furthest from the front door, and how her father had been severe to the point of madness about Anya's schooling, particularly anything to do with history or social studies. If she didn't feel like reading something or called a topic boring, he would berate her for it. Their upbringings have warped them, Anya had said, almost scathingly.

After I returned from Solovetsky, we never really spoke about our idea of writing together. Anya loved her job at the TV station and said that she sometimes thought she could stay in the Soviet Union and be happy. We even spoke about every Soviet couple's dream of having our own place, a room and a half somewhere that was just our own. It was more of a laughing dream, though, with the wait for any apartment likely to be a decade.

Still, even if we weren't to write the stories of our fathers together, I wanted to continue my conversations with Mikhail Sergeyevich. I felt a connection with him that I couldn't really explain. It was as though a link existed between him and my own father, and I couldn't stop trying to find a pattern, to join things together somehow. It could simply have been that Mikhail Sergeyevich knew what it was like inside those hospitals that often occupied my thoughts.

We didn't meet again until the autumn. Anya said that his health hadn't been good for a few months, so he wasn't up to going out during the summer months after I returned. When we finally did meet, we walked in one of the parks, as we had the previous year, and then once again sat on a bench.

Mikhail Sergeyevich spoke about the mass-gravesite discoveries. That year it had felt as though we were witnessing a re-emergence of the dead. A branch of the Memorial Society in Novosibirsk sent an open letter to Ligachev at the Politburo. He'd been Party leader of the Novosibirsk region in 1979, when the banks of the Ob River burst and the torrential waters flooded the site of a former prison of the NKVD, the secret police, releasing from the earth a mass of mummified corpses. It was all hushed up at the time, the bodies reburied. The letter from the Memorial Society called for those responsible for the cover-up to be held to account.

Burial sites were being uncovered everywhere. A mass grave on a building site at the Rutchenko fields in Donetsk province.

On Golden Mountain near Chelyabinsk they found the remnants of bullet-pierced skulls. Diggers in a sand quarry in Poltava in Ukraine found another site filled with the unknown dead. It was as though they were all coming back, that they knew *glasnost* had arrived.

I feel an almost incomprehensible horror, said Mikhail Sergeyevich. It seems there is so much *work* to do—the work of memory, if there's such a thing. Your work, the writing you and Anya want to do, it is a good thing.

I told him how, in the past year, it had been my hope to contribute in some way, to record from my outsider's view, as a child of dissidents, what I knew, what I'd learnt. But, I confessed, I wasn't getting anywhere.

He nodded. You're still young, Pasha; there's still time. You feel empty, sometimes, when you're young.

I nodded, looking down at my knees.

I've long felt a similar sensation of emptiness, he continued. Feeling a void, I suppose it's kind of a paradox—it's not something you can comprehend other than through knowledge of an absence. I can attest that I'm here, as a man, with a body right now sitting on this seat, but I cannot say I am sure what I'm made up of—what is going on inside. Whether, by virtue of the system I grew up under, the very household in which I was raised, my mind has been conditioned. That's how the Marxists would have it, in any case. Material being determines consciousness.

We sat in silence for a while, both looking ahead, over a path and to a view of trees, a few people walking through them and near us. I had the sense that Mikhail Sergeyevich and I were preoccupied with similar questions: whether we were products of our upbringing—for me, whether I really could carry on the work, preserve the life, of the apartment of my childhood; for him, whether he could estrange himself from his upbringing and still know who he was. Unsure if our mental lives really came from within us or outside, whether the things we did because of those thoughts were even under our control, we were perhaps both haunted by causation.

I think there's something more, I said, as much to myself as to Mikhail Sergeyevich, more than just conditions that make us think things. Well, I hope there's more. I look at the apartment I grew up in, and I think that it was the other way around—*thoughts* made that apartment. Our inner life, consciousness or whatever, made the apartment a place where that manipulated and censored world couldn't get in.

Mikhail Sergeyevich gave a slight smile. I certainly hope there's some truth in that, Pasha, he said. Because otherwise it's too tempting for us to destroy our bodies to protect our minds from further distortion.

I looked down again at my knees, not sure what to say. We sat there, in the silence of our separate thoughts. Afternoon sun elongated our shadows and the air began to cool.

One freezing winter morning I returned home from some-where—maybe Anya's, maybe a night out with Ilya—and saw my mother sitting at the kitchen table, silent tears racing down her face. I'd never seen my mother cry before, not about anything.

It was 15 December 1989, and Andrei Sakharov—dissident activist hero—had died the night before, died at his desk, at which he'd been writing a memorandum to take to parliament the following day.

I went over to my mother and put a palm on her back, ran my hand over her spine, like I used to as a boy when she'd sit there at the table, working at the typewriter. Her black hair, streaked with a little grey, was tied in a loose bun, a few wisps around her ears. She nodded as if in thanks, stood up, poured a glass of brandy, poured me one too. We drank and her tears stopped.

It feels like my whole generation has died, Pasha, not just poor Sakharov.

New Year arrived, 1990. Anya was staying at our apartment more and more. She and my mother got along well—better than what I'd heard from friends about their girls and mothers. Anya was still studying, I was still working at the library, and so our days were long.

Anya's research was moving in a different direction, she said. Lately she had been researching the life of the first female psychoanalyst, Lou Andreas-Salomé. She had mentioned her the first night we met, I remembered. That had been almost two years ago.

As we loved to do, we just lay on the divan talking, smoking and thinking together. Sometimes my mother would sit across from us, on a chair she brought in from the kitchen. My mother said she missed the long conversations around the kitchen table. Gatherings were still sometimes held at our apartment or the apartments of other dissidents, but there was a different structure to things now—public discussions and lectures, meetings held in halls and offices in the city. It wasn't a negative change, my mother said, it was just different.

I think the idea of the subconscious is important, Anya was saying, but I think we're closer to it than people realise—we just don't tell others about that inner life. My mother, you know, she lives with this whole world of Stalinism in her still. This ongoing state of fear. It's conditioned her to think a certain way. It's not that she just keeps thinking about the past; to me it seems like she is *still living* those moments.

Then Anya mentioned how she would prefer to study those ideas abroad, travel to the places where Freud and Lou Andreas-Salomé had been.

We both were quiet; a pause that held unsaid things. Often we used Anya's hypothetical journeying out of Russia as fuel for our thoughts, our conversations. It had become very abstract to me; more of an opinion of hers than a plan.

One day in the spring we were sharing a meal—Anya, my mother and I. My mother had left the room for a moment— maybe to go to the bathroom or the living room. The radio murmured in the background and I could see a square of blue sky through the window.

I've applied for an exit visa, said Anya, looking straight at me for a moment and then back at her plate. She pulled at her thin cardigan as though securing it over her.

Anya and I broke up for a while. She said she just didn't believe in the idea of love being transcendent, of it being something more powerful than other desires. She could feel love for me, she said, and at the same time feel fine about being alone—making her own path, as she often called it. It was as if she felt a stronger love for the things she couldn't have: the places she had never been and the unattainable fullness of art. Of course, such a maddening paradox just makes the one left behind, made me, feel more drawn to the thing that was constantly leaving me. For it always felt, in some way, like a circular, never-ending sort of loss.

And so I didn't see her parents for a while, either, though I often thought of Mikhail Sergeyevich. He was, like Oleg, someone older for me to look up to and think aloud with. The spring passed and summer arrived, and it felt far removed from the summer of 1988. A feeling of muteness crept into me, like a growing bleak landscape. I wasn't sure where to look anymore for the things that inspired me. Probably it was the first fraught realisation I had that I was so attached to that group, to Anya, for my own meaning, and without them I was just a step away from feeling like nothing at all.

Then one night Anya called me. She was crying.

He's dead, she said. He died. He's gone. Tsoi is dead.

Our musical hero, Viktor Tsoi, had died in a car accident. He was driving alone, on his way home to his wife and son after a tour, and was thought to have fallen asleep at the wheel.

Come over, I said. I was surprised that my voice sounded as it always did: low, quiet, steady, without any hint of the absolute need I was sure would saturate it.

She arrived less than an hour later. I hadn't seen her in a few months. For reasons neither of us really understood, the death of Tsoi drew us together. As if we were looking back at what his loss represented—the loss of our generation's voice—and we wanted to preserve something of it by salvaging whatever was left of us. We each had a glass of something, probably brandy, and then went to bed and had silent and sad and fast sex. I held her and stayed inside her for a long time, and then we just lay there, and at some point fell asleep.

The night Tsoi died, someone started a memorial wall on the corner of the Arbat and Krivoarbatsky Lane. Anything could be a memorial, it seemed, once we made a mark, inscribed pain into a thing. We went to the wall: Anya, me, Ilya, Sukhanov, Lena, Yura. It had been so long since we'd all been anywhere together. I kept glancing at Anya, thinking of the night; her presence beside me again made every place feel as though it contained more. Other people sat or lay down nearby, some murmuring, most just staring or sleeping. We each lit a cigarette, pressed them against the wall, each at a slightly different time, till the fags were bent in half, then we left them on a plate put there by someone before us. The thin drifts of smoke joined one another until each shaky grey thread was indistinguishable from the next. Then we sat down, closer to each other than usual, quiet, the girls crying soundlessly, and we let our offerings burn their ends.

It was that summer, or maybe once autumn started, that Sukhanov and Lena started having troubles, and we didn't go there so often. At first we would drink in the park, or have quieter nights at the apartments of others we didn't know so well. But losing that place, we lost some spirit. A time passed after which I knew we would never go back there. Sukhanov wasn't painting much anymore, he said. I think I'm losing the heat, he said. His wavy blonde hair looked ragged somehow, his eyes bleary. He said he still tried to paint sometimes after work, but the effort was wearing him down. It made me feel stranded in a way hard to describe, to think that he, Sukhanov, artist of colour, child of Kandinsky, could in some way feel the same slow spiral as me.

In October 1990, the memorial stone was finally laid in Dzerzhinsky Square. I walked through the city with Ilya—none of the others wanted to come, or maybe we didn't ask them—among a long chain of people. Gathering darkness tinted the sky dark blue, towards night. Candlelight glowed stronger in its wake, while incense hovered, invisible, in the air. We had gathered first at Sretenskaya Gate, and then proceeded down Dzerzhinsky Street. Each person held a candle, some also a photo of a lost relative, or banners bearing the names of labour camps—Karlag, Bamlag, Alzhir—and walked to the square. A woman read out names, and after each one the word *shot* followed with the strange resonance of an echo from a moment that had taken place much earlier, perhaps even before our births. It also felt as though, with her voice, she was in some way re-enacting the shots that needed an honest witness.

On reaching the square, thousands pressed towards the memorial stone brought from the Solovetsky Islands. Something in the quality of the near-silence, disturbed only by murmurs and footsteps or the light wind, created the impression of a funeral. The stone was the body laid to rest in the open, cushioned by the mass of red flowers falling one on top of the other. The statue of Dzerzhinsky, the grandfather of the KGB, was an unwelcome and almost spectral presence in the square.

It was like a slow process of mourning in those years. *Glasnost* had taken us up, hardened our hopes to gold. We knew what we wanted—memory and suffering recognised, real change—but what to do with such memory once it is unrepressed, that was the uncharted course, the unanswerable question.

In the winter of 1990, McDonald's appeared in Pushkin Square. Enormous queues, ridiculous queues, persisted weeks beyond the restaurant's opening, more devout even than the lines to see Lenin in the Kremlin mausoleum. The square seemed to absorb it so quickly: the facade, MCDONALD'S in thick backlit letters, glowed boldly as night came. The restaurant seemed dirtied overnight, the remnants of meals on the tables looked withered; sagging napkins, tall drink cups tipped over.

We had an argument, Anya and I, when we went to it. Everyone was going to try the food and see what it was like, so we decided to go as well. We stood outside, waiting, just as we had in the long lines we'd grown up with outside grocery or clothes stores elsewhere in the city.

There's your West, I said to her, half joking. You don't need to go now.

I knew by then that she was going, that we were in a vague relationship, like the twilight of togetherness.

You're not even giving the country a chance, I went on bitterly. Have some faith.

I want to go. I want change.

At night we were calmer; we seemed to thrive in darkness.

I wouldn't mind talking to your father again, I said as we lay in bed one night. I hate that I never did anything with all the notes I made, all the things he told me and the research we did.

Anya was very still, and I wondered if she was sick of me talking about her family, about the past, and that old plan we had of writing something together.

You can talk to him, she said. But you can call him yourself to arrange it. I don't want my mother using this as yet another thing to hassle me about.

When I called him the next morning, Mikhail Sergeyevich asked whether we could walk through the city instead of the usual parks. And so we met at Frunzenskaya Embankment and walked through a few streets, fairly quiet, and eventually reached Kotelnicheskaya Embankment.

Ah yes, he said, sighing in a sad sort of way. Yes, these huge buildings. I've kept away from these for a long while.

He meant the Stalinskie Vysotki, Stalin's skyscrapers; the Seven Sisters, they were called. White-and-cream monstrosities, like disproportionate versions of other 1930s buildings—straight lines, towers, countless windows.

They're just cruelly enormous, he said. I used to walk here a lot, as a young teacher. Every weekend, first thing in the morning. I loved that grey time which seemed like no time, at the start of a day, when you know that nothing has happened yet.

He turned to me. I feel as if the *weight* of things is catching up with me, Pasha. I don't know which has come first, really. Whether my talking has begun because of *glasnost* or whether I helped start *glasnost* itself by talking about the past.

He shook his head in a strange, irritated way that I wasn't used to.

A couple of years ago, when you first met my Anna Mikhailovna, I was very disturbed to hear that the history exams had been cancelled in schools. It reminded me of the Secret Speech that Khrushchev made back in fifty-six.

Suddenly he admitted Stalin did wrong. Suddenly they want us teachers to explain the unexplainable, answer unanswerable questions. I was sure I'd freeze in front of my class of students. I had no idea what would happen in there, that dreadful classroom. I wondered, at the time, whether I could explain things to my students by likening that past, the Stalin years, to a cut—a single injury, which could heal, which could be overcome. That was what the newspapers and Party statements at the time seemed to encourage. But I felt I couldn't say that. It seemed more honest, more true, to call that past a disease. Something that spreads to others, which can be passed between families and colleagues and generations. I can tell you, Pasha, that it kept me up at night, the worry of how to get things right; the question of how to tell the right story. My desk at home—covered in all sorts of papers and books, history textbooks and newspapers, novels and memoirs. Piles of notes, but no matter how often I ordered them the piles seemed to sneak themselves back into a hideous mess overnight.

What a mess, he said, sounding irritated. What a horrible mess it was. Someone needs to set this right, I told Yevgenia at the time. I felt as though nobody in this godforsaken place would tell the story right. I was difficult, then, said Mikhail Sergeyevich, glancing once at me. And I feel like that time—like that certain time in my life is a place to which I have recently returned.

I had a bad fall then, Mikhail Sergeyevich said a moment later, and his voice went strangely dreamy, even wistful. In 1988. Tripped on the escalator at Kirov station. My body was a bit off then, and I lost my balance. There I was . . . lying on my back at the foot of the escalator. I just stared upwards for a while, at those sharp silver steps coming towards me, and then at the people who began to glide down too. So still, they were. So still.

My father, he said abruptly, my father slept with a gun beside his bed. He was close to the power. You don't want to be too close to the sun, Pasha, or it'll burn you. He came out of the 1930s, the Purge years, alive, rose up in the forties, working with Kaganovich here in Moscow, as I've told you, helping to direct the construction of the Moscow metro and the collectivisation campaign in the provinces and Ukraine. There was a bad purge over in Leningrad at the end of the forties. Lots of top officials killed. It scared my mother no end. No matter how loyal you were, no matter how loyal you felt *inside*, death could come for you anytime. Fear was a constant presence, a *state of being*, Pasha. A constant background sound, like a high-pitched violin note.

I listened but I felt powerless to help him and wasn't sure what to say. It was as though so many old moments, the night-time of his thoughts, were returning. His present was punishing him now but began so long ago.

CHAPTER 24

From Leningrad station in Moscow I walked to the metro at nearby Komsomolskaya. It was early in the morning, October 1999. A few men and women in business clothes sat or stood in the carriage. A couple of elderly people held bags or baskets for shopping. The voiceover at each station called out names so familiar to me. *Krasny Vorota*, it said, *Krasny Vorota*. And then, *Kuznetsky Most*. I listened so carefully, as though it was the voice of all meaning. *Kuznetsky Most*. I didn't want to go straight to the empty apartment, so I changed at Kuznetsky and then got out at Tverskaya.

At the top of the escalators I met a light wind, clear sun. It was early autumn when summer seemed close but then so did winter. The lime tree leaves were yellow on Tverskoy Boulevard and the wind was cold. At the end of the boulevard was Pushkin Square, where my mother took me as a boy. In summer I'd see girls with orange or red umbrellas, white socks to their knees and braids down their front like golden knots. I would devour an ice cream, pure white, from the round-bellied man in a navy-blue apron, whose cart stood near the Pushkinskaya metro. In the winter, I'd see the old ladies in headscarves walking together, hooked at the elbows, and through the fog the curved iron arms of streetlamps holding up the light. I'd hold on to the hem of my mother's coat so I wouldn't slip on the red bricks, a crimson ice lake. Pushkin himself would be cloaked in snow. I'd hold the iron chains around his statue and stare up at his tall figure. I had to brush away the snow, and the chains were cold. Then it was summer again and in my hands the coils were warm, and as we walked on, my sweaty palms would smell of rubbed *kopek* coins. I was sure that Pushkin himself felt the seasons.

When I was a young boy, my mother taught me to memorise poems. She spoke often about the Poets who lived and died for words under Stalin. *It's important to remember their words, Pasha.* In my mind I saw those Poets as tall figures with long cloaks and sad eyes and white hands gripping their pens. Like a silent citadel they stood in the back of my mind while I heard their poems, a dead choir who somehow still sang.

I sat beside my mother on our sagging divan and she coaxed the words from her memory to mine. She never wrote the poems down. At the height of Stalin's Terror years, she told me, the Poets could not risk the ink drying on their pages and those pages being found. They would memorise each other's works, and in that way the poems moved from one person to another. And if at rare times they did put words to paper, the lines were to be read in the moment and then burnt in the stove. From ink to ash to memory.

During *glasnost*, a group of activists led by Lev Kopelev worked on drafting a constitution for the Soviet Union, to take to the Congress of People's Deputies in 1989. Oleg called that constitution the new poetry. From my earliest years I learnt that language was a thing to both love and fear.

From Pushkin's my mother and I would sometimes take a white-and-red tram, or a blue bus, along the boulevard near Red Square. As cars flew past, I felt as if we might have been aboard a ship, sailing the concrete expanse. I'd never seen the ocean. In the winter, sometimes the sun couldn't rise. Streetlights and windows in the distance looked like dusty lamplight. We might stand in a queue for a while, edging our way up to the women in striped dresses, white aprons and hats who would weigh potatoes on enormous scales. If we saw a street seller with slabs of meat in deep silver trays, my mother would inspect the quality, and sometimes she would take home a piece.

I couldn't see my father in those memories. It was a strange thing. As though because he was in my life for so little of it, he faded even from the memories he was actually in. The precise years of those images in the square, I couldn't say; 1968, perhaps 1970.

And then, years later, the square with Pushkin's statue was a place to meet Ilya and Yura, to meet Anya, to read poetry in circles or listen to Billy Bragg on black-market Walkmans. Let's meet at Pushkin's. Pushkin's at midday. Always there were people waiting, reading a book, savouring a cigarette, always someone waiting for another. In spring and summer the fountains soared, long veils of white water hanging in the air. Groups of us, students dancing, awkward and in love in the open sun.

My life in Moscow, layered like stacked slides of an old magic lantern. And I could see a little of each transparent slide through the others, somehow making the whole.

I hitched my rucksack straps over both shoulders. Though I zipped my coat against the wind, the chill stayed inside for a while. I lit a cigarette and walked across the square. The old Rossiya Cinema which had stood behind Pushkin's statue was now a casino. It looked both dark and festive, neon and cold, as the coloured lights shone beneath the sun. A young couple walked past me, the girl holding a single rose. Three or four young guys sailed by me on skateboards with wheels softly growling. The boys held out their arms, graceful, the unzipped sides of their baggy hooded sweaters spread like the wings of large birds.

I walked over and stood at the statue. Pushkin had one hand at his chest, half tucked into his jacket, as if thinking or feeling deeply, though Tolstoy said he looked like a footman about to announce dinner. At the foot of the statue was his poem 'The Monument'.

Perhaps it was from Pushkin's words, glinting gold in the summer, frosted over in the winter, in the background of so many days in the square, that I absorbed the idea that literature could be a kind of memorial.

Come on, Pasha, it's time to go to Pushkin's.

CHAPTER 25

It was winter, I was woken by the ringing of the telephone just after midnight. It was Anya and her voice was thick with tears.

Mikhail Sergeyevich took his own life in February 1991. Anya came over very early the next morning, and she and I sat on the divan in the living room, my mother across from us in a single wooden chair, silent and grave. I felt as though I was holding the dying; sometimes Anya cried, but mostly she was still as if frozen.

I pulled the yellow crocheted rug that had been on our divan for so many years over Anya's knees. When I tried to comfort her, with one arm around her body, the palm of the other hand at the back of her head, I had a strange feeling, like the echo in me of a moment from very long ago, a moment still resonating, trying to come to an end: I was a boy, my palm rested on my mother's shoulder. I couldn't see her face or remember her expression, but I knew she was pained. Her sadness was linked to a quiet terror for me. And so maybe that was why I had a horrible feeling, when I held Anya, that some grievous crime was behind her sadness. It was a strange thing to feel, but then again if that was my first grief, watching my mother cry, then perhaps I would forever circle back to it.

Mikhail Sergeyevich's suicide was a question never answered. For a while—the first few months after, at least—I assumed it was something that would come up, at some later date. I took it for granted that Anya would one day be ready to speak to me about it, or that the history of his illness would one day be unearthed. But it was like a constantly missed moment; I never asked, she never told.

We stopped mentioning anything to do with the psychiatric repressions or psychiatric hospitals, especially our now distant plans to write together. And because those topics were connected to our artistic and activist hopes, those too seemed to be muted by the cover of silence we pulled down, together and between us, after her father died.

In the next months, fraught and fractured, I no longer saw the expectant white canvas of *glasnost* and the eighties, but rather a kind of murky pool we had to wade through, unsure. After years of stagnated stability, the leadership of the country, things going on *up there*, seemed shaky. It was exciting but at the same time we weren't used to such uncertainty.

Anya would sometimes raise her shoulders in a stiff shrug and say, bitterly, that she couldn't believe she was still in the country. I was so sure about leaving before, she said on our way to a concert one night. We were walking through the city on dusk and she spoke ahead as if to the streets and sky. I wondered if she regretted staying with me; maybe she saw me as the cause of her inaction.

On the anniversary of Viktor Tsoi's death, August 1991, we went back to the wall and lit our cigarettes again. It was as if we were mourning our own lives, or that's how it felt to me then; how it feels when you're young and you learn those first pangs of loss for things that haven't happened. In horror you realise that it doesn't take long for you to transform into a person with regrets. People can fall from the heady precipice of nascent art, feeling the ashy death of burnt-out desire.

A few weeks later, I was sitting in the apartment, on the divan, watching TV. I changed from one channel to another, the state news, and saw a single white figure, a woman, spinning on a black surface like a dove in the night. It was unspoken knowledge that when something was happening in the country that they, up there, didn't want us to know about or didn't yet know how to present to us, the news stations would abruptly broadcast ballet instead of news. And so as I sat on the divan in the living room that August and saw *Swan Lake*, I knew something was up.

That night, Ilya called me.

Something's up, he said.

I know. I saw the ballet dancer.

We went to the city centre. One of Ilya's friends had called and said things were happening in Dzerzhinsky Square: Anya, Ilya, Sukhanov, Yura and I were there, but not Lena. It was madness. Protestors everywhere, shouting, jostling crowds. There had been a failed coup against Gorbachev, started by devout Communists horrified at the changes wrought by *glasnost* and *perestroika*, by openness and change.

That uncertainty from above seemed to shake people into seeing a true alternative: the end of Communism. Felix Dzerzhinsky's statue had stood over the square in front of the Lubyanka building since 1958. He, founder of the Cheka, was hauled by a crane to the ground that night, after the failed coup.

The square was floodlit by the lights of surrounding buildings—or maybe they were car headlights from afar. I looked at the faces of my friends in the ill gloom. Anya had her arms crossed, a cigarette in one hand resting on her elbow, her mouth a straight line of wariness, her blonde hair tinged a strange green-gold. Yura had his hands in his pockets, his glasses reflected white dots, he moved his head slowly as if searching for something. Sukhanov, in his denim vest and jeans but without Lena at his side, Ilya with his gelled hair and leather jacket—both stood smoking and staring, their eyes creased a little by unasked questions, and it made them both look older than their twenty-seven years.

The light shed a green glow over Dzerzhinsky's figure. The rope around his neck was like a coiled snake. I later saw on TV similar scenes across the Soviet Union as other statues—Lenin, Stalin, heroic workers—were hauled down. It was an eerie sight, to watch the way that stone giant, Iron Felix as they called him, did not crash to the ground nor break into pieces, but instead glided on the flight of his noose with an ethereal, birdlike grace; not a hangman's dance but a spectral hovering, stone face high in the air as though looking ahead to his next destination. I didn't want to get too close. It felt unfamiliar to me; I was used to protest waged by words, not barricades and ropes. A few people ran over to the statue and scrawled graffiti on him: *antichrist—bloody executioner—shit in a leather coat.*

And across the concrete sea, at the edge of the square, as though washed ashore, was the Solovetsky Stone, resting low in the view of the Lubyanka building.

Things spiralled from there. The Soviet Union dissolved in December 1991. We now lived in the Russian Federation.

CHAPTER 26

late lunch at a cheap bistro and then kept walking. Like St Petersburg, Moscow was now full of small chain restaurants. A lot of the old *kommunalki* apartment blocks had been knocked down. Tall, modern buildings, with countless reflective sheets of grey glass, stood in their place.

I went to Gorky Park. It was barely recognisable. I was a stranger. The place had become so dirty, full of fast food stalls. The carnival rides looked worn out, broken or old. There were people with wild animals—a crocodile, a puma, and I thought I even saw a woman holding a young lion. A thin old *babushka* with a bent back saw me gazing at the zoo, the old rides, and muttered to me, It's like a madhouse, nowadays.

I thought of my meetings with Mikhail Sergeyevich in the same park, the conversations about our fathers and the past, about Moscow and all that was beneath the city. I looked up to the trees. In the wind, their beseeching twigs scratched the sky.

Dzerzhinsky's statue, a ghost of stone, now stood in the park. That same statue I had watched soar down, with the frightening silence of heavy stone falling, from his height in Dzerzhinsky Square—soon to be renamed Lubyanka Square—in 1991. It was full of statues, that graveyard of memorials, full of other former leaders, former Soviets, now toppled and probably cracked in places, with a missing limb or crushed cheek but otherwise intact, while some were stunted half-bodies removed from their plinths. All lying or standing together in apparent repose.

Looking at those malformed statues, I told myself that if I could make some kind of shape out of the memories of the men and women of my life—Mikhail Sergeyevich and Yevgenia Fyodorovna, Vera Sergeyevna and the neighbour, my parents and friends, Oleg and Marya—then somehow, impossibly, the broken past could be given form. Not put back together so much as refashioned into a kind of warped, fragmented sculpture. But nonetheless it would be something that I could hold, at least in my mind. I linked all things—Anya leaving, our group drifting away from one another, Mikhail Sergeyevich's suicide—with this lack of a form, our collective failure to make art out of what had happened. We didn't make what we set out to create. None of us did.

I was ready to cry out for all that had happened, but at the same time I felt that my eyes, my cheeks, my face had slowly hardened just as concrete sets. My numb chest hid a heart gone grey, as if the sadness, too old now, couldn't come out in the usual way.

I thought of men and women moved to take their own life in old age, those who are not far themselves from a natural death, but who nevertheless decide to take their leave by their own hand. And in thoughts I would probably not have shared with anyone, for they seemed to ask unforgivable questions,

I wondered whether in those cases the long road towards the final act, sometimes the years and years of consideration, as in the case of Mikhail Sergeyevich, in some unspeakable way made the act intelligible. The death which was to come was perhaps always inside them, attached to memories repressed and to a past that was latent, due to arise at some future time. And when that death did rise up inside them, the confrontation with all that was dormant proved too overwhelming for a single mind to comprehend. But then I thought they perhaps failed to see the impermanence of death. With the death of one, countless others then carried it inside them, the dead lingering and emerging at certain times, like the stars which at times are not visible yet never disappear.

If I died now, as a thirty-five-year-old man in Moscow, I supposed certain important memories would die with me. I wasn't ready to kill myself, I just felt indifferent about death. It made me wonder about the value of a thought. Those men—my father, Anya's father—thought about something to the point that they died because of it. Their minds had thoughts that came from beliefs that came from somewhere else, or maybe from them. They had let their bodies die because of their thoughts. And if nobody knew that, those thoughts might as well be the ash of the names once written on paper around the kitchen table of my childhood. Ash to memory to oblivion.

I had the sense of those other things being in me—the shot that might or might not have killed the neighbour's father, and the weight of never knowing, which was itself like a well-lodged bullet; the camps where Oleg and his father sat, and the moments of their return, when they started again as though newly born from the grave. The shiny-floored asylum rooms, the white-sheeted beds where my father, Marya, Mikhail Sergeyevich were confined. I felt stuck at the moment all those things happened. To go forwards left them behind; to go back only made them happen again and again.

I thought to myself that we are all merely fractured creatures, forever wanting, always in search of our story. Our memories joined with every missed moment and unspoken utterance, and together those things lived in us as did the people we once were. Every little failure, the things never done and the memories forgotten, they too are upon the maps we draw, the maps we are.

CHAPTER 27

After the fall, life became less understandable. We'd lost our story, our cause, after 1991, as though the spinning white ballet dancer on the black TV screen a few months earlier was a pointer on the dark compass of our lives.

I didn't want to miss the Soviet Union and hated feeling nostalgic for the excitement and hope felt behind the bars of Communism. But when I was a boy, a teenager, a twenty-year-old, real life for me existed between the lines, in the novels and poems given to me by paper and voice, in the line I followed within the walls of our apartment near Arbatskaya. There was clarity under oppression. After the fall, those lines were entrails strewn about, like the insides of half-destroyed buildings when wires and cables emerge as if from wounds.

During the repressive years, official censure told us we were doing the right thing. If they, *up there*, didn't like our works, we knew we were right. In the nineties, we were just ignored. Editors would laugh sadly and say there was no space anymore for articles about the Gulag or someone's shot relative. And scathing articles about Yeltsin dragging the country into mud, calls for him to go, didn't make a ripple with the censors. Academics stood in the street wearing placards demanding months of wages. There wasn't even the respect of censorship.

On the street, people were tired of the past. Inflation ate pensioners' life savings overnight; though people were struggling just to eat, the price of vodka plummeted, and so it fed a void. People could barely think beyond each day, let alone carry their thoughts above the city, to cloudy heights, to the abstract or the ideal.

Sometime in the new year, 1992, we went to see Ilya perform, and we all got filthy drunk. It was winter. I couldn't remember much from the night, except feeling wretched about everything, how we all looked like disoriented children left in the playground. Just four years earlier we had been, apparently, capable of anything. Ilya screeched out lyrics I couldn't understand. Girls tripped on high heels, like statues nearly toppling over. Guys hovered around as though longing to catch them. It had been over six months since Mikhail Sergeyevich died. The Soviet Union was no more.

Anya said she wanted to go home, she was sick of Ilya's music. I was determined to stay out, as though the night could be salvaged somehow. After a couple more songs I agreed to leave. It was freezing outside.

Nothing here inspires me anymore, said Anya. Her mouth had an expression I'd come to know, tensed with worry. I don't know what anything means, and everything feels worthless, she said.

She pressed the heel of her palm to her chest. Her eyes were dusty black, blurred by alcohol and smudged make-up, or maybe she was just tired. I noticed that she hadn't put her hand on my shoulder or hooked an arm through mine like she used to.

CHAPTER 28

Finally I started walking to the apartment of my childhood. At least three of the other large Khrushchev-era apartment blocks in the street were gone. New towers stood in their place, either apartments or offices, while shops—glass-fronted with mannequins or computer products on display—occupied the ground floor. All evidence of the sixties, my childhood, was now built over.

I went into the foyer, walked up the steps to the fifth floor. The lease was now in my name. I could afford one more month, I thought, but after that I'd have to either terminate the lease or give up my place in St Petersburg and move back in there myself. It seemed inconceivable to me that the people I'd known, the moments, looks, sensations and feelings I'd once had there, were really gone. Such memories seemed just beyond my immediate vision, no less real than what I could actually see. When I saw those rooms, I was in company with my boyhood self, and together we saw everything, as if perceiving and remembering were twin currents overlapping in a sea.

There was a bottle of brandy in the cupboard in the kitchen. I took a glass from a wooden shelf. I sat down at the table, put my glass on the cream tablecloth with its orange, brown and yellow flowers. Large utensils still hung from small spokes in the wall. On top of the refrigerator was the mint-green radio. I drained my glass and went to turn the radio on. For a moment I thought there was a voice emerging through the static, but as I twisted the dial this way and that, it seemed to get further away from me.

I went to the bookshelf as though looking for some kind of guide. In the final chapter of Radishchev's *Journey from St Petersburg to Moscow*, he describes how, during an evening walk to Alexander Nevsky Monastery, he came across the grave of Mikhail Lomonosov. He scorned the mere cold stone of a graveside monument. Stone could not carry a name into future centuries. Only the Russian language could do that, according to him. I remembered my own walks to Volkovskoye Cemetery, where Radishchev himself lay beneath an inscribed headstone, and where the old trees bent down as though tending to his memory.

I lay on the divan in the living room; beneath me was our yellow crocheted rug. I watched morning arrive while I lay there, listening to music. Our old record player was still there. At first I put on Kino, Viktor Tsoi's band, classic Russian rock as if that would mean I was in the old Moscow. I craved something gentler but didn't know what. I tried Liszt's 'La Campanella', from his suite *Years of Pilgrimage*. Like sounds from childhood. I pictured the latticed metal of the speakers of our radio I listened to as a boy, captivated by the bodiless sound. Music is loneliness and company at the same time, someone said once, or maybe I just thought that as I lay there.

I got up, went to the kitchen, poured a glass of brandy, went back to bed. I drank that morning with a distant thought of my boyhood friend Dmitry, our secret brandy, showing him that forbidden record made *on the bones*—that old friend who might now be getting older too.

Once the morning had fully formed, I went to a supermarket because there was no food in the apartment. I had thrown out the milk and a few other things in the fridge, my mother's lasts. At the checkout, I took my wallet out of my pocket to pay for the bread and whatever else, and on the five-hundred-ruble note was the Solovetsky Monastery. The thick, tall towers, the swathe of sea and stone. I couldn't get away from any of it, that ever-rising past. As I put the note on the tray in front of the grim-faced teenage cashier, I wondered if she was looking at me like that because I'd given her such a reminder of old violence. And then I thought about how we were all passing that note around, how it had travelled and would travel through a thousand hands and more, and of course there were countless copies of it, each made from unique fibres so they were all different while appearing the same.

I went home, ate a little, then read, slept, smoked. I didn't know why I was there, whether I had actually returned to Moscow or if it was a brief pause before a permanent goodbye. I did think of Sonya, that bare life we shared, apart, in Petersburg.

I woke in the early evening. I got out of bed at some point, half-heartedly chewed some bread while standing at the window, alternating a bite with a drag. Then I called Ilya. I had seen him only a couple of times on my few trips back to Moscow. But really we had drifted away from one another even before I left. Around the same time as I stopped going to concerts, after Anya was gone, he had taken his band touring Russia. And he'd still moved with politics, following elections and going to rallies, while I retreated from that world.

We met at a cafe near Pushkin Square. The sky was overcast, the light low. Ilya looked a lot older. His hair was cut short, black flecked with grey. He had a thin, short beard, also a mix of black and grey. He wore a band t-shirt (NAIV), and had tattoos on his arms, an earring in one ear and several rings on his fingers. His enthusiasm was foreign to me. He listed show after show at clubs I'd never heard of, proudly rattled off collaborations with bands whose names meant nothing to me.

Ilya asked me about Yura. I said that he was now married to Piia from Finland. They'd had a child. Ilya nodded, but I couldn't help but think he seemed disappointed in Yura for not making a bolder statement by leaving the country, for not fighting anymore. Neither of us had seen Sukhanov or Lena in years. Ilya said that Sukhanov was still known around Moscow for his artworks. For no real reason we had lost contact, and I didn't feel like trying to find them; perhaps I didn't want any more meetings that felt like reckonings with all that I had once wanted but failed to do.

We walked afterwards, across the square, and I saw Pushkin's statue. When Ilya asked me how it felt to be there—back on the old ground, he said—I merely shrugged and didn't say that I'd been in Pushkin Square the day before.

We've lost something, he said. Russia's definitely lost something.

He told me about a woman he had been seeing who earned money reading palms and tarot cards. Her customers were mostly old ladies, who returned again and again, as if the prospect of multiple futures reassured them. I imagined she wore long gold earrings, this woman of Ilya's, and had long painted nails like pink talons, clattering bangles on her wrists and was dressed in layers of coloured silky scarves.

Ilya told me about the day of the bombing below Pushkin Square, just a month earlier. Eight people had been killed.

I wasn't in the metro, he said, but I wasn't far away. I saw the smoke coming out from the underground. And then all these people came up, covered in cuts and dirt and blood—the ones who could walk, anyway—like damned zombies.

He described how, all around Pushkin's statue, the ground was glazed with blood, littered with bandages, torn clothes, a woman's shoe.

The papers and TV stations had all reported the same story: Chechen terrorists were blamed for the bombing and for several others in the previous year, including those of two apartment blocks in Moscow.

I don't know, brother, said Ilya. I don't want to leave Russia, no way, but there's no telling where we're going.

We sat down on a bench. Ilya lit a cigarette, scratched the side of his face, shook his head. He still bounced his leg like he used to, as if to an ever-present beat.

I teach guitar to some young kids, he said, leaning in. They don't care about anything. Their only hero is Tsoi and their only salve is marijuana.

We made tentative plans to meet again while I was in Moscow. Ilya mentioned an upcoming show and I gave a vague answer before we parted ways.

Across the square, McDonald's glowed in the low light. I walked over, hands bunched in my jacket pockets, went inside where it was warm and ordered a coffee, which when it arrived was watery and burning hot.

Thinking of that woman Ilya was seeing annoyed me; tarot cards and fake fortunes, *babushki* delirious on incense, giving all their coins to a future killed already by our past. I saw, too, the wavering calm on Sonya's face, imagined her sad eyes looking up at her saints: Feodor Kuzmich, a king who had faked his death to become a hermit—even non-believers like me had read about him—and John of Moscow, called Blessed John the Fool for Christ. And my mind bathed Sonya's hair in light from candles I'd never seen in churches I'd never set foot in. The void of Communism had been filled, the maps of dead futures rewritten and the ghostless ghost towns populated.

I sat drinking my weak, hot coffee under the fluorescent light. Each moment, every memory of the place I was in, were piled one on top of the other. I felt heavy, somewhere in me, to think that I was in every moment and none. In nowhere but the place of every moment.

I went to the Tsoi Wall, as it was now known. I remembered us all leaving our bent cigarettes on a tray on the ground, our travesty incense, how close we'd sat together. Graffiti lovingly coated the walls, words warring to grieve, layers and colourful layers of it.

Viktor Tsoi died today.
You were our voice, you were us.
Listen listen listen forever.

We fucked to your music, now we can't even kiss.
Tsoi is alive!

I lit a cigarette and walked away from the old words. Around the corner, another line of graffiti in thick black lettering said, *Don't travel with a corpse—the point of life is to ponder the cross on your own grave.*

CHAPTER 29

The last time I saw Anya, we stood in Pushkin Square. It was early 1992. We stood oddly apart on the red bricks, still as stone, like stage actors frozen at the point when the curtains should come down. That hair I'd touched, blonde to the shoulders, hidden away in a brown felt hat. She looked at me as though from another shore.

You don't even know why you're going, Anya, I said, or yelled. You say you want to search for something, but you don't even know what.

She just looked at me. Whatever I said seemed to confirm something for her. It had rained. There was a persistent wind, or maybe my memory just thought that seemed fitting.

I must have yelled, because her voice went softer, a calm that unnerved me, and she took my forearm and sat me down on one of the benches near Pushkin.

She said she knew somehow that there was more out there, more that she could feel.

I can't make myself feel it here. I know this is a horrible thing to say, she said. That a person isn't enough for your capacity. That you know somehow you are capable of feeling more, but you can't feel it with them, can't feel it here.

She spoke as if about some hypothetical other person.

It's like you're talking about Russia, not me, I said. I'm not a country, I'm not a *city*, Anya.

I stood up, moved away from the bench.

Anya came over. From a distance we must have looked like a duo in a strange call-and-answer dance, the one slowly following the other's movements. She lit a cigarette, passed it to me, and then just stood there.

When I'm alone to think, I feel alive, she said. I want to start a life of my own, away from here, away from my mother and this country, the dragging past.

I said something about having met her too soon. That's what I said: I've met you too soon, Anya.

She said again that she was leaving, as if to confirm it for me. We remained there for a while longer, performing our strange, slow choreography of sitting, standing, yelling, silence. Then she went. I couldn't remember our final words. A heavy night rain had stopped and nearly every surface of the ground was obscured by polished reflections of the sky.

It's dangerous to your own sense of calm when a person, when she, stands for more than she should, for a life, for a country that didn't happen. She was a time that was over, and a place that time had changed.

If I'd happened to be afflicted with some illness not long after she'd left, I probably would have also associated losing Anya with all I couldn't do anymore because of that illness. Circumstances and people that are separate from each other can join if the mind tries hard enough. I really did wish that we'd met later, when we were both older and those years had become the past.

Two days after our Pushkin Square scene, I went to the Frunzenskaya apartment. But Anya's mother, Yevgenia Fyodorovna, was there alone. I knew I was just going there for some self-paining confirmation.

Yevgenia Fyodorovna had lost the tension or spark of previous visits, before her husband's death and at the height of arguments with Anya. We had a brief, quiet conversation, dull voices in the hallway. She leant against the doorframe, holding the edge of her red cardigan in a desperate sort of way. She told me Anya really was gone. Her flight had left from Domodedovo airport.

The next months were a mess of days without meaning. My wretchedness was probably just as much about failing to really do anything as about Anya's leaving. I told myself that Anya and I could only understand each other in that old world, the one we grew up in. Our world had changed but our inner selves hadn't caught up with it.

I looked at my mother and Oleg, and was sure they must have thought me hopeless. I went out with Ilya a lot. Slept with a few girls. Being out with him, drunk, experiencing weeks of night-time wakefulness, not knowing the city during the day except for blurred hours at work, removed me from the normal time of others, and that was just what I wanted. But even Ilya started to bother me, with all his plans and ambition. He organised a tour with his band, with bookings in St Petersburg, Murmansk, Yekaterinburg. He had lost his job when the stock delivery driver had to shut down his business—mafia blokes monopolised all now, Ilya said—but had chased work with a radio station, organising interviews with musicians, helping write the scripts. Yura worked all the time now, and went to St Petersburg for a few weeks to teach a short course. Sukhanov and I went out drinking sometimes. He and Lena were patching things up, he hoped. They had a kid, a little girl. If ever we all caught up—Ilya, Sukhanov, Lena and I, the only ones left—it just seemed to emphasise who wasn't there. And any talk of the old days, trying to revive moments in which we'd laughed or loved, just left an ashy bitter feeling in me.

Listlessness wrapped me in her sweet, grey arms. I didn't want to want anything anymore.

Even as I tried to avoid the lag of the past, the trial of the Communist Party pushed its way into every form of media and I couldn't get away from it. It was a filthy hot summer, 1992. Crowds were out in the sun reading the *stangazety* newspapers.

While the trial began as an appeal against Yeltsin's banning of the Communist Party, Yeltsin's supporters argued that the Party was itself unconstitutional. Yet the Party was included in that Constitution. And the judges had all been Party members, since only Party members could be appointed, and so they were judging the system that gave them their careers. It was a legal labyrinth and I could not see how any trial would offer a way out. Party supporters argued that defeating Hitler and making the Soviet Union a great power were reason enough for a decision in its favour. Yet such reasoning only judged the actions of the Party, not the issue of whether it was a criminal state to begin with.

A couple of months later, Yura said he was moving to St Petersburg. I met a girl, he said, looking away as though expecting a caustic reply.

Yeah, she's from Finland, he continued. She just got a permit to work here, works for a Swedish furniture company. You should come too, Pasha. Have a change.

I shrugged. I'll come visit sometime.

I helped Yura with his bags and waited with him at Leningrad station, bound for the newly renamed St Petersburg. Autumn 1992. I thought about what was lost with a name and felt that the silence of that loss extinguished something in the very depths of me.

When it was close to the time the train would leave, we made our way to the platform. People all moved in the same direction towards the train; there must have been nearly twenty carriages. The engines hummed, voices rose, suitcases scraped, the platform full of the energy of departure.

Yura seemed excited. Come visit, brother.

I nodded, we shook hands, he picked up his two heavy suitcases, one in either hand, and stepped onto the train. I stood there while others rushed on, suitcases or carry bags in hand, coats and toys, food and presents, until eventually the doors were slammed by attendants, hands waved inside and out, and with a great groan the carriages began to move. I couldn't see Yura inside, but I held one hand up anyway, for a moment.

I wondered if it would be another permanent farewell; whether, one by one, I would bid goodbye, goodbye, goodbye, until Moscow was empty of everyone I knew.

CHAPTER 30

One morning, after another unsettled and slightly nauseous walk through Moscow, I stood on Frunzenskaya Embankment. I was holding a newspaper—Sunday, 3 October 1999. If I hadn't had that pinpoint, it could have been any year, any time.

I went to a payphone in front of a tall pink building. It took Yevgenia Fyodorovna only a moment to place me.

Pasha, she said, I didn't ever think it would be you. Yes, you can come. Come for tea tomorrow.

I walked past the mustard-yellow building where they all used to live—Anya, Mikhail Sergeyevich, Yevgenia Fyodorovna—with the strange, connected but separated feeling of knowing I had just called those rooms. I kept walking. I walked until midnight and then went home to uneasy sleep.

Twelve hours later I arrived at the apartment building near Frunzenskaya Embankment. Perhaps because I hadn't eaten breakfast, I felt weak, slightly disconnected from my body.

The wooden door of the building had been replaced by a thick heavy black door, locked and alarmed. I pressed the button and, shortly after, the door clicked unlocked. The dim wooden elevator was empty; its slow shudder felt familiar. I pressed the doorbell of number eighteen. Yevgenia Fyodorovna looked pale. Her hair, once deep brown, was now lined with very light grey, tinsel threads in a thick bun. She wore a brown cardigan, a constrast to the strong magenta and purple and reds I remembered her wearing.

Pasha, she said, come in, come in, Pasha.

On entering the apartment, I tried to reconcile the place with how I remembered it. I was in the place where Mikhail Sergeyevich had died. Whenever I returned to that thought, his death shocked me anew. As though I'd forgotten entirely and it may as well have occurred that very day. Though even my memory of his death was a chimera. When I thought of it, I didn't only remember the moment Anya had called me, or the words she had used to tell me. Cutting across that real memory was my own reconstruction of the scene. I saw the discovery of his body and the imagined, possibly real, cries of shock—all of the things that may or may not take place at such times and which those who were not there try, in vain repetitions and slight variations, to see in their minds. And with this, my imagination made memories of its own, memories of moments I didn't witness myself.

We sat in the kitchen. With the curtains drawn over the windows the light was dim, and in the air was the lingering suggestion of a small breakfast, bread or porridge and tea. I thanked her for inviting me over. Yevgenia Fyodorovna seemed to have trouble sitting down and I asked after her health. She told me she had arthritis in the spine. Bekhterev's disease, they call it.

On hearing the psychiatrist's name an uncanny film of recognition passed over my mind. I'd seen his statue in stone at Volkovskoye Cemetery in Petersburg. He had discovered the place where memory was thought to be stored in the brain.

Yes, Bekhterev's disease, she repeated. It's genetic. The doctors tell me my spine will fuse together, and I'll either be walking like this, tall as a tree, or like this, at a mountain angle—she laughed, first holding her arm up vertical, then at an alpine slope, to show me.

Next I asked Yevgenia Fyodorovna if she had heard from Anya.

Anya's far *over there*. She waved an arm. I hear a word from her sometimes, but she has been moving around. Europe mostly. Working. Always working.

I tried to ignore the twin arms I felt reaching out, like snaking branches, of bitterness and longing interest. Maybe she had found someone else, someone from *over there*. Time condensed and I felt I was a bare second away from our final meeting in Pushkin Square.

Maybe, I thought, she just keeps running, settles in a place only as long as nobody knew much about her or asked after her past. A fragment of a long-ago conversation found me. Anya said she enjoyed first meetings, and the second, but after that it was hard. You have to show too much, she said.

I explained to Yevgenia Fyodorovna that I'd come because I was trying to write a sort of history, a book about life in Moscow. And because Mikhail Sergeyevich had been eager to share his story, I thought maybe she would be willing to talk to me about him.

Yes, she said, Misha had an interesting and difficult life.

She asked me to wait a moment, went to another room and returned with a small pile of loose notepaper.

You hear of people leaving papers behind when they die, she said. And those of us still here have to grapple somehow with the job of *working through* or *sorting out* those papers. Well, in Misha's case what he left were maps and his classroom notes. Yevgenia Fyodorovna sat down, holding the papers as she spoke.

A lot of men play chess, it seems, when they retire, she said. In the courtyards of the apartments here you see them all the time—she waved a hand—sitting there, facing one another across a table. And in the gardens and parks around Patriarch's Ponds, too. But Misha preferred walks. He didn't want to sit there playing chess *like the old Bolsheviks*, as he said.

She held up a map, very worn, crinkled but soft in the way of well-handled paper.

This one, said Yevgenia Fyodorovna, Misha drew himself, shading in all the dark spots—see there, and there—to mark the areas where the Great Fire of Moscow wiped out most of the city last century, in 1812.

The map showed, in black-shaded masses on the paper, how three-quarters of the buildings in Moscow were lost.

And Misha told me about the different accounts of who was to blame for the fire. How some said the invading French, under Napoleon, were responsible for setting the city alight when they arrived. Others said that it was actually the Russians who did it, when they knew the French were coming. The *scorched earth* method, he said. When people set fire to their own land. Killing the city to save it from invasion. But many Russian historians hated that theory, saying we would never carry out such an act of suicide on our own city.

Misha was fascinated by the history of the fire. First he would read and research, then make his markings on the map, and set out on his walks, seeking out the old borders of the city, as though he might somehow find a trace of them there, even though there was probably nothing left to see.

Yevgenia Fyodorovna stood up slowly, as though with pain, went to one of the high wooden cupboards over the sink and brought out a packet of sweet biscuits. Gratefully I ate three of them. The food eased my nerves, somehow warming me too, though I hadn't known I felt cold.

At some point, Misha decided to add a second layer to his original map. It would be a layer that showed the world beneath all of us, he said, the hidden, buried world, which he could now make visible.

I thought of my own conversations with Mikhail Sergeyevich, and his meeting with the man who explored the underground and met people resident in that world. We were in Gorky Park at the time. They *live* down there, Pasha, down in that reversed world, Mikhail Sergeyevich had said to me. Almost as if they are people from the past who lost their way many years ago and can't live or die, they only keep on walking beneath Moscow.

Yevgenia Fyodorovna said she felt it was time she had a rest, but that I might come again to visit, if I wanted to talk to her again. Here, you can have his maps, she said forcefully, as if purging herself. Take them, she said. I've had enough of papers for three lifetimes. And take these pastries, I have too much food here, and clearly you need some, Pasha.

CHAPTER 31

I arrived in St Petersburg alone in the winter of 1993. When I moved there, to my apartment by the gulf, it was as though I was walking outside, never to go inside again. I barely read a thing. I didn't care what was going on in the country, didn't care for the bland movies and music from the West, the bad novels, the overflow of brand names and things and labels and nauseous varieties of every object or food.

I did not bring many relics with me. I left things behind at my mother's: a photo or two and my beloved books, and newspaper articles on the Memorial Society, its petition for a monument, and the demonstrations on the Arbat. But I wouldn't have been able to say with any certainty what I had thrown away, or what I planned to throw away and perhaps kept out of longing or to protect against forgetting. In the end there was so much forgetting and I had come to fear its potential contagion, its incubation in the heavy smog-mist in Moscow, breathed in, or picked up on the soles of shoes in the caked ice and dirty snow.

We only have the photographs that survive, just as we only have the memories we remember. A choice was made by someone, or some part of us, or by circumstances.

After a few days in the new apartment in Primorsky, which felt sparse and grey, cramped in a different, soulless way to my childhood concrete block in Moscow, I walked through the city. It was freezing. At first my walks usually took me along the gulf or from one edge of Vasilyevsky Island to the other. The steely, flat, purplish water was so wide, perfectly poised in a tenuous balance—just a little wave and it would overflow.

As I ventured further into the city centre, I got lost so many times, as though Petersburg was determined to hide herself from me. I'd only been there once before, with Oleg in 1989.

Canals crosshatched the city. Bridges arched over them, connecting footpaths and boulevards. Something about a city riddled with water, it seemed colder than landlocked Moscow. I thought of those stories about the city just after the revolution. Aristocrats threw their swords into the Neva River, breaking the ice and hiding the evidence of their identities beneath the freeze. I wondered if Mikhail Sergeyevich knew that. His death was raw in those first months in Petersburg.

Then I started to take *elektrichka* suburban trains further out, to dilapidated suburbs where I'd wander for hours. I saw people begging or selling on the streets, it was hard to tell which.

I went outside. Often I walked till the late hours. The sky's was a darkness I could deal with. I wanted to stop living by the measures of everyone else: before and after, death and life, sea and self. Being out there—in towns where I spoke to no one, in green deserted parks, along the edge of the gulf's water—allowed me to turn inwards. It reflected the silence I felt in me. I wanted to be outdoors for good. Yes, I went outside.

Before I left for St Petersburg, Oleg had given me a copy of one of Shalamov's books. I thought of that night on Solovetsky Island when Oleg quoted Shalamov, so fluidly his quotes were like breathing. *I believed*, says Shalamov's narrator, *I believed a person could consider himself a human being as long as he felt totally prepared to kill himself, to interfere in his own biography. It was this awareness that provided the will to live. I checked myself—frequently—and felt I had the strength to die, and thus remained alive.*

The trip to Leningrad in 1989 was fresh in my mind when I first arrived in 1993. There were certain flashes, scenes of the city, shades of past moods, that followed me. I remembered walking through the city by myself, staying with Ivan and Susanna, who I should've contacted but didn't, and I remembered the gaping skies, Solovetsky, the sea bathed gold, Vasily's fires at the water's edge.

I sometimes spent time with Yura and his girlfriend Piia, who eventually became his wife. She was a quiet, kind woman with long dark hair always tied in a high ponytail. Their gentle routines, their generosity and shared meals, somehow both increased my sense of isolation and eased a pain somewhere in me.

Oleg and I exchanged a few letters, and I called my mother sometimes, but I detached myself from them, because they were Moscow to me, just as Anya had been. Or maybe also because they were a reminder, for me, of what I hadn't done, and my failures were amplified by their efforts, their work and the constant struggle that had been their lives. I was lonely but never really wanted company.

Sometimes I wondered if I really wanted to be there anymore, to be anywhere any longer. Thoughts of suicide strayed across my mind, like the shadow of a skulking fox gone before I could really look at it. Mostly I thought of my mother, back in Moscow, and that it would be a crime for her to lose both her husband and her son to self-inflicted deaths. And so I just persisted, drifted, and the years kept going. I met Sonya in 1998, at a social event at the university, something to do with Yura's work. She was there with a friend, neither of us really knew anybody, a condition which always seems to bring people together, the brief solidarity of the lost ones, the extras, at gatherings like that. And so we had begun to see each other after that night, every few weeks and then a little more frequently. It suited me that Sonya didn't seem to want me to stay for long. I reasoned that she looked at me in the same way as I did her: another person adrift, who for brief times is willing to cling to shore. There was a kind of closeness born of that sense of detachment—I never felt the need to fill silences and she seemed content with the same. Neither wishing to turn in for light or warmth, in a sense we were both outside and wished to stay there.

CHAPTER 32

I went to the entrance of the Frunzenskaya apartment building for the second time since my return to Moscow. The mustard-yellow paint glowed in the afternoon light. I pressed the button at the street entrance and was again let in with a gentle click of the door. I crossed the foyer, entered the wooden lift and travelled upwards, walked down the hallway and pressed the doorbell for number eighteen. Yevgenia Fyodorovna opened the door. I must have looked desperate. She invited me in with a grave expression on her face.

I just want to know what happened, I said. The last time I saw him, he was talking about the year the history exams were cancelled. He seemed so agitated.

After what felt to be a never-ending moment, heavy and silent, Yevgenia Fyodorovna started speaking. Her voice was stern, low, almost curt, as if to let me know she would tell me things in her own order, and only as much as she decided to tell me.

I remember when Stalin died, in 1953, she said. March the fifth. My mother seemed to believe everything would change for the worse, that it would mean chaos. She lit a candle beside Stalin's portrait on top of our bookcase. She was sure something would happen to my father, that he'd lose his job or worse. For three days and three nights there was a stream of mourners queuing for the House of Trade Unions, where they could see his body and pay their respects. I did not go, but saw photographs. Above the entrance of the building was a gigantic portrait of him, draped in curtains. Gorky Street looked transformed, with huge crowds. And there were photos from Prague, from Riga. A stampede in Trubnaya Square, right here in the city. They say thousands were crushed.

Then they buried him. I remember the funeral well. It was March the ninth—Anya was born on the same day, nine years later. Even though I was not there, of course, at the funeral, I recall very well the reports and photographs, the endless mourning. I can see his portrait, cradled by red flowers, absolutely everywhere, and I think it has given me the impression that I in fact was there. And then there was Khrushchev's Secret Speech, three years later. Well, nobody knew what to think after that.

I stayed quiet, letting Yevgenia Fyodorovna find the memories. I thought of how lost the Secret Speech must have left teachers like Mikhail Sergeyevich feeling. The speech blamed Stalin's *cult of personality* for all ills and criticised only the losses under Stalin. As though an errant child had made a mistake and its parent, Communism, couldn't be held responsible. This new official line had to be propagated to the next generation without undermining the system as a whole. But even Soviet officials were horrified, either because they hadn't known the scale of death under Stalin, or perhaps because it could now no longer be called necessary sacrifice. I thought of how Fadeyev, the head of the Soviet Writers' Union under Stalin, had shot himself in the heart the same year, 1956. He wrote a suicide note to the Central Committee, lamenting the death of literature as much as his hopes for Communism.

Misha even wrote to the authorities, continued Yevgenia Fyodorovna, as he said many teachers had already done, asking for guidance, asking how on earth to acknowledge the speech in their lessons without denying the history they had been teaching all along. But in reply he received nothing more than token statements, re-renderings of the speech. The pedagogical council at the school held agitation meetings, as they were called, to discuss the situation, but the meetings were so frustrating, Misha said. The committees spoke in circles, *tak tak tak*, tapping their pencils like schoolchildren who had been given a complex equation with the wrong formula to work it out.

As I listened to Yevgenia Fyodorovna, I wondered if the cancelling of the exams in 1988 brought it all back to him again, had caused Mikhail Sergeyevich to revisit past anxieties.

Buried on Anya's birthday, it's a funny thing, said Yevgenia Fyodorovna. Anya was always a sad girl. I worried that she was somehow absorbing her father's melancholia, his preoccupation with the past. She surely heard him speak about his own father. *He was a butcher, Yevgenia!* poor Misha would say to me. Children's ears are sharp, and I could never be sure quite how much she heard or understood of the things her father spoke about. But then there's also that special ability of children to take on things that they have not actually heard or seen for themselves, as though they are somehow born with certain traces in them. As it is, I think that perhaps children of these times are born with too much memory already.

I say this because Anna Mikhailovna, even as the delicate little girl that she was, sometimes had such a heaviness to her mood, a brooding that seemed beyond her years. She never threw tantrums or had the silly little wants of most children, but when she was unhappy it seemed to be on such a deep level, what should be beyond a child, that I worried she was already showing signs of the darkness that lived within Misha.

Yevgenia Fyodorovna took a long breath, utterly silent, or so it seemed to me. I sat holding a glass of tea. I caught myself turning one ear towards her, as if terrified I'd miss something.

Anya said to me, not long before she left, that she didn't want to go that way, the way of her father, said Yevgenia Fyodorovna. It was as though she was convinced his memory was going to . . . invade her, pass on to her, like a disease she might catch.

The last day of Mikhail Sergeyevich's life, the first of his death, was relayed to Yevgenia Fyodorovna by a former colleague of her husband's.

Misha had spent that morning wandering the boundaries of the school at which he'd taught for over two decades, she told me. A few students and this teacher looked out the window and saw him. At intervals he would stop and look through the wire fence. Then he'd begin walking again with an appearance of lightness. He was holding one of his maps and didn't seem surprised to see his former colleague, who had walked around to the entrance of the school and now stood on the same side of the fence.

Mikhail Sergeyevich then said, according to the teacher, that he hadn't planned on visiting the school that day. He had merely been following certain lines on the map, letting them lead him around the city, but now that he had arrived at the school he couldn't quite bring himself to leave. *One always wonders*, he said to his former colleague, *whether the students remember the things you have said to them. How much they remember.* He then seemed to lose what little balance he had and swayed towards the fence, holding his head, then his stomach, obviously overcome by nausea. A film of sweat on his face and neck. He was very disoriented. The colleague helped him home, by bus, to the apartment. He assured the man he would be fine. Yevgenia Fyodorovna found his body in the bedroom when she arrived home that evening.

When she was finished, Yevgenia Fyodorovna took my hand and blinked so heavily she might have been sleeping. We stayed like that for a long time. Then I said I should be going.

Yergenia Fyodorovna nodded, went to a wooden dresser in the living room—I thought of the portrait of Anya's grandfather there watching—and returned with a photo.

Here. I would like to give you this photo of Misha and Anya and me. *Na pamyat*—for the memory. Look at our smiles, how happy we look! I suppose there is no one after me . . . and I don't know, it is a funny thing, Pasha, that in the end we feel we must leave something behind.

She followed me to the door. It has been good to see you, Pasha. I wish you well.

I left the apartment, took the tremulous wooden elevator down to the ground floor.

I stood outside for a while, leaning against the mustard-yellow building. I lit a cigarette but forgot and it burnt out. The teal-green treetops of Neskuchny Garden and Gorky Park stroked the sky. Watching leaves sailing and falling onto the pebbly footpaths in Frunzenskaya, I thought the city could have been falling apart. I thought of 1988, the summer. Though I couldn't recall the summer heat, summer sun.

CHAPTER 33

I woke up very early, when it was still dark, in the apartment of my childhood. I made a cup of instant coffee and sat on the divan.

I couldn't get back to sleep, the coffee had begun waking me up, so I made another and started rummaging through my mother's files to decide what I would keep and what I would discard. There were lots of old *samizdat* documents, sheets of onionskin paper, journals with scuffed covers, books in manuscript form. I came across an old envelope, opened it and saw it was empty except for a smaller envelope enclosed. I was tired and agitated from sorting through all those objects heavy with memory, but after my shaking hands had dropped it once or twice, I finally opened the second envelope and held two photographs. Colourless, the first was of my father. He looked young, a thin figure with a beard, in patched jeans and a woollen jumper, standing with his hands in pockets outside a rough wooden building that seemed to blend into a crop of mountains behind. *In exile* was written on the back.

The other photograph was of only a building. A wide multi-storey structure, most of it was white and the grounds surrounding it were covered in snow. Wire was strung between high poles, although I could not decide if it was a barbed-wire fence or a powerline. I realised after a moment, as if they had only just materialised, that there was a column of huddled people walking in front of the building, while the right-hand side of the view was obscured by something thick and dark, perhaps a tree trunk in shadow. The left side of the image had a misty, grainy shadow, as though the photograph was being slowly overtaken by the mist, gradually obscured until the figures and the building were softly obliterated. *Oryol, 1973*, said the inked scrawl on the back, labelling the place of my father's death.

I sat down at the kitchen table and wrote for a while. Writing everything that I had been, the past and the present. Time was running into itself, events folding inwards as I wrote. The closer they ran together, though, the less sure I was of the meeting point.

I wasn't going to get the answers I needed. My father and my mother, together they were dead. Learning about Mikhail Sergeyevich's death filled a void that took me nowhere; nothing was complete, because time is not a thing that ends.

I called Oleg and arranged to visit him later that morning.

He opened the door, hugged me.

I didn't expect to see you back in Moscow so soon, Pasha.

He led me down the hallway. The apartment building hadn't changed in the decade since I had last been there.

Thin cracks trailed over the decorative cornices in the old hallway, the ceiling and walls were still painted pale green. In the kitchen, a middle-aged woman stood cooking at one of the stoves. Socks hung in a row along the window.

In his living room, we sat for a while, quiet; it felt like a silence of understanding. Oleg made tea, looked up at me every so often with his stark blue eyes.

Then he began to describe his recent trips retracing some of our journey in 1989. With a group of Memorial Society volunteers, he again took the *Arktika* along the shores of Lake Onega. And he told me how, around nineteen kilometres from Medvezhegorsk, researchers had discovered a mass gravesite at Sandarmokh. There were thought to be at least ten thousand people buried there, telling a long history of state murder. The earliest graves were from prisoners held at Solovetsky—including hundreds of Ukrainian intelligentsia—taken into the forest to be shot. Thousands of bones were thought to be from 1937–38 alone; victims forced to dig their own graves beneath the pine trees.

Awkwardly, briefly, I explained that I hadn't had much contact with the Memorial Society since I left Moscow. Oleg didn't seem to take much notice and instead showed me into the study, still covered in its wallpaper of maps. I looked over the walls and realised eventually that Oleg was repeating the same trips, following the same maps, going over and over to the same remnants of the camps.

I never feel I'm any closer to accurately representing all the camps on the maps, Oleg said.

Different maps and sketches were laid out on his small table or pinned to the walls of his study. They were everywhere.

I've started using a pencil, he said, rather than ink, since there were just too many changes to make in my mad pursuit of absolute accuracy. He grinned. And I keep thinking of different ways to record the camps—symbols to show their present condition, whether any original buildings remain, how many people were imprisoned there.

The maps seemed to become a never-ending palimpsest, the erased lines still faintly visible beneath his corrections and additions, and he was too afraid to mark anything in permanently lest he get something wrong.

I never did, in the end, return to the Perm camp where I was taken in 1968, he told me. It has been closed only since 1986, a fact which has somehow given me the notion that it would still resemble too closely what it looked like back then, when I knew it as a functioning prison. It would perhaps be too recognisable. There was something reassuring in the decay of Solovetsky. As if it cannot come back.

I pictured the stone that had been laid in Moscow, in Dzerzhinsky Square—Lubyanka Square now—not long after we got back from Solovetsky ourselves in 1989. Veniamin Ioffe from the Memorial Society called the stone *a question mark that asked about the meaning of this tragedy.*

As I was leaving, Oleg told me to wait for a minute, then went back into the apartment. He returned a moment later and handed me an envelope.

Here are some journal entries of mine, and photographs I'd like you to take with you, he said. They might be useful. The photographs are of Kolyma in 1995. My father's camp. I spent five days there in the winter. I'm still not sure that I ever really *saw* anything.

Oleg's blue eyes were bright as he smiled at me. We hugged goodbye.

Outside, it was a terrible day, with a fitful wind. Shifting veils of dust and leaves flew everywhere, into my eyes, down my shirt collar. I revelled in it, in a strange way, encouraging the wind to try to knock me over. Ridiculously, I held my notebook open, determined to write a few things down. Passers-by looked at me briefly as they hurried on, coats held tightly around their bodies. I pulled out the envelope in my rucksack and looked at what Oleg had given me. There were only three pages of diary entries from his trip to Kolyma.

> Four days of snowstorms. Stranded at Yakutsk airport, on the way to Magadan. Sitting in hotel in Magadan, thinking of the dead beneath the grounds beyond here.
>
> They still speak of Kolyma as an island here. Once, it could only be reached by sea. Stood a frozen morning at the Bay of Nogayevo, the gateway into Kolyma. Seen as the threshold into hell.
>
> I recall once reading that Kolyma's permafrost so preserves corpses that the faces of the dead keep their expressions. Shalamov said they are faces of people who saw that which man should not see. I cannot help but try to picture their faces. Especially their eyes. I think, perhaps, that I will never fully regain the sight of my own.

The photographs, there were six of them, showed bleak landscapes, all coated in snow, sometimes fenced areas or depressing buildings that might have been abandoned, but it was hard to tell. One was entirely white, as though the camera had failed to focus. A sense of heaviness, helpless anxiety, slowly crept at me when I thought of all the things I had been given—the neighbour's maps of aborted roads and ghostless ghost towns, Mikhail Sergeyevich's maps of Moscow, and now Oleg's journal and photographs. As though I'd been given everything I needed and yet I still would keep searching for the rest of my life.

I woke the next day feeling that I didn't want to be in Moscow much longer. Each morning I woke with an increasingly numb feeling, ever closer to the stone-like man I always felt on the verge of becoming. A man who didn't care about either living or dying. Aside from writing, and the couple of visits to Oleg and Yevgenia Fyodorovna, I'd had little to do but walk by myself through the city. I was aware of an alternative path: that if I stayed there I would be more alone and wretched than ever. I had loved the city, but I was no longer in that version of it. I wondered whether the routine of work in St Petersburg, so mundane a lot of the time, had actually held me together all of those years.

That morning, after I made tea, I sat at my desk. At times I felt I'd come close to finishing what I had been writing since my mother died. The only time I didn't feel numb was when I was working at the desk. I had a few hundred pages that I'd handwritten in Moscow and at the *dacha*. I hadn't reread any of it and was not sure whether that was something I wanted to do. I didn't really want to know if it was finished yet. I thought of Bitov's saying that writing was a state of being, and thought perhaps I just had to keep writing forever, to remain in that state of being, because I didn't know what to do without it. Sometimes, surely, a writer feels as though the thing they are staring at cannot go on any longer. And maybe sometimes a writer wishes with their all that instead of producing thousands of pages, they could plunge into the well of themselves and come up with something that translates their overwhelming innerness into a single painting, or one wordless song, and in that concentrated form their art would be realised.

I finished my tea, took up the papers of Mikhail Sergeyevich, Oleg and the neighbour, and left the apartment.

I stood on the old Arbat, beside a lightless streetlamp. Looking at Mikhail Sergeyevich's map, I could see that where I stood had been completely destroyed by the Fire of Moscow. Every building around me, in pastel green, pink, yellow, or dark grey, was in fact built on ashes.

Beyond the Arbat, it was impossible to tell whether a building stood before me because it had survived the fire or because it had been rebuilt to look just like the earlier, burnt building.

I walked to Patriarch's Ponds, another significant site in the landscape of my life, like a man paying last visits. I walked to Tverskaya metro, which used to be called Gorkovskaya. After a moment's hesitation, I took out a pencil and put a neat line through the word *Gorkovskaya* on the map, marking in the new name but making sure the old was still visible. An uncanny feeling passed over me and I kept on walking.

In Red Square, which I had rarely visited at any time in my life, I overheard a tour guide speaking about the rumour of the hidden underground library of Ivan the Terrible, which had been the subject of renewed interest lately from academics and researchers who were sure that it was located somewhere beneath the Kremlin. Ivan III had married Princess Sofia of Byzantium, and she brought with her a dowry of ancient books and scrolls. To protect them, the newlyweds employed a famous Italian architect to design a hidden library underneath the Kremlin. Her grandson Ivan the Terrible was apparently the last to know the location of the library, and the tyrant took the secret to the grave.

The tour guide told her listeners how Khrushchev had permitted some investigations into that hidden past, but the searchers didn't find anything beneath the Kremlin. When Brezhnev came to power, the investigations were shut down, and everyone was quiet about it until new investigations began in Gorbachev's years. By then it wasn't only historians and architects searching beneath the city, but also people who could apparently detect the presence of gold or silver beneath the earth's surface, as well as psychics to guard against dark forces preying on the investigators, since those who searched for the library were said to be prone to misfortunes, accidents, disease or premature death.

A city would see a stranger if it saw itself as we describe it. So much would always remain unknown to us. We lived there for the briefest of a place's moment, our lives mere stones falling through a lake's surface, leaving a quickly forgotten ripple. I wondered if, with all those maps I now had, all those layers, the country might finally recognise itself in all those attempts to represent it, amid our collective, desperate scrawls.

I had lunch at a bistro, and then went to a public phone to make a call to terminate the lease on the Moscow apartment. Averse to returning there, almost guilty, as though I'd betrayed those rooms, I had a compulsion to go to the psychiatric institution where my father had once been incarcerated, a place that had long haunted my imagination. To reach the Serbsky Institute from the Arbat District I took the metro to Smolenskaya. From the station I walked about ten minutes to Kropotkin Lane. Along a grey-white wall, seemingly endless, was a small recess, just wide enough for two wooden doors. Above, the number twenty-three was written in white on a blue oval sign.

I felt I'd returned to a place I'd never been.

What little I knew about the institution came from books. I remembered the account by Leonid Plyushch. He wrote of how he felt increasingly that the tranquillisers and pills administered daily against his will were deadening something inside him, the will to read and think, the very idea of politics. His memory, he felt sure, was slipping away. And it was particularly painful to have his children come to visit; forcing smiles, making jokes when his heart was as grey as could be. And worst of all, he said, was the increasing fear that his mental condition was in fact deteriorating with each day in that oppressive ward, and that perhaps the job of his torturers would become easier if he went mad.

And I remembered Nekipelov's recollections of awaiting the ride in a Black Maria truck from Butyrka to the Serbsky, the desperate etchings he saw scratched into the prison wall with pencils, nails or burnt matches: *K, they're taking me to the Serbsky, V* and *Waiting for transit to Serbsky* or simply, *I've been committed.* And of Serbsky, he recalled the tranquillising drugs administered to the prisoners; how the most passionate, aggressive, stubborn inmates would suddenly fall onto their beds, and thereafter move about as though dazed, empty vessels with no will or want.

I could see us together, sometimes, my father and me. It was a feeling, an impression, more than a memory. Lying on his bony chest (to me he was always thin, maybe because I knew he'd starved to death, maybe because he never was very big anyway), I could smell tobacco, thick and strong; he might have been smoking, or it could have been an old scent buried in the fibres of his shirt, or even just the association of that smell with the dissident aunts and uncles I so loved. And on his chest I rose up and down with his breath, moved as he talked (maybe my mother, or Oleg, or someone else was in the room), as if together we rode light waves. I wasn't asleep but maybe close to sleep; all I could see was the edge of him, his shirt, and a section of the floor, the linoleum sea streaked with light from the curtained window.

But then I could also see us as if from a distance. I could see my childhood self, a boy of five or so, lying with my face turned to the right, lying on his thin body as he talked, gesturing with one hand, maybe smoking with the other, or patting my back. It couldn't be a memory, but I didn't know what it was, other than perhaps the image of a memory.

He was first arrested in 1968, when I was four years old. Then again, for the last time, in 1970. I was six. The fact that I was likely in the room when my mother was told he had died and when the circumstances of his death were spoken about, but that such things were either buried so deep in my mind or were entirely forgotten, horrified me on some level. I hated to think of how words dissolve like smoke.

Countless past conversations emerged, speaking over one another but somehow together all at the same time. Mikhail

Sergeyevich saying to me, I can attest that I'm here, as a man, with a body right now sitting on this seat, but I cannot say I am sure what I'm made up of—what is going on inside. Whether, by virtue of the system I grew up under, the very household in which I was raised, my mind has been conditioned . . . It's too tempting for us to destroy our bodies to protect our minds from further distortion.

Oleg reciting Shalamov, who wrote that if he had the strength to die, if his mind could still decide that, it was still *his* mind. He still had intellectual freedom though his body was confined in a prison camp.

And memories of my own thoughts emerged among the other voices. Art should tell us of life, but in a place where the official perception of reality had been so manufactured by the state, in some ways art was the only thing that was real. Art represented the truth of our inner lives.

Maybe when we are pushed to the limits, art and death are so similar. Maybe art, like people, cannot escape the conditions around it. To consider whether my father's death was art might have been the ultimate unspeakable question, born of a system that crushed all logic. You cannot ask why, the poets said.

Perhaps they were all artists of memory, something I had failed to be. Oleg, my mother, the dissident aunts and uncles, Mikhail Sergeyevich, the neighbour. Forgetting was their thread and with it they constructed a gauze-like tapestry, an image of how things might have been. Memory was, after all, made by what forgetting let us have. It must have pained them, to feel the limits of their knowledge and the insubstantiality of it all; it must have felt as though they were using the dust from moth wings to paint a vast canvas. The pink-blue glimmers were beautiful but always nearly gone.

I walked away from the Serbsky Institute. I took a metro back to the centre, walked down a few side streets until I found a tattoo parlour. Sitting in the chair, feeling the sharp sting of the needle on my inner forearm, the left, it occurred to me that I was the same age, thirty-five, as my father was when he died. The tattoo I had inked into me that day was just a small grid, straight lines. I had in mind that they stood for the street I grew up in with the apartment I had just given up; the Arbat, where life seemed to open up in 1988; Kropotkin Lane, where the Serbsky Institute stood; and Frunzenskaya Embankment along Moskva River. Nothing like true to scale, but that wasn't the point.

No street names, for they could change as easily as the seasons. Just the lines, the roads I'd walked down as a boy and then as a man. Eight lines showing four streets and their counterparts beneath the ground; whether there were pipes or drains or rivers or train tracks, I didn't know, and it didn't matter. That below-ground reflection was probably for the memory of Mikhail Sergeyevich as much as it was the echo of my old life, as a child of the underground, a life existing between lines now gone. A couple of crossroads gave it a kind of pattern. It could've been depicting the streets in any year, season, minute. Just midnight-blue lines, lines as good as veins, veins of my city etched on me, all time gathered and returned to write itself on the body.

CHAPTER 34

I took a return train to St Petersburg at the end of October 1999. I had left Moscow on dusk, but because the trip took me north, the sun was only just going down when I arrived in Petersburg five hours later. However, the light did not mean warmth, and it was far colder than Moscow. By the time I reached my apartment in Primorsky, it was dark. I put the picture of my father on my bookshelf, behind the glass.

I returned to work, and the city grew colder seemingly every day. After a week of brisk air and sun, the city was then beneath endlessly grey skies. Most mornings a low fog obscured the buildings as I looked out the window of the bus. Nothing about my daily routine changed. In a pile on my desk were the pages I had written. I felt time soundlessly circle me back to the same place each morning.

I met with Yura for a drink at a bar in Primorsky not far from my apartment. He wanted to know about my trip to Moscow, what it was like to see Ilya again, and all the places we had once been.

I was thinking about the place a lot the last few weeks, he said. Knowing you'd gone back. If I could go back anywhere, it'd probably be those nights at Sukhanov's.

Yura looked down at his drink; I wondered if he did in fact want to see Moscow again. I considered telling him not to bother, that it wasn't there anymore—our Moscow wasn't there.

Maybe you should try to publish what you've written, said Yura.

I shrugged. The kids don't care what we leave behind, I said. It's not interesting anymore to hear our memories of standing in long store lines with our mothers, or that we only got candy, and only one type, at New Year. That you can see the crackling coloured wrapping in your mind and feel like you're nostalgic for a dream you once had is of no interest to anyone anymore.

I drained my drink and we sat in silence for a while. I was thinking that I wanted to know where it had all gone, the memory that rose up, like plants after heavy rain, during *glasnost*. Maybe some people had told their children, *This was Grandma, this was Russia*. Or maybe by 1999 they were in a new apartment, and as the *kommunalki* walls were knocked down, as the old witnesses fell, the memory was lost in the move.

One night, a week after I returned, I was surprised to receive a phone call from Sonya. She said that she wanted to meet. The next day I took a metro into the city centre and we met near her work. It was late afternoon. I realised that I felt a sense of relief to see her. The sky had remained grey all day; the light was already tinted dusky blue. We walked for a little while and then she took me into a church. I could smell the sweetness of incense, see patches of candlelight in the gloom.

I know you don't believe in all this, she said, gesturing to the interior of the church. Her voice was hushed but clarified in the wide, cool space.

I nodded, and without speaking we both took a few steps to the pews, sat down beside one another, facing the altar. Sonya's hands were folded neatly over one another, and she looked utterly at peace.

Let's go to this *dacha* that you so like, she said after a long moment. And then, as I listened in the quiet, Sonya began to talk about her husband. Just a few words: she spoke his name, Andrei, and told me how they met at high school, how he had been shot—she didn't tell me the circumstances, but the omission told me that such things were perhaps not yet for her words—and she recalled a few disparate moments, memories of her boys and her husband: how he had worked too much, as she always told him, but that he could get carried away spending time with the boys, taking them to the playground in the apartment yard, or mushroom picking in the autumn. Sonya told me these things in a relaxed way, looking ahead and occasionally smiling, as if the moments were rising up on their own and she was happy to tell me what she saw. And then after a while she went quiet.

I nodded slowly, struck by a strange muteness. I still felt a sense of relief, sitting there next to Sonya, but wasn't sure what to say or whether she wanted me to say anything. I looked up at the mournful face of a woman in a painting in the church, and remembered reading, just a few weeks before I left for Moscow, an article about a new artwork in St Petersburg, a memorial sculpture. I hadn't been to see it yet, but right then I very much wanted to. There were a few others sitting in the quiet church, so I silently motioned for us to stand up and leave.

Outside, the cold air struck at our skin and it was nearing dark.

I said that I would make arrangements for us to go to the *dacha* as soon as possible. Sonya said that maybe her boys would come one day, too. We didn't say anything more about it then. I briefly explained about the sculpture I wanted to see, and we took a metro to Chernyshevskaya. In the quickening dusk, we walked down an intersecting street to Robespierre Embankment. After a few minutes we reached the river. We faced Kresty Prison, a cluster of red-brick buildings across the river. It looked like an old, low-built temple newly excavated. On the embankment near where we stood was the artwork by Chemiakin, of two sphinx sculptures facing one another on thick plinths.

I heard about this a while ago, I said to Sonya, but I didn't really want to see them, for some reason. I haven't been here before either.

Sonya stared at the sphinx face closest to us. She put one hand up to her mouth, like a slow movement of mourning.

Unlike the graceful, feline sphinx statues over on University Embankment, brought over from Egypt hundreds of years before, these sphinxes were new, just a few years old, and they looked half dead. Their bodies were emaciated; soft creases in the greenish metal showed ribs emerging from the skin. Half of each face was that of a woman, looking ahead, the other half a skull. Poems and quotations, from winters and dissidents like Allmatova and Sakharov, were inscribed on the plinths. Maybe, I thought, these sphinx-women are the memory of the *dokhodyagi*, the soon-to-be-dead, set in stone so that they neither die nor live.

Sonya let me stand there for a long time, looking out from the sphinxes' view, over the water, across to the prison that was gradually receding into the dark. We walked back to the metro together in a comfortable silence. The night was cold and I put my arm around her shoulder.

That evening I called Sergei Ivanovich and arranged for Sonya and me to stay at the *dacha* that weekend. I was glad to be going there. The city was too familiar to me, too connected to the unsettled feeling I still had since my return from Moscow, a feeling that I was still searching for something.

We took the *elektrichka* train, as I had in August. We arrived at Repino station and walked the forest road to the *dacha*.

Summer had gone. The feel of the *dacha* and that quiet place, of dusty paths, hidden houses, the always-silent forest, had changed. In the shade of the largest trees I could see a thin coating of white, the first snow. There was a new whisper, heavier, in the trees, and the wind felt thicker as it travelled along its own wild corridors, straying onto the road as we walked. Sonya pulled a scarf high up to her mouth and we both wore thick jackets. On the way, we went to the *produkti*, where the woman greeted me familiarly, putting my cigarettes, bread, ham and tea into a bag. She had blue-painted nails this time.

The key was under the brick at the front of the *dacha*, and I opened the door and let Sonya walk in. I looked over at the neighbour's house; it was lightless and locked, as though long unoccupied. I thought about leaving a note, in case he or Vera Sergeyevna returned there soon. I went inside, and after we had unpacked our things, we went out walking. The beach was as deserted as ever. On the stretch of damp sand, along the wet trails of the Gulf of Finland, the colours were so different now; there was more grey and uncertainty, the tide seemed thin and stretched, receding almost as if the ocean had turned its back, turned away.

A slow tide pulled lazily over the sandbanks, caressing lines into the sand when it left. Further out, the small waves looked hard, freezing and inviting all at once.

We should swim, I said.

Sonya was unconvinced, but I told her that plenty of people jump into icy oceans during winter. It was tradition.

They do it in Moscow, I said, in the river.

Yes, but they have somewhere warm to go afterwards, she said. A hot spa.

We each took another few steps towards the water, and I took her hand.

I'd had swimming lessons all through primary school. My school—in fact, probably every school in Moscow—was adamant about participation in sports. I didn't like the games but enjoyed the pool. Swimming felt solitary, even among twenty-five rowdy classmates. I loved the aloneness allowed in the echoing warm water.

Salty air moved in a cold breeze. I took off my clothes, Sonya did the same. Her skin was ashen, striking, reflecting the cloudy sky, her blonde hair paled, as though her body was blending with the sand, the landscape. There was no way I could walk in slowly, so I ran in waist-deep before the water had a chance to hurt—then I dived in. Ice and pain. Sonya was right behind me. The weight of nothing, nothing but the cold, crushed my chest. I heaved in a breath and kept my arms moving. I both loved and hated the feeling.

Oh, this is ridiculous! Sonya was laughing, her deep voice rising. Her wet hair was dark, coating her head as if on a sculpture. Gasping laughs, she waded over to me, wrapped her arms loosely around and kissed me with her gentle, sad force.

The house was cold when we returned; it had a small gas heater in the kitchen, so we sat on chairs beside it, Sonya wrapped in a blanket from the bedroom, and we sat smoking, occasionally talking with an ease that I'd not felt in our fragmented relationship up until then.

I woke in the night with a strange feeling that I'd been imagining, or dreaming about, a funeral. It was a night scene, and I had no idea whose burial it was, nor why I was there. I couldn't get back to sleep and so got up, lit a candle and walked out of the bedroom. I stopped at the front window. My reflection was weird in the uncanny shadows, my face all battered and broken up by the orange glow, the flicker of the flame. I was almost unrecognisable. It was so dark beyond the window and in the room behind me that I could see nothing of either. I walked in cautious, measured steps, expecting in the darkness to mistake a wall for a doorway or knock over a vase. And for a moment I felt I could've been back in Moscow, in October 1990 on a cold afternoon, when we walked through the city, holding candles, for the ceremony honouring the dead at the memorial stone near the Lubyanka. It could've been a walk that never ended and I was just re-entering it for a moment with those night-time steps. I imagined the sounds of the marching feet of the crowd, growing louder; then the woman's words came

back: one name—*shot*—another name—*shot*—the dead the
dead the dead, her voice a latent echo of the gun, but then
the names were cruelly indistinct, too many for memory.

I went to the desk at which I'd written during the summer.
I was disappointed; I had been sure that coming back to the
dacha would begin a course of rest, of decent sleep at the very
least. I thought about Moscow, the dead there. Not all the pain
and horror and loss began with us; much of it came through
the past to the time we called the present. Perhaps those
emotions not born with us were among the most vital and
we didn't know it; maybe to forget past pain was tantamount
to a grievous, criminal blindness. When there were breaks in
the thread of the past coming to us, if our understanding was
severed in some way, by denial or silence or a loss of knowledge,
surely we would meet consequences somewhere. I wondered
if I'd ever write anything else.

I lay down back in bed. At the first sign of grey light, while
Sonya slept peacefully, I left the house and walked to the
beach. I needed to see the gulf again. I thought of Sonya,
her body naked now under the blanket, bare on the sand the
day before, how natural she looked there, running easily over
the sand, the gentle white skin on her upper thighs moving
soft, loosely.

I daydreamt about spending winter at the *dacha*, with
Sonya, though there was no way I could afford to stay so
long. I imagined the *dacha* locked in the absolute silence of
snow. Even the birds and moths would be buried until the
sun finally uncovered them, their damp and fragile wings, at
some later time.

I went through the forest towards the coastline. It was a bright wintry morning, just after dawn.

I walked along the compacted, icy tracks, over snow and spiky knots of twigs towards the beach. An old jeep was parked at the top of a small hill, where the forest floor gave way to sand and the eventual path to the shore. Snow coated the sand. Three or four men, a dog, the remains of their campsite fire, came into view. One of the men raised an arm in a vague gesture of greeting; the others stared. The dog ran over, barking but unsure. The man who had waved came over and took the dog by the collar. On his arm was a large tattoo of a bird among twisted branches and a woman's name. As his arm tensed, holding the dog's collar, the bird seemed to move. It was a strange sight of beauty on the man's rough red skin, and I thought it looked trapped, on that ugly muscle.

I passed by the campsite and watched thin grey smoke trails rise like the ghosts of tree branches from the remnants of the fire. The air had the uncertain silence of isolation. I stood for a moment, struck by the sudden contact with those strangers who had appeared like nomadic wanderers braving the onset of winter and who had woken to another day, slowly tended their fire and blinked tiredly out at the early dew, unsure whether they had yet made it through.

I continued walking, over the small rise that was the threshold from forest to sea. Sand fell around my feet as I descended towards the water.

ACKNOWLEDGEMENTS

First to my parents and my sisters: if there's one thing writing teaches me, it's that the most powerful things I feel can't be written. So I'll just say—thank you for every day and everything.

Much love and thanks to Angela Keating for a deeply treasured friendship; to Maya Klauber, my sister in New York and friend through all pain, and to the Klaubers—who show me that family can be anywhere. Thanks to Myles and Linda Ashton for your love and support. Thanks and love to my Nonno, Alfonso Rossi: *vale*, I wish you could have been here for this, and to dear family Luigi, Maria, Eleonora and Maurizio Rossi.

Thanks to my dear writer friends: Angela Savage, Rosey Chang, Jen Anderson, Sophie Torney, Nancy Chen, Brian Lance, Alyssa Watson, Kathy Merrell, Beverley Eikli and Kellie Flanagan. You all continue to inspire me. Thank you Hugo Bitte and Kseniya Melnik for advice on the earliest draft and for telling me to keep writing. Thanks to Rob and Sam for always encouraging me and inspiring me with your lives. Thanks to great friends Leif Louwen-Skovdam, Ally Richardson-Siemon, Alexandra Haydock, Olivia Yelland, Nicole Buss, Kylie McDermott, Alexandra Adams. Thanks to Ed and Tina Kasparek in Connecticut—I'm so glad to have met you.

Much love and thanks to my Oxford family: Simon Mee, Junyuan Xue, Leanne Tse, Lyndsay Stecher, Judith Weston, Norihiro Yamada, Alex Moran, Lennart Garritsen, Mikołaj

Barczentewicz, Nate Jingze Niu, Fabian Baumann, Kusha
Baharlou, Adam Lapthorn, Julia and the Brouard family, Kris
Palmieri, Saskia Läubli, and too many more to list here. Thank
you University College for being home and the place I began
to research this novel. Thank you Catriona Kelly for your
encouragement, wisdom and incredible knowledge of Russia
past and present. Thanks to Robert Horvath in Melbourne
for sharing your deep knowledge of Russia and particularly
the dissident movement. Thanks to Ekaterina Polyakova for
a warm welcome in St Petersburg and to Elena Cherkasova
for your patience over many Russian lessons while drinking
coffee on Swanston Street.

Thank you to Monash University and the Literary Studies
program for ongoing support, particularly from Ali Alizadeh,
Marko Pavlyshyn and Chandani Lokuge. Thank you Adrian
Jones at La Trobe University for your infectious enthusiasm
about Russian history and your support over the years. Thanks
to all my teachers, I value your work so much. Thank you John
Sutton for my first Russian history classes; Branka Shallies
and Bernadette Noonan for sharing a love of literature. Thank
you to Bill and Jane O'Callaghan for friendship and support.
Thanks also to the Yale Writers' Conference for a great ten
days in 2014. Thanks to everyone at the Trading Post at
Mount Macedon, Ben Oost and Phil Holgate in Woodend,
and to many more locals—our small town community means
a great deal to me.

And finally, enormously, to all those involved in *The
Australian*/Vogel's Literary Award: thank you to the late
Niels Stevns for establishing and funding the award, and to
his son Alan, who continues his father's admirable legacy of
supporting the arts. Thank you to the judges, and to Allen &

Unwin for taking me on, for having faith in the manuscript, for encouraging me. Thanks particularly to Ali Lavau for incredible insight, advice and encouragement, and to Annette Barlow, Christa Munns and Henrietta Ashton.

I gratefully acknowledge the use of the following texts and translations: Elena Bonner, *Mothers and Daughters* (translated by Antonina W. Bouis, Vintage Books, 1993); Joseph Brodsky, *Less Than One: Selected essays* (Farrar, Straus, Giroux, 1986); Mikhail Bulgakov, *The Master and Margarita* (translated by Richard Pevear and Larissa Volokhonsky, Penguin Classics, 2007); Fyodor Dostoyevsky, 'The Dream of a Ridiculous Man' (first published as 'The Dream of a Queer Fellow' in *A Writer's Diary*, 1877; this translation by Kenneth Lantz, 2009); Nadezhda Mandelstam, *Hope Against Hope: A memoir* (translated by Max Hayward, Modern Library, 1999); Viktor Nekipelov, *Institute of Fools: Notes from the Serbsky* (translated by Marco Carynnyk and Marta Horban, Farrar, Straus, Giroux, 1980); Andrei Platonov, *The Foundation Pit* (translated by Robert Chandler, The Harvill Press, 1996) and *From the Notebooks of Andrei Platonov* (translated by Alex Miller, Encyclopedia of Soviet Literature at sovlit.net); Alexander Pushkin, 'The Monument' (translated by Catriona Kelly in *Russian Literature: A brief insight*, Sterling Publishing, 2001); Alexander Radishchev, *A Journey from St Petersburg to Moscow* (translated by Leo Wiener, Harvard University Press, 1958); José Saramago, *The Year of the Death of Ricardo Reis* (translated by Giovanni Pontiero, The Harvill Press, 1992); Varlam Shalamov, *Kolyma Tales* (translated by John Glad, WW Norton & Co., 1980); Viktor Shklovsky, 'Art as 'Technique', in *Russian Formalist Criticism: Four essays* (translated by Lee T. Lemon and Marion J. Reis, University of Nebraska Press, 1965); Alexander Solzhenitsyn, *The Gulag Archipelago, 1918–1956: An experiment in literary investigation* (translated by Thomas P. Whitney, Harvill Press, 1975).

Other works of immense use and influence include the following: Anna Akhmatova, 'Requiem' (translated by Nancy K. Anderson in *The Word that Causes Death's Defeat: Poems of memory*, Yale University Press, 2004); Fyodor Dostoyevsky, *Crime and Punishment* (translated by David McDuff, Penguin Classics, 2003); Alexander Etkind, *Warped Mourning: Stories of the undead in the land of the unburied* (Stanford University Press, 2013); Vasily Grossman, *Everything Flows* (translated by Robert Chandler, Elizabeth Chandler and Anna Aslanyan, New York Review of Books Classics, 2009); Robert Horvath, *The Legacy of Soviet Dissent: Dissidents, democratisation and radical nationalism in Russia* (RoutledgeCurzon, 2005); Catriona Kelly, *Russian Literature: A brief insight* (Sterling Publishing, 2001); Martin A. Miller, *Freud and the Bolsheviks: Psychoanalysis in Imperial Russia and the Soviet Union* (Yale University Press, 1998); Rebecca Reich, 'Madness as a balancing act in Joseph Brodsky's "Gorbunov and Gorchakov"', *The Russian Review*, vol. 72 (January 2013), pp. 45–65; David Remnick, *Lenin's Tomb: The last days of the Soviet Empire* (Vintage Books, 1994); Hedrick Smith, *The New Russians* (Vintage, 1991); John Weaver and David Wright, *Histories of Suicide: International perspectives on self-destruction in the modern world* (University of Toronto Press, 2008).

Also: the art of Boris Sveshnikov, Antanas Sutkus, and Wasily Kandinsky, and the works of W.G. Sebald.